# The Witches Walk

JEANNE ADAMS

# DEDICATION

*To those people who, throughout history, have fought for religious freedom for all peoples. The Witches Walk is dedicated to the pioneers in so many areas from religious freedom, to personal choice, to gender equality. Many of those upstarts and whistleblowers and way-showers lost their lives because they were different, "other" or just creative, inventive and brilliant. We will persevere. Walk, Witches, walk.*

# CONTENTS

# ACKNOWLEDGMENTS

*This has been one of my favorite books to write, partly because of the fabulous people I've connected with in my research on witches and covens, as well as direct research in and around Massachusetts. My deepest thanks go to Ellen Dugan, Garden Witch extraordinaire, for her help and counsel when it came to witchy endeavors. Thanks are also due to Jean-Marie Ward, and Barbara Devlin, for their unending patience and amazing friendship.*

*And to witches everywhere, fly on!*

# PROLOGUE

*April, The Year of Our Lord, 1691*
*Salem, Massachusetts Colony*

L ifting the bloodstained blade in exultation, he bowed toward the small fire and the little altar he'd set up. He offered the blood and soul of his sacrifice to his Master. He had been given the knowledge he needed to bring down the mighty, to set himself up as the leader of the Massachusetts Bay Colony, to gain wealth, power and all the other desires of his heart. And no one would ever know he'd been the one to bring them all down.

Knowing that, no task was too brutal, no sacrifice too great.

The young native girl lying before him, bleeding from a hundred cuts and slashes was slack-jawed and her eyes were glazed. Her chest rose with the last jerky breaths of life. He must take her and her soul for his Master before she died of her wounds.

It must be now.

With a shout of triumph, he plunged the blade into her heart. Within minutes his body convulsed with pleasure equal to nothing he'd ever felt before.

The rapture of it was overwhelming. He shouted with exultation.

There was nothing he could not do in this magnificent new land. Unlike his journey on the boat or his time in London waiting for the papers from the King, allowing the Salem petitioners to claim their portion of the colony, he didn't have to cloak his activities, he didn't have to hide his lust for killing. Here, there were bond servants and natives a-plenty to slake his Master's thirst for blood—and his own.

Now, he would be able to subvert the Aldens, the Mathers, the Webbs and all the leaders of the Colony, and in so doing bring the meddling witches to their knees and burn them all. He would support the rabble rouser, Samuel Parris, the less than modest man fighting for the post as Salem's highest citizen, which, as an officially sanctioned, ordained minister, he could be once the witches were dead. Then, as he humbly denied any skill, allowed the credit to go to lesser, but more vocal men, all the glory and power would be siphoned away to make his Master stronger.

What did he care for titles or position, as long as he had the power?

Cleaning the blade, he straightened his clothes and pushed the girl's body into the deep ocean pool. The changing tide would carry her out to sea before morning broke, and the strong current offshore would wash her deep into the ocean's depths. Any blood he'd missed on his clothes would be explained by the deer he'd killed and dressed to bring back for the larder.

Soon, he would begin. The witches would die.

####

"Hurry, Sarai," the eldest of the Colony's witches snapped at her daughter. "We must be gone before he returns. If we are not, it will be the trials for you and for me."

Sarai picked up the full pack and the mule's leading rein. She didn't pay any mind to the older woman's tone. They were all on edge.

The other members of their group fell in behind the mule. They were the last party to leave, even though theirs were the members of the community in most desperate need of escape. Those with foresight had seen the coming storm of trouble for all Salem's herb witches, healers, seers and weather workers.

If they stayed, they would die.

The moon's full light made the silvery frost glisten where it lay on the weeds that lined the deer track they followed. It was cold, but without the true bite of the forthcoming winter. Fall had begun to spread her colorful cloak over this amazing new land, and they needed to be resettled before true winter set in.

At the crossroads, four other witches waited, their families with them. They had left by a different, more circuitous route, with their loaded wagons and much of their household goods. Those with outlying homesteads had the benefit of being hidden from prying eyes, and could pack more for the journey.

Miles later, following the faint signs left for them, they found the camp of the few who had left the night before.

Within two days' walk, they caught up with the witches who had left earlier in the week. None of them could stay in Salem. Not with the evil that lurked and hunted there. For those with magick in their blood, Salem held nothing but death. While each was powerful in his or her own Gift, none of them had the skill or strength to defeat that kind of darkness.

It hurt them all, with a bone-deep pain, that they would be unable to stop the growing accusations and the trials they knew would come. All they could do was remove themselves and pray that in doing so, they removed the target of Evil's wrath. With them gone, there would be no one to accuse, no one to kill, and the Evil—a demon, or so the most experienced thought—would go unfed, at least by blood with Power.

Between certain death and walking into the unknown, they had all chosen to walk.

"How far are we going, Mother?" Sarai asked, into the hushed darkness.

"We'll walk until we find safety. There is surely a place that we're meant to be," Rachel Mathers said firmly. Her uncle was among the most supportive of the witch hunts, believing everything those deluded young women said. He'd always scared her, but she hadn't thought he'd had such hate in him. Sallie Hestworth said something drove Uncle Mather, like he was a horse, and the same with Samuel Parris and the others, even the girls.

Rachel wasn't so sure. Rachel was pretty sure they liked killing, liked hunting, and found people to be the most interesting prey yet. There might be something helping them toward evil, but the drive was theirs alone.

"Will we make it, alive?" Sarai whispered.

"Unless we're killed by the wild people of this land, or attacked by wild animals, or killed by an act of nature or the gods," Random Miller said curtly. He was keeping pace with them, pulling along two laden mules and a string of four cows. "Same as in the settlements, young miss. We're on a new road, beyond any Seeing."

Frowning at his pessimism, Rachel added, "Death follows the will of the Gods, more often than not, and not the hand of man." That was the way of things. They could live with that.

"Unless someone pulls some strings," Random added darkly.

He knew, as they all did, that the evil stalking Salem was beyond their power. The fact that he couldn't stop it ate at his soul, though, more than most. Random was a fair and honest man, and had been a noble in England. Rachel knew he felt that he should have protected those the tribunal had already taken, already accused. It hit him hard that he couldn't help.

"Time to go." Their leader, young James Hestworth, lifted the slitted night lantern in the signal that their brief rest was done. He'd said that his father, Levi, had found a place that they might settle. So they would go and see.

They rose with no protest, shifted packs into reasonably comfortable positions and set off. There would be pursuit, no doubt of it, for they held knowledge and position and some wealth that was useful to the Salem Colony.

Most had to leave things behind of course. They'd slipped away by twos and threes to escape. But some, like Ransom, had managed to bring livestock. Others had ridden, bringing along useful things since they had the horses' strength for it. And the others, from outlying farms and homesteads, had managed wagons.

They would make new, or do without. Better to live sparse and barren of any luxuries than swing at the end of a hangman's rope. Or be pressed to death with stones, gasping out a last breath, as the Seers had foreseen for many of them.

They'd make their appeal to the colonial government for new settlement on their own terms. If that failed, they'd trade northward with the Acadians or the French. They'd survive.

"Close up the ranks," Hestworth called softly. "Let's keep together."

Together. Yes, they would go into the darkness, into the unknown together and hope to outdistance anyone who would follow.

For now, they would walk. It was dark and cold and they had far to go.

# CHAPTER ONE

*August 15, The Year of Our Lord, 2016*
*Haven Harbor, Massachusetts, USA*

"Why the hell did you take this job, Mari? You've moved to the back of beyond."

Marisol started to say something, but her friend Babs just kept going. "Anyway, where's the potential dating pool? Where's the action? You've never been one to sit home on a Friday night, so where ya' gonna go out when you live in a backwater suburb? Boston's an hour's drive at least, maybe closer to two, with the traffic and all."

"After the Las Vegas contract fiasco, I'm so not looking for dating pools. The Haven Harbor Council met my very substantial pay requirements, despite the fact that the event's still regional." Mari smiled at the memory of that coup. "Anyway, the event's a good one, a stand-out," Mari said as she tucked the phone in the crook of her neck, and ran the box cutter along the top of one of the endless stack of moving boxes. She'd no more than waved the movers off than Babs had called.

She wondered if she dared tell her friend the real reasons she took the job. Hell, she wondered if she even *knew* all of the real reasons she'd come to Haven Harbor.

"Yeah, but the other job in Nashville, that would have been so much fun. It was a total slam-dunk, and would have put you in the spotlight. You'd have only been an hour away from me, two from Cynthia," Babs added, citing their other sorority sister. "It would have been like old times."

Right. Old times. Not a bit like "old times" with both Babs and Cynthia married with kids and Mari the only singleton in the group. And not with Terrence, Cynthia's husband, constantly watching her, trying those one-armed *gosh-its-good-to-see-you*, boob-grazing-hugs every time they got together.

"I know," she managed, when the silence drew out. "But the Nashville job wasn't as appealing in the long run, and the money wasn't as good. This job, The Witches Walk, has lots of room to grow. The Tennessee event was only a one-year contract, you know that. This is two with an option for a longer term if I can grow the event."

And she would. She felt it like a hum in her bones. She was meant for this event. Sometimes it worked that way—she'd get that *feeling* and if she followed it she was never sorry.

Mari decided to leave the full disclosure for another day. Hunches and weird feelings didn't count when it came to business, not the way Babs understood it. And some things were too crazy to tell even your best friend, like how at home, how welcome, she'd felt, just driving over the bridge into Haven Harbor.

The Nashville gig was also too close to the reputation-damaging event she'd done in Memphis. Not her fault, as everyone in the event world reassured her. But on the surface, it looked bad when two major sponsors defaulted and an event dripped red ink. It didn't matter that the defaults were problems in the companies themselves, not the event. It was the event—and its contracted event director—who took the hit.

"I'm going to make it a signature event, Babs," Mari said, turning her thoughts back to the positive. And for her, the Witches Walk was positive in a way she couldn't entirely define. "I mean, really huge. You know I'll pull it off." A surge of adrenaline hit her at the thought. She was so damn excited about this gig. "Once I put The Witches Walk on the map, I can get any event I want. When this breaks big and grows, I'll get more calls, at an even higher level."

"Of course you will, but damn, girl, Haven Harbor, Massachusetts? Dullsville. C'mon, tell me the real reason," Babs pressed. "You know I'll dig it out of you in the end."

The doorbell rang, distracting her from unpacking and from her friend's pressure tactics. "Hang on a sec, gotta get the door." She popped her barking, wiggling Corgi, Pepper, back into his travel crate and did a quick check of her looks in the mirror propped against the wall. Her dark, curly hair was escaping the clip, and there was a smudge of dust on the tanned skin of her cheek. Great.

She wiped at the mark but had to let the whole messy hair thing go. It was too hard to tame anyway. At least her jeans shorts and t-shirt fit her petite frame without being too skimpy or too frumpy.

Marisol opened the door just as Babs asked again, "Tell me the truth. Why did you take the damn job in nowheresville?"

Six women and two men stood on her porch, straggling down the front steps of the tidy rental house into which she'd moved. To a person, tall and small, fair-skinned and dark, they wore black or rusty brown robes. The familiar, tiny, silver-haired lady, with her hand outstretched to push the doorbell again, smiled beatifically. Lucille Birkland, council member and head of the biggest bank in town, was on her doorstep. With witches in tow.

Mari hadn't known Lucille was one of the actual witches on the council.

Mari remembered the woman from the endless council session where she'd grilled Mari about her proposal to turn the town's annual five-day festival event, complete with three-day-walk, a 5K run and celebratory Faire with vendors and bands and performers, and a wrap-up Gala, into a much larger, nationally recognized event.

Lucille might look harmless and sweet, and be tinier than Mari's own five-foot-three, but her shark-like cross-examination of Mari's proposal had been incisive and thorough. No wonder half the council had deferred to her every pronouncement.

"Hello dear," Lucille said. "Well here we are. These are some of my friends from the main Haven Harbor Coven. We're here to officially welcome you to Haven Harbor and to bless the house."

Beyond them, to her shock, she also saw picketers across the street. Four people stood holding signs that said things like, "Just Walk Away." And "No Witches Walk."

"Hello," she said to the group, phone pressed to her chest to stifle Babs's chatter. "And thank you." What should she do? "Would you like to come in?"

"Oh, my God," she muttered, standing aside to let the group file in. As she watched, another couple of people picked up signs across the street. "I have protestors outside my house."

Babs must have heard it because Mari could hear her muffled shriek. "Protestors?!"

She didn't think Babs would take *I have no idea* as an answer, in terms of why she'd taken the job. While it was true that Mari had no real clue why she'd uprooted her life in St. Louis to move to the relatively small town of Haven

Harbor, Massachusetts, instead of taking the more prominent, more "known" type of gig in Nashville, she didn't want to admit it. That was the kind of thing that Babs would hound her about forever.

Instead of dwelling on it, she motioned Mrs. Birkland into the house and watched as the petite woman gathered the others into the foyer.

"I'll just be a minute," she said, and as two stragglers shifted inside, she stayed on the porch and held the phone back to her ear.

"Lord have mercy," Babs said her voice ringing with concern. "See? See, I told you to take the Nashville job. What would possess you to want to go run a charity event for a bunch of witches? You're Unitarian, for heaven's sake."

"Oh, don't mind them," the last woman in the group waved an airy hand toward the protestors as she passed Mari and headed into the house. "We know them. The picket's more for form than any substantive dislike of us, or the Walk. I sort of think CAWW is more like a book club. They get together to chat and drink and talk about those of us who are witches."

"CAWW?"

Another woman answered, looking pained, "Citizens Against the Witches Walk. Acronym, CAWW. As Adele said, they're fairly harmless."

Marisol looked more closely, with that in mind. The men held neatly lettered signs and were drinking soft drinks as they chatted together. They weren't very intimidating, but they were still protestors.

*Witches on the doorstep and protesters in the yard. If this was her first full day in town, what were the next two years going to be like?*

"Mari? *Marisol?*" Babs spoke in her ear. She was getting irritated now. "Are you still there? Are you going to answer me?"

Mari smiled at the coven people. They were all trying

not to eavesdrop but were obviously curious too. She pointed to the phone mouthing, "Be right with you."

They all nodded and smiled, talking to one another.

Mari stepped further out onto the porch to finish the conversation. "I have to go, I have company. Some of the folks from the town are here. Uh, I guess it's kind of like a Welcome Wagon." Marisol managed not to giggle as she said it, but it was a funny thought. The Witchy Welcome Wagon.

She could hear Pepper yipping and scratching at the crate to get out and greet everyone; she could see the picketers laughing and joking; and she had a Coven in her foyer. It was just a little freaky.

"Would you feel better," Marisol said to her friend as she turned away, masking the phone with her hand, "If I told you I had no idea why I did it?"

Babs's rant started the moment the words left Mari's mouth.

"Babs," she interrupted, immediately, already sorry she'd admitted moving on a restless impulse—that *feeling*. "*BABS!*" it took the firmer, louder tone to get through. "I have to go. Some of the ladies are from the Haven Harbor Town Council, I need to make nice." Well, at least two of them sat on that august body. "I'll call you back."

"You damn well better."

She said a hasty, "You bet, love ya, bye," and hung up. She'd call Babs back.

Maybe sometime next month when she figured out how to answer the questions.

Or not.

"Oh, no need to cut your call short, dear," Lucille said. "We're in no hurry."

She saw several of the other people roll their eyes, as if to say that they didn't have all day, even if Lucille Birkland did.

"Hello, Mrs. Birkland," she greeted the small woman again, setting the phone on the still-bubble-wrapped hall

11

table. "It's lovely to see you."

"Hello dear. These are my coven brothers and sisters. This isn't all of us, of course, just those who could get away in the middle of the day. I'll introduce them in a moment. First, let me say that it's traditional in Haven Harbor to have us bless the house of any newcomer, and we certainly wouldn't want to break that fine run of good luck with you, now would we?"

She said this as if it were the most normal, Welcome-Wagon-y thing to do. "Especially after we went to such lengths to get you here." She turned to the others, and Mari saw her smile turn a little bit sly. "Right everyone?"

"Right," agreed the brunette decisively. This was the one Lucille had called Adele.

Unsure of the undercurrents in the group, most of which seemed to be amusement, she just smiled, motioning everyone forward. "Please come into the living room. I think I've gotten most of the furniture unwrapped."

Pepper barked furiously now, scratching and yipping to get out.

"Oh, you have a dog!" Adele exclaimed. "What breed?"

"Adele is our local veterinarian," Lucille explained, introducing her to the thin, dark-haired woman with an intense smile. "You'll be connecting with her over your...?"

"Corgi. His name's Pepper."

"Spicy," quipped Lucille and one of the ladies tittered. "Excellent. Why don't we let him stay where he is for now since Dolores and Jim aren't that comfortable with dogs, shall we?"

"I'll move him—" Marisol began.

"Oh, no," Adele chimed in. "He'll be fine once we get started."

"Started, yes. Ah, what's involved in blessing the house?" Mari had to ask the question. She knew very little about witches, witchcraft or Wicca, although she'd bought and read several books before she did her proposal to the council on how she planned to improve the event. Heck, one of the only solid things she knew was that the terms witch and Wiccan were *not* interchangeable.

As a military brat, she'd traveled all over the world, but she'd never stayed anywhere long enough to go to the same school more than one or two years at a time, much less get very involved in church. While she knew from her research they wouldn't be doing any dark rituals or spirit calling or whatever, she wasn't sure where the line stopped on that sort of thing.

"Nothing sinister, I assure you." Lucille patted her arm with a warm hand. "Just a little chanting and harmless smoke. A few candles and some salt, water and oak leaves. That sort of thing." She waved expressive, fine boned hands in the air.

"What Lucille means is that we won't do anything you don't want," a good-looking man chimed in, smiling. Blonde, brown-eyed and serious, he looked to be only a few years older than Marisol herself, perhaps thirty-five or six. "But if you'll let us, we'd like to clear the house of any negative influences and give you a good start."

Marisol held out a hand. "Thanks, I'd like that. I don't believe we've met."

His handshake was firm and Marisol felt warmed by the contact.

"I'm Dan Nutter," he said. "I'm director of the town and school libraries."

"Ah. And you?" Marisol turned to each person in turn, gathering names and impressions. She'd sort them out later, make what notes she needed to remember each person. It was one of those skills she'd picked up, one that made her one of the most sought-after community development and major-event planners in the country. She remembered people, connected with them. Got them to volunteer and make events work.

Jim, the only other man, last name, Stansfield, was tall and wiry, but broad-shouldered enough that he seemed to loom like a giant when he shook her hand.

"You've met everyone now, I think? Excellent." Lucille Birkland clapped her hands together and all the chatter ceased. "Good. Okay, let's get started." She turned to Marisol. "With your permission?"

"Um, sure. Is there anything you need me to do?"

"It will sound very…interesting," Adele chimed in before Lucille could speak. She winked and added, conspiratorially, "I thought they were a bit different when they knocked on my door the first time. The best thing to do, if you can suspend disbelief in witchcraft, and in the blessing and clearing, is just keep an open mind and focus on good things happening. If you can't do that, just try and keep your mind clear of any negative thoughts."

"Pessimist." Another woman, who'd briskly introduced herself as Lydia, shot the word towards Adele with a smile. To Mari, she added, "Seriously, all you need to do is think positively. Imagine a good future here with us in Haven Harbor. For however long you're here, we want you to be happy, so just focus on that."

"On being happy?"

"Happy, content, settled, comfortable, successful," Lucille rattled off the list. "Whatever feels best to you."

"I think I can manage that," Mari said, trying to keep a straight face.

"Wonderful!" Lucille enthused. "We'll do the rest."

Lucille clapped her hands once more and everyone opened satchels and purses to pull out implements; candles, string, herbs and a very small iron cauldron.

"You're not allergic to anything, are you, my dear? Plants or herbs?" another older woman asked. She was neatly coiffed, and her shoes gleamed a patent leather black under her hem. She'd introduced herself as Winona.

"No, ma'am, I'm very healthy in that regard."

"Be glad," she heard Lydia mutter, but when she

looked over, Lydia was smiling. "I get the worst hay fever once we hit spring. Ugh." She rolled her eyes to express her disgust at the condition.

Mari grinned. Although she was having a hard time getting past the robes and paraphernalia, she already liked these people. The two men in the group were as pleasant and personable as the ladies.

"All right with you if we shift your table a bit?" Adele asked.

"Go for it."

"Excuse me," Dan said. He didn't look like any librarian she'd ever met. He looked like a cover model. Adele evidently thought so too, because she blushed a little and helped him move the table and angle the sofa.

As the group moved to stand in various places in the room, Lucille took out a compass and nudged everyone again according to what she saw on the dial. The others followed her lead.

"Are you ready, Ms. Beecham?" Lucille said to Mari.

"I guess," Mari said, frowning as the group stood in a ring around the room. "And please, call me Mari." How was she supposed to think positive thoughts with random strangers in cloaks, stood in her barely unpacked living room, holding candles and herbs and whatnot?

"Very well Mari, just focus on good things, on a successful event, success for you, for us. Keep your mind on how wonderful it is to be here, and if you like the house, how much you like the house and the town. From that, we'll do the rest. Okay?"

"All right, I'm ready." Mari was always up for an adventure, albeit that was usually a night out or a new recipe. She settled onto the bench she'd placed in the foyer and watched the show. Given that Haven had boosted its economy by claiming to be the refuge created by the *real* witches who'd fled from Salem's infamous witch trials, she might have expected something like this.

*You never expect the Spanish Inquisition.* The wry Monty

Python line leapt to mind. You could always count on the Pythons to get you through the weird moments in life.

"Ladies, Jim and Dan, call the quarters," Lucille commanded, and Lydia, Winona, Jim, and Dan-the-hot-librarian called off the points of the compass. As a group, the ladies then chanted in unison about earth and air and fire and water. "Positive thoughts, Mari," Lucille encouraged.

*Positive thoughts. Okay.* Settling her back against the wall, Marisol set aside her worries about CAWW, about the fact that the town council president hadn't voted for her, and all her other worries. Instead, she focused on the Witches Walk, her skills and what she'd bring to it. She thought about the house and how much she liked it, especially the kitchen. She'd already been dreaming about a trip to the local farmer's market, fresh tomatoes and late summer fruit. Next to the bench, Pepper had quieted down in his crate, so she slipped her fingers into the grooves in the plastic sides to caress his thick fur.

Marisol smelled fragrant smoke and opened her eyes. Lucille held a lit bundle of what looked like a mini-broom full of herbs and tied with string. Nothing was on fire, but there were faint embers at the tips of the herbs, and sweet smoke floated around the room.

Mari absently hoped it wouldn't set off the smoke detectors.

Within a few minutes, after a few passes with the smoky bundle and some more chanting, bell ringing and a few passes with what looked like a really long letter opener, the ladies wrapped up.

"This circle we open, though it remains unbroken," Lucille intoned with solemn pomp, though her eyes were smiling. "With the grace of the Lord and the Lady, and of all those deities upon which our members call, we willingly release all power, all energy, all deities summoned today. Merry meet, and merry part, and merry meet again."

There was a moment of silence then the group began

to move from their places, gathering everything up and putting the room back in order.

"Oh, that was wonderful." Lucille clapped her hands together like a pleased child. "You were very open," she beamed her approval at Mari. "Just the right attitude, don't you think Winona?"

"Perfect," Winona agreed with an equally pleased smile. "You have a very tidy skill there, my dear, of focusing. You were quite engrossed in your own thoughts, which were very positive if I do say so." She patted Lucille's shoulder. "You were right. She is a very contained sort of person, and perfect for the job."

Winona now patted Mari's back; evidently patting was Winona's thing. "Lucille has had nothing but the best reports about you from council meetings. She told us you were her candidate when you first presented." Winona shot a look of amusement at another, younger council member, who'd given a snort of disbelief. "I think Dolores, who found you this house by the way, was more partial to the young gentleman from Ohio. Isn't that right Dolores?"

Dolores, a sixty-ish, trim woman gave Mari a smiling nod. "Well, he was more my type, being a bachelor, but I think we got the right woman for the job in the end. She got my vote."

There had been three dissenting council votes when Mari and the other final candidate had battled it out. Out of the thirteen council members, in the end only the council chair, a church deacon and the at-large member had voted against her.

Winona now patted Dolores's back. "Yes, of course you voted for her. That man wouldn't have done at all. If we wanted sloppy, and a ham-fisted backslapping type," she said seriously, but with a genial tone totally at odds with her words, "we could have stayed with Gus."

There were a combination of snorts and gasps from the group as they all moved to leave. Tactlessness was evidently another of Winona's traits, since no one looked shocked, only amused.

Mari had a hard time keeping back the snicker. The at-large member council, a local businessman, Gus Wilkinson, had been the director of the Witches Walk for the last five years. He gave considerable lip service to being glad to get the Witches Walk on a more professional footing, having neither the time nor the energy to do the job full time. As the event grew—and it was growing—the job became just that. A job. Unfortunately, it was also obvious he didn't want to let go of the power and control being the director of the event gave him. A good-old-boy type, as Winona had so bluntly put it, so it hadn't surprised Mari that Gus had voted for the guy from Ohio.

"And you know," Winona now seemed puzzled, "young Peregrine didn't vote for you. I'm sure he had his reasons, but he's usually so sensible. Obviously he was having an off day," she concluded, with one last pat.

An off day. An interesting conclusion. The council chair, Peregrine Hestworth, was an imposing man. He was a dangerously attractive and sexy, and the fact that she'd even noticed those traits puzzled the hell out of her. He was tall, at least six feet or maybe more, and quite striking with his raven-dark hair and crystal blue eyes. Mari had been drawn to him from the moment she laid eyes on him. At first she thought it might be a problem, but when he so obviously disliked her, her proposal and everything else, she decided it wouldn't be an issue.

The real problem was that she'd have to work closely with him. He had an intense personality and obviously commanded respect in town. All the non-verbal clues said he was someone to reckon with. Throughout her presentation, she'd felt that he looked right through her and found her wanting. He'd dissected the proposal with a sharp, clear and precise technique that found the smallest hole in her planning methodology. It had been obvious he'd disapproved of her. That said, Hestworth hadn't actually listed any reasons why he preferred Mr. Ohio's proposal over hers, so Lucille's equally forceful personality and specific reasoning *for* selecting her had turned the tide.

She could guess, of course, why Gus didn't want her. It had been obvious that he really didn't want to relinquish the post of director to anyone, much less a woman. She had no clue why Hestworth had voted against her. As to the deacon, she figured it was a church thing to oppose the Witches Walk on principle, since he'd been very pleasant to her personally.

Jim came over to say goodbye. "I've got to run. Dentist appointment. It was great to meet you."

"Of course, thank you for coming," she said, imprinting the face and name. Jim Stansfield. According to her research, the Stansfields were another prominent local family.

"Is there anything you need, dear?" Lucille asked, as she came into the foyer with her bag.

"Thank you, ma'am, but I haven't gotten far enough into unpacking to know what I need," Mari demurred. It was true. She'd been in town less than forty-eight hours. With yesterday's marathon session of cleaning and today's directing of the movers, she was weary. When Lucille had called to ask if she and a few friends could come by, she'd agreed more out of form than desire. Being greeted by picketers and witches today added to the feeling of disorientation.

"Well just let us know if you think of anything we can do for you," Adele offered, as she too prepared to leave. "Here. This is a list of our names and numbers. We're happy to help."

Mari took the list and thanked her, opening the door for them. Dan stepped aside for Adele and three other women. Dolores Webb and the younger woman, her niece, Lydia Webb, along with Lucille Birkland, were the last to go.

"Now, where did you say your people were from,

dear?" Dolores-who-wasn't-a-dog-person asked.

"Dolores is one of our local realtors, and our local historian. She runs the historical society," Lucille added helpfully. "She's always asking people where they're from. I believe you mentioned being from Hawaii, didn't you?"

"You don't look Hawaiian," Lydia blurted, then blushed. "Sorry. I dated a guy from Hawaii for a while, and they have a distinctive look…" She trailed off, grinning. "I'm going to shut up now before I stick my other foot in my mouth."

Mari laughed, liking her immediately. "Not to worry. I did spend several years there, Mrs. Birkland," she answered Lucille's question, returning Lydia's grin as she did so. "But I'm a military brat, I've spent a few years in a lot of places. I was born in Oregon, but my grandparents were actually from here in New England."

All three women stopped and stared. The silence stretched just long enough to make her wonder. Then Lucille's beaming smile broke forth.

"There, now if that's not vindication that my spell worked, I don't know what is," she said to Dolores, in a "so there" tone of voice. Turning back to Mari, she said, "You're just what we need, young lady. Absolutely perfect."

Mari could feel her cheeks warm up. "Thank you, Mrs. Birkland. I appreciate your support."

"Yes, yes," Dolores brushed that aside, her eyes bright. "We've all heard you go on and on about that spell. Obviously it worked a treat. Now, Ms. Beecham, what's your family name?"

Lydia broke in, "I don't remember any Beechams in your books, Aunt Dolores."

"No," Dolores dismissed that with a wave. "That must be your father's name, yes?" she demanded of Mari.

"Yes, my mother was an only child."

"What was her maiden name?" Dolores was waiting with an expectancy usually reserved for celebrity news.

Mari wondered why everyone seemed so interested in her family background all of a sudden. She hadn't thought about her grandparents so intensely since they died five years before, and even then, she'd not considered their background.

"Hachette. My grandfather—" she began.

Dolores interrupted her with a triumphant "Aha!"

Eyes closed, finger tracing an imaginary line in the air, she declaimed, "Your grandfather had to be Morgan Hachette of the Myron Standish Hachette family. His original ancestor, Myron Hachette married Stewart Alden's fourth daughter, Marguerite." Her eyes popped open. "Well, goodness, Mari, you're a local." Her family bombshell dropped, Dolores looked like the cat who ate the canary with special sauce.

The other women gaped.

"Well, now that's even better news," Lucille said, beaming once more. She looked beside herself with glee. "Wait till everyone hears this. They'll be over the moon," she assured.

Lydia rolled her eyes at her aunt. "Aunt Dolores, you talk about these people as if they're still alive." To Mari, she said, "The way Aunt D talks about some of our long dead ancestors—like Marguerite Alden Hachette who died in 1799—you'd think they'd just stepped out for a smoke. You'll have even more visitors now," she added, hefting her bag of supplies and shaking Mari's hand again. "You've got Hachette aunts and cousins around here, and since the Aldens had those four daughters and what, three or four more sons in that generation?" She looked to her aunt for confirmation.

"Yes, yes, at least. They're not in my direct line, so I don't keep them in my head." Dolores waved a hand. "You can be sure I'll be looking them up."

Lydia finished her sentence, "Well, then you'll have cousins coming out your ears."

"Do you remember their Gift lines?" Lucille

interrupted, her gaze keen.

"Gift lines?" Mari finally remembered to speak. The whole discussion had taken on a life of its own in these lightning exchanges about family. The feeling of disorientation returned full force. It had never occurred to her that she might have family here. Her parents had been such nomads before they died.

She remembered her grandfather as a tall, stern, white-haired old man and a slightly less stern, bun-and-glasses woman whose house was one of the only constants in her young, roving life. No matter where they lived, they'd always gone home to Grammy and Gramp's house for at least three weeks during the year. But she'd not given much thought to where they were from originally.

"Oh, yes." Lucille clapped her hands again. "Most of the families here abouts have a distinctive set of magickal Gifts. The Hestworths—you met Peregrine at the council, dear—usually have the Sight. The Prescotts, his mama's people, are mostly weather workers. My family line is frequently Gifted with strong spellcasting skills." She beamed at this statement, still visibly proud about her supposed spells working well. "Dolores and her niece, Lydia, descend from a long line of herbalists and healers. Lydia owns the Besom Shop, you know. Right down in town?"

Lydia grinned again, explaining, "The one with the enormous broom over the door."

"Ah, yes," Mari managed. "I did see that." How could you miss a sixteen-foot-long broom suspended over the front of a building?

"Ostentatious, but come Walk time, I get tons of business," Lydia said proudly. "You wouldn't believe what people ask for, though. It's amazing."

"Eye of newt." Dolores snorted. "As if," she said, rolling her eyes. "Idiots."

"My favorite is still the fat, old guy who came in the limo," Lydia said, and both Dolores and Lucille chuckled.

"This guy," she said to Mari, shaking her head. "Black limo, long black cloak in August, all in black right down to the boots. Lots of silver jewelry, even the whole Goth thing with the black fingernails." She mock-shuddered. "Shades of Ozzie Ozbourne. Ugh. Anyway. He wants Real Herbs for Spells," she said, emphasizing the words. "Like I run a shop for brooms, herbs, spell products and lotions and potions and I don't know what those are."

"Hadn't done enough homework," Dolores added, shaking her head again.

"Yeah, well, his kind never do."

Lucille sniffed, a superior look on her patrician features. "Amateurs. I'm all for people exploring the Craft," she said to Mari, her tone indicating she wanted to be sure Mari knew she was open minded. "However, posturing is just that. Posturing. Idiotic."

"He'd driven all the way from Boston, you see. Salem wasn't Witchy enough for him, so he came here."

"Well to his credit, he knew where most of the real witches are."

"Now, Dolores, there are some fine witches in Salem."

"I know, I know, but the Blood is really here," Dolores insisted.

"I'm telling a story," Lydia protested. As an aside to Mari, she said, "Old argument. The Salem versus Haven Harbor deal, and hey, basis of the Walk. Anyway, he asks for all this stuff in what he thought was this scary sepulchral tone." She dropped her voice an octave and put on a menacing face. Problem was, on her snub-nosed, cheerful features it just looked silly. Mari struggled not to laugh.

"Yeah, you laugh, but I had to set this guy straight, and not laugh in his face. He asked for the same herb by three different names, thinking they were different items."

"Wanted to know if she had 'one of the special whetstones' for his athame," Lucille chuckled. Mari didn't understand why that was funny.

Dolores must have seen the puzzled look because she smiled and said, "An athame is traditionally an unsharpened dagger for spellwork, no sharper than a letter opener. A boline is the sharp version, used for harvesting plants and herbs."

Lydia grinned. "You look at sea over all this. I'll get you a book with the basics—a good one——you'll need to read up anyway, to handle all the witches, both real and the wanna-bes, that show up for the Walk and for Halloween and Yule every year."

"That would be great," Mari said, meaning it. She'd read some, and said so, but added, "Obviously I have a whole lot more to learn."

"So are your grandparents still on this side of the Veil, Ms., Beecham?" Dolores interrupted.

"The Veil? And please, call me Mari," she reiterated.

"She means are they still alive," Lydia translated.

"Ah. Unfortunately no. Both my parents and grandparents passed away several years ago." Mari didn't like to think about the four-year span where she'd lost everything—everyone—that meant family, in quick succession.

"I'm so sorry for your losses, child," Lucille said, laying a warm hand on Mari's arm. "That's very hard."

"Thank you." Mari kept it simple. If she said any more, she usually ended up crying. And most people didn't expect more, which saved her both tears and the headache that followed them.

"Well, that's a terrible note to end on," Lydia said, frowning. "Somebody needs to tell a joke or something."

"Three witches went into a bar," Lucille began, merrily.

Dolores and Lydia groaned in unison. "No, not the witch-witch jokes."

Lydia opened the door and waved the older women out. "If you get them started on those old jokes, they'll be here for hours trying to top one another."

"Mari," Dolores said, pausing on the threshold. "May I

tell your family hereabouts that you're kin? Or do you not want that?"

"I'd be happy to know them."

"Most of them," Lydia muttered.

"Lydia," Dolores scolded mildly. "They are fine families. Founding families. Show some respect."

Unrepentant, Lydia grinned. "Like I said, most of them are respectable."

Lucille leaned in and pressed her soft cheek to Mari's. "We're distant cousins, my dear, on my mother's side, several generations' back, so I'll say welcome both as a witch, a member of the council, and as an honorary aunt."

Warmed by the thought, Mari returned the embrace, smiling at the other women. "Thank you for coming, and for the welcomes."

Lydia let the older women go down the steps, and she turned back, whispering, "Want me to drop by later with a bottle of wine, tell you about your kinfolk?"

Mari didn't hesitate. "Absolutely."

Lydia waved in answer and followed her aunt and Lucille down the steps, her robe billowing as she hurried to catch up. While they'd been inside, the picketers had wrapped up. One lone sign remained, planted in the grass like a warning. "Citizens Against the Witches Walk," it read. In smaller letters it said, "Christianity first!"

Sighing, Mari closed the door. Leaning against it, she spoke into the silent house and to the listening dog, "Well, that was freaky."

What in the hell had she gotten herself into?

####

"Yes. She came in yesterday," he whispered into the phone. His office door was closed, but it felt like someone could still be listening. "Yeah, the coven biddies went over to bless the place. No, my mother didn't go." He was pretty sure she hadn't, but they weren't talking much these days. He waited as his business partner made a few comments, but he really didn't care about excuses. "Yes, of course the shipment will go on to Boston tonight. Nothing going on that will stop that."

More comments through the phone that he mostly ignored. One thing caught his attention however.

"Hell no, she can't just disappear. What are you thinking? Gods, man, we're not so far gone that we'd resort to…" he stopped, listening to the reasonable voice explain why it might be necessary to do away with the new girl in town. "Shallow grave, my ass. You know the damn witches would find her. They'd know immediately."

He listened with growing agitation. He hadn't planned on this kind of thing. Spells of concealment were difficult, and he wasn't a master of them. "I'll fix it. We won't have to go that far. Really. I'll fix it. Just give me a couple of weeks."

The threat came through, loud and clear, and it wasn't something he wanted to contemplate. If grave digging was in order, it sure as hell wasn't going to be *his* grave.

"Yeah, yeah. It'll be fixed by the time the Witches Walk rolls around. Promise."

Shuddering, he hung up the phone. He thought longingly of the bottle of whiskey in the bottom drawer.

No, he'd have a drink later. For now, he had to think. He had to plan. He had to figure out how to get rid of Marisol Beecham. Before somebody got hurt.

# CHAPTER TWO

Mari unpacked six more boxes by the time it got dark. She was in the groove. She'd just gotten back inside from taking Pepper out to do his business when she heard another knock on the door.

Restraining the wiggling dog, she opened the door on Lydia's smiling face and a waft of warm, delicious scents. "Hey, you still up for some company?" Lydia asked as she waved a bottle of merlot in one hand and take-out bags in another. "I brought Chinese."

"Food and wine? Oh, yeah. Come right in," Mari said as she moved aside. "I poured some cereal, but never got around to milk."

"Cereal's good. Chinese food's better." Instead of coming in, Lydia put down the food and wine and pulled a long package from where she'd tucked it under her arm. "Let's do this right, though." She put the paper-wrapped package across her arms. "From a new friend to a new friend," she said solemnly, but her eyes were twinkling. "A new broom sweeps clean, and in a new space, you need a new broom. So, here's one cleared and cleansed and ready for your use."

Mari wasn't sure what to say or do. Lydia grinned.

"All you have to do is say thank you and take it. It's just another little ritual we like around here."

Mari picked up the package. It was heavier than she'd expected, and weightier at one end. *Of course it would be,* her brain caught up with the words. *It's a broom.*

"Thank you."

"You're welcome, and now you can invite me across your threshold."

"What, you can't cross? Like a vampire?" Mari joked.

Lydia grinned but didn't rise to the bait. "You'd be in trouble, since you invited all of us in earlier, but no, just a kinda cool thing associated with the broom. I gave you the means to sweep anyone or anything out of your life by handing you a broom. So, you invite me in, I'm not one of the ones who gets swept."

"Seriously? That's cool." She hefted the broom. "Man, I could've used this a lot on other events I've done." She grinned at Lydia and bowed with a flourish. "By all means, be welcome and cross my threshold, since you drink...wine."

Laughing, Lydia picked up the food and wine and stepped in.

"Hey, pup." Lydia greeted the ecstatic Pepper who was bouncing on his hind legs sniffing at the bag of food and generally dashing about in doggy greeting. "He's a cutie. What kind of dog did you say he is?"

"Corgi. Technically, a Pembroke Welsh Corgi," Mari explained. "There're two types. Cardigan Corgis have tails, Pembrokes have that ridiculous little nub that wiggles their whole back end instead."

Laughing, Lydia trailed Mari to the chaos that was the kitchen. The bucket of soapy water sat in the sink and empty boxes and packing paper sat neatly stacked in the corner waiting to go to the attic. Mari moved often enough that she had it down to a science.

"Wow, you're an organized soul," Lydia complimented. "When I moved into my house, I was so indecisive I left my dishes on the counter for three weeks until I figured out how I used the kitchen."

"I move a lot, so it helps me to get it all put away, even if I move it around later. The sooner I get the boxes out of sight, the happier I am," Mari explained, wiping down the small bistro table so they could sit.

"I pretty much took the smorgasbord approach with the food." Lydia's tone was a bit apologetic. "No idea what you like, so I got the variety pack. We can split the leftovers."

Noting the amount of food Lydia was setting out, Mari laughed. "Variety pack, indeed."

Lydia grinned. "When you live alone…"

"Yeah, I get that. Thanks." Mari pulled out plates and wine glasses. "So what's it like growing up in Haven Harbor?" That seemed like a safe topic with which to start.

"I didn't," Lydia said, laughing as Mari winced. "Aunt Dolores and my mom grew up here, of course, but my mom married a Boston podiatrist and got out of Haven as fast as she could. She's not a witch. She's from the firmly Presbyterian side of the family, so she didn't really like the whole Haven Harbor scene. She'd probably have been out there with the picketers this morning." She grimaced. "It's not that she really objects to the Craft, but appearances and feeling like a Normal are really important to her."

"A Normal? Ha!" Mari laughed little at the apt description. "I guess my grandparents were like that. There were a lot of undercurrents," she explained. "Being here," Mari waved a hand to indicate the town, "makes sense of a lot of stuff that got discussed over my head when I was a kid."

"Same here." Lydia clinked her glass to Mari's in salute of that mutual experience. "The first time I came here and visited Aunt Dolores," Lydia said with wry humor, "I was twelve. Aunty D had always come to visit us before that. You know, holidays and stuff." Lydia piled food on her plate and opened a pair of the mass-produced chopsticks the restaurant had included.

"Here, try these." Mari handed her an elegant set of polished ebony chopsticks. At Lydia's surprised look she said, "Military brat, remember? Those are from Shanghai."

"Cool!" Lydia seemed delighted with the chopsticks. Plunking down in a chair with her wine, she clicked them together with an experimental tat-tat-tat of sound. "Most excellent."

Taking her equally full plate to the table, Mari prodded her to continue the story. "So you came here?"

"Oh, yeah. Well, during Mom and Dad's twentieth anniversary trip to Italy," Lydia said, easily wielding the chopsticks. "My older brothers went to my Uncle Todd's cabin in Maine for the week, I came to Aunty D."

"And?"

"Oh, well, I started my period, and then had serious cramps, you know." Lydia's eye roll was expressive of that womanly pain in the ass. "Aunty D hauled out herbs and brewed up a wickedly strong pot of weird tea, which actually tasted pretty good, and whammo-blammo, I felt better. Then I started asking questions." She lifted her wineglass in toast to that event. "And I haven't stopped yet. Read a lot of books and drove my science teachers crazy until college, visited here every chance I got, then went to Boston College and snagged a degree in business and botany. Kicked around the corporate scene for a while then came back here to live."

"To open the shop?"

"Not at first. When I came back, I got a job at MicroMechanics Gamin, out on Foundry Road. That's

Pere Hestworth's gaming and tech company."

Mari had done her homework on Hestworth, so Mari knew all about MicroMechanics and his rise to gaming-tech fame, but all she said was, "You're a computer type then?"

"I hack around. Mostly I did research, which I'm really good at." Lydia grinned again. "If you need information, I can find it for you. I almost took a job with the Feds."

"Really?" Lydia seemed too cheerful and free-spirited to want to work for the government.

"Too stuffy, too many rules," Lydia said, confirming Mari's guess. "Unlike retail. The first year I lived here, I made up all these soaps and lotions to do a booth with, you know? I'd been playing around with stuff in the greenhouse at school, and sold things on the sly to classmates. Anyway, they put out a call for everybody to pitch in, make the event a success." She gestured with her chopsticks. "The Walk had only been going a few years. It struggled, at first. Everybody *did* pitch in, including me. I had so much fun. I sold out of everything, took orders for batches and batches of stuff 'cause I'd kept my testers, so people kept buying brooms, stopping to try the lotions and potions. I sold every packet of herbs I had. The only things I had left were a few broom charms and a little bit of jewelry. I was so psyched."

"I'll bet," Mari said, dropping a crisp water chestnut to the eagerly waiting Pepper. "What then?"

"I came back to reality with a thud, you know? I had no production capabilities, no suppliers, no capital." Lydia shook her head, ruefully. "I remember sitting down in the middle of my dinky starter apartment, looking at all the orders and panicking. I called my dad. He was wonderful, but he basically told me I needed to call the customers and tell them I couldn't fill the orders. He told me I had a job and that this was a hobby gone mad."

"Oh, Lydia, that must have been hard," Mari sympathized.

"It was," Lydia admitted, her smile returning. "But in a good way, because it was all or nothing." She smiled. "I do better with those kinds of decisions than the ones where you have seventeen choices, you know?"

"So?" Mari waited eagerly for what came next.

"I went in to work the next day and asked for a meeting with Pere," Lydia said as if that were self-evident. "I knew him a little from working the local ice cream parlor together one wicked-hot summer before the foundry mill closed. They'd have these specials for the mill workers, half price for a two-scooper and stuff, and we'd work our asses off. The parlor's still over on Yew, round the corner from my place. Anyway, I felt like I could ask for a meeting."

"I take it Mr. Hestworth said yes to the meeting."

Lydia laughed. "Jeez, that makes him sound so old." She grimaced again, a funny squinching of her cherubic features. "Anyway, I told Pere all about it. I figured he'd done it." Mari must have looked as puzzled as she felt, because Lydia added, "You know, started a business. I figured if he told me I was nuts, it might mean something." She paused. "Aunty D read runes and cards for me, and said go for it. My dad said I was nuts. So, not that I didn't trust Aunty D's readings, but, well, you know, it was about business, so...Pere."

"If it's any consolation, my folks were worried as hell when I started my business too," Mari laughed. "My dad kept talking about security and stability. I was at a company in San Francisco, putting together high level meetings, portfolio junkets, that sort of thing. Nice and secure."

"I guess you decided security was overrated?"

"Yeah, I guess," Mari agreed, remembering how bored she'd been. "Or I'm certifiable. Either way." She waved around the kitchen at the boxes. "It worked and eight years later here I am in Haven Harbor."

"There you go," Lydia agreed. She topped off their

wine, then clinked it again with Mari's. "Here's to insanity."

"So what did Hestworth say?"

"Ah, well, it was funny. Long story short, he asked me one question." She paused dramatically, and dropped her voice into the bass register, like a man's voice. "He said, *What does your gut tell you to do?*"

"Wow, perfect impression. I'm guessing your gut said *Go for it.*" Mari stated it as fact. She'd had the same feeling about her own work.

"Yep. So he gave me outstanding advice and a week off with pay to get my crap in a pile, then co-signed a loan at the bank so I could get started. I filled the orders and within a year, I'd opened The Besom Shop. Within two, I'd paid back the loan."

"Whoa! That's outstanding!" Mari said, awed not only by the leap of faith, but by the speedy success. "You must have great margins, and excellent marketing."

"I'm pretty proud of it, and yeah, the internet is my friend when it comes to marketing." Lydia looked down at her empty plate, then up at Mari. Cocking her head, she said. "You know, you're really easy to talk to. I don't think I've ever told anyone else that story, not all of it anyway."

"I enjoyed hearing it," Mari said, clearing her equally empty plate to the sink. She'd definitely have to get the number of the Chinese place. "I'm looking forward to coming in, seeing all your wares."

"I'll show you around myself." Lydia beamed. "It's a lot of fun, hanging out, creating a business here. It's a good town," she said, reflectively. "So, I'm looking forward to what you're going to do with the Witches Walk. It's been awesome for me, so any way it gets better helps my business."

"I didn't realize there were so many people who were against the Walk, though. Your friend Pere, for instance."

"Oh, Pere's not against it, not like the other group,

CAWW. He just is wary of it getting too big, too commercial, I think," Lydia said, carrying her plate to the sink as well, absently rinsing it and adding to the dishwasher just like they'd been friends for years. "Not that he's confided in me." She shot Mari a crooked grin. "We're not that close."

"Really?"

"Co-signing a loan kinda put us on a weird footing. Besides, he's not my type." When Mari glanced over, Lydia laughed. "You should see your face. Oh, Pere's hot as a match, but he's intimidating, you know? Besides, it's like I borrowed money from him. Sort of. So I couldn't see him as dating material after that. Its more big-brother-ish, I guess. And he goes for the hot-model-from-out-of-town type."

"Hmmmm. I can see that. I think."

"Why? You think he's hot?" Lydia asked, leaning on the counter, eyes gleaming with mischief and interest.

"I have no idea," Mari denied. "I mean, he's certainly attractive, but I hear you on the intimidation factor." No way was Mari letting on that she'd had sweaty dreams about Peregrine Hestworth, town council chair, CEO of the largest business in town and one of the fastest-growing game tech companies in the country and scion of one of the oldest families in Haven Harbor. She wasn't confiding that to anyone, no matter how much it felt like she and Lydia were long-lost pals.

"Aunty D and Lucille said you didn't back down for one minute though, even with Pere. Hell, if you stood up to Lucille, you're made of sterner stuff than I am," Lydia admitted with cheerful self-deprecation.

"I like her," Mari admitted, remembering the fiery exchanges she'd shared with the silver-haired matron. "She's got great ideas."

"She's stubborn as a goat. Once her mind's made up even the Gods couldn't change it."

"I can see that. So before you tell me about the

relatives, tell me about CAWW and their picketers," Mari said, topping off their glasses and leading the way to the living room. "I'd best get the lay of the land on that one, right away." She wanted to know more about Pere, and the hot, male-model-like librarian too, but wasn't sure how to ask.

"Well, I guess I'd better tell you about the lawsuit too," Lydia said, settling into her seat.

####

"She's a determined young woman," Lucille Birkland said with satisfaction. Her best friend, Estelle Hestworth, was pouring them both a gin and tonic, adding the requisite twist of lime before bringing the drinks to the antique dining table set with lovely old china. "I'm very pleased. You should have felt how clear she was. She's got power, Stell, and a lot of it. I can't wait to get home. I'll bet I'll have an email from Dolores about the Hachette Gift line. I'm dying to know."

"Well, Peregrine seemed set against her," Estelle commented neutrally. "Interesting that she didn't mention her local connections in her presentations. You'd think she'd have played that card in her bid." A businesswoman herself, Estelle was curious about that. Lucille had kept her apprised of the whole process as it happened, even though Estelle wasn't on the council herself. "It certainly might have swayed those votes more quickly her way."

Lucille harrumphed. "Your son wasn't ever going to change his mind about her. And the heavens only know what Del Morton was thinking in that secretive head of his. We know Gus wasn't going to like anyone we did choose, so that was moot. Good Lord and Lady, Gus still doesn't think we need a professional even as he says yes to giving up the power." She rolled her eyes with comic annoyance. "So I'm sure that's going to be fun both this year, with Marisol observing and learning the ropes, and the months afterward when he has to turn over the walkie-talkie, so to speak. That explains Gus, of course, but I don't know what Peregrine or Del have against her."

"I don't either, Luce. He didn't confide in me," Estelle said, regretfully. The rift with her only son was a painful topic. They spoke, of course. He came to dinner on Esbats, Sabbats and holidays as he'd always done, but the connection wasn't clean or clear. There were harsh words between them, and harsher feelings. It was a constant source of pain.

"To be frank, I don't think the girl considered the family connection," Lucille continued on the earlier thread of their conversation, oblivious to Estelle's wandering thoughts. "I don't get the impression she's had a lot of family support even when her parents were still alive."

"She's all alone then?" Estelle knew what that felt like and sympathized. She, at least, had had a community surrounding her. If she'd read young Marisol Beecham's situation correctly from her son's vague comments, the girl had no home base to speak of.

"She won't be alone for long. Not anymore," Lucille said smugly. "You know Dolores. She had Caroline Hachette Webster on the phone before we'd gone a block. Mari isn't going to know what hit her when the Hachettes descend." She giggled. "Oh, that sounds so funny, but you know what I mean."

Estelle laughed. It did sound funny. "You're right. I hope it'll help her settle in. It could have the opposite effect of course, given Paul Webster's disposition, but maybe he'll lighten up some. He stands to make a lot of money if the Walk gets more popular. It'll give him the boost he needs to expand. You know he's wanted to for years."

"Bought all that land, yes. He's a smart one, for all he's pickle-sour most of the time."

"Luce, about Peregrine, I think I know why he voted against her." When Lucille turned a surprised gaze her way, she sighed. "He thinks I'm trying to marry him off, and that I've set some sort of spell to make women come here, to court him. He thinks Marisol Beecham is one of them."

Lucille choked on the sip of gin she'd just taken. "Court him? Oh, my goodness, Stell. Why on earth would he think that?"

"I swear I didn't do anything, but I let something slip, something that I'd done a long time ago," Estelle began, her heart pumping faster and faster as she prepared to reveal a long-held secret. "And there's the apprentice thing. He thinks I'm running them off so he'll work on his Gifts. I swear, Luce, I can't even find one to run off. You see—"

Both women turned at the sound of a knock and the door opening in the foyer.

"Mother?" a deep, masculine voice rang through the house.

"In the dining room, son," Estelle called, looking over at Lucille. "What do you reckon?" she whispered. Lucille knew about their estrangement, and now she knew a little bit of the why of it. Pere hadn't come over uninvited in more than a year.

"No idea," Lucille whispered back, her eyes a-twinkle, but her expression was sober when Pere's tall form cleared the kitchen door. "This should be interesting."

"Hello, darling," Estelle greeted her son. He crossed to her, dutifully bending to kiss her cheek. The warmth they'd once shared was absent. The kiss was perfunctory, cool, and it broke her heart. "What brings you over tonight? Would you like a gin?"

"I was in the neighborhood," he said briskly, turning to the liquor cabinet. "I think I'll have a whiskey. May I?" he inquired, his hand on the cabinet knob. Her heart pinched. Until last fall, he would never have felt he had to ask, never had been so formal.

"Of course. Please. Then come join us."

He nodded, pouring a short, neat glass of the amber Irish whiskey into a cut crystal tumbler. "Thanks," he said, pulling out a chair, but his posture was stiff, even after a sip of whiskey. "I understand you went and did the usual at our new Walk director's house. I came by to see how it went, how she took it." He glanced at his mother, but focused most of his attention on Lucille.

"Of course we did, Peregrine," Lucille answered amiably. "We not only want her to succeed, we believe we need her to."

"Really?" He drawled the word, but his eyes were keen. "And why is that?"

"Really, Peregrine," Estelle chided. "I'm sure she was fine with it. As to why we want her to succeed, don't we all want the Walk to prosper? There's nothing sinister or odd here. Lucille tells me she's a nice young woman who stands a good chance of making the Walk a nationally recognized event."

"You chose not to go today," he said, turning to his mother.

"No, I didn't go. I didn't want her to be too overwhelmed, and frankly, I wasn't feeling well."

Pere's gaze sharpened now, lasering in on her. "Mother?" He put a world of query in the single word.

She dismissed his concern with a wave of her hand. "It's nothing to worry about, son. I was just tired. The weather's been unstable all over New England, and calming it has been challenging."

"You take on too much, Mother," he said softly.

"I'm still looking for an apprentice, you know that. I'll back off, as soon as I can find one," she said, keeping her voice level. This was an old argument, and her promise was true, even if he didn't believe it.

Problem was, finding a weather-working witch willing to come to Haven Harbor to apprentice and then stay, was difficult. The last and only lead she'd had on someone hadn't panned out. The boy had had a viable talent, but he'd stayed in California and apprenticed there.

"Besides, if I'd let that last storm brew into an August

gale it would have devastated the fishing all over the northeast. As it was, I meddled more than I should have. I was lucky," she said, remembering her worry, her real fright, when the National Oceanic and Atmospheric Administration took far too much notice of the nor'easter's sudden loss of power. "That nice young woman from NOAA called me, let me know it was too much, so I backed off."

She could see Lucille's surprise. She'd not shared that little nugget of information, even with her best friend. Just one more little secret in a lifetime of secrets.

Pere sat back in the chair with a jerk, the whiskey in his glass sloshing up to the rim. "Mother," he said, setting the glass down, then leaning forward to take her hand. "You need to be careful. Don't jeopardize—"

She cut him off, slipping her hand free. The turmoil of his emotions was too much for her to bear. "I'm not going to jeopardize the town, Peregrine James Hestworth. I know better than you what's at stake." She laughed, and it sounded brittle, even in her own ears. "All witches do, and I'm no exception."

"Very well, Mother." Pere's words dripped icy restraint. She knew his temper, volatile since childhood, was straining to break free into angry, hurtful words and he, strong as he was, was using every trick she'd ever taught him to keep it leashed. Obviously, his distrust and her dismissal of his concern were just making things worse. Her heart broke even more, because she didn't know how to mend things. "Thank you for the whiskey," he said, downing the whiskey and setting the empty glass down with a snap. "I'll see myself out."

Without another word, he rose, nodded to Lucille and left.

"Oh my," Lucille breathed, reaching for her gin and draining the glass by half. "I thought he was going to catch on fire there for a minute."

Estelle sighed and closed her eyes against the pain in

her heart. "So did I."

"Stell, you're my best friend. Won't you tell me what caused this terrible rift between you? You said he thought you were meddling, but surely you told him you weren't? I've tried to stay out of it, let you mend it or not, as the Lady wills, but…" Lucille let the words trail off, as Estelle opened her eyes and the tears tracked down her cheeks. "Oh, Stell," she said, rising to come around and offer a supportive hug. "You can't keep this up."

"I feel like I'm going to fly apart, Luce," she told her old friend, nearly sobbing the words into her shoulder. "In addition to everything else, he believes he's let me down, let his father down, because his Gifts only show him how to make his business succeed. He believes that something he did—" She tried to draw a breath, hiccupped over the words and nearly laughed at how stupid it all sounded. "Something he did in college, with a woman, that it somehow changed his Gift, stunted it or shut it down."

"Did he…did he…" Lucille seemed unable to spit out whatever she was thinking. Obviously she was imagining something far worse than what had occurred.

Estelle shook her head. "No, no, nothing terrible. In fact, it's ridiculous, Luce. He got hooked on this woman, told her all about Haven Harbor, about his Gifts. He was going to ask her to marry him."

"Ohhhh," Lucille drew out the word. "Natalie. Brown hair, big boobs, blue eyes."

"That one, yes." Estelle managed a watery laugh. "We all knew she was wrong for him, but I never thought he was so far gone in infatuation that he'd actually tell her anything. Really." She wiped at her cheeks, and Lucille handed her a tissue. "Thank you. I didn't think that much of it. When he came home, he was sad, and seemed very disappointed, but at the time he said nothing about his worries about his Gift or anything else. He only said that she wasn't the right one after all."

"Then he told you differently?" Lucille prodded.

"Last fall we had an argument, you know that."

"The whole town knows that. Even the non-witches are tuned in to gossip, Stell. For heaven's sake, he's the head of the town council, and our most eligible bachelor. Everyone watches him."

"Perhaps that's the problem. He and his father never got along. Too much alike. Then there was Natalie rejecting him and telling he was a freak, and then his father up and died." She said it with some asperity, still annoyed with her late husband for not planning better. He'd left everything a mess and not only did she miss him terribly, she'd had to deal with the sheer drudgery of clearing up their tangled and astonishingly messy financial picture, much less his other affairs. "Then Peregrine left for a while, which you already know, but when he came back he was different."

"Again, dear, preaching to the choir as the Christians would say. I well remember when he strolled back into my office and told me he was opening business accounts. Then all the real estate too."

Estelle had to smile at that memory. Peregrine's return had been the talk of Haven Harbor for over a year. His company, MicroMechanics, had revitalized the economy, giving it enough of a shot in the arm that at least ten other businesses survived just because Peregrine came home to build his gaming company. His election to the town council had been anticlimactic.

Rising to its leadership was on his own merit, of course.

"He believes, though, that somehow I expect more. That I expect him to be his father, reestablish the family business, Lord and Lady forbid." Estelle wiped her eyes again and managed a laugh at Lucille's unladylike snort of laughter. "You know I loved James, but his flaws were glaring at times."

"No more so than in his handling of his estate or his

son," Lucille said dryly. "Remember, I was there. Nothing like telling your son he's a carbon copy of you on one hand, just as he's trying to establish a separate identity, but telling him he's worthless in the same breath because he was the only child, and hadn't manifested his Gifts yet. Then yelling at you because he decided he should have married someone who could have given him more children."

Estelle winced over the memory of that top-of-the-lungs, drunken argument between her husband and son. Lucille had been an embarrassed witness to the whole thing.

Peregrine had defended her, then.

"Well, it's all part of the problem," she sighed as she admitted it. "He believes in the Craft, of course. He believes in his Gift, even though he's hemmed it in so tightly I'm surprised anything gets through. However, he believes that I set a love spell for James and that I've been trying to do the same for him. He thinks I want him married off and producing little Hestworths so I can find an apprentice."

Lucille's O of surprise would have been funny if the whole situation wasn't so painfully undignified. "You mean he thinks that you…" she trailed off, wiggling her fingers in the air, to mime a spell.

Estelle imagined the paths and thoughts running through her friend's mind. "Yes, exactly."

"He stopped dating that woman that runs the temporary agency last fall."

Estelle nodded. "He's sure I was trying for a set up because I said she was lovely and so practical." She couldn't help it, she sighed again. It was all so stupid. "I know, and before you say it, I know it was an idiotic thing to say, but at the time I had no idea he thought I was meddling."

"You told him you didn't set a spell on James?"

Estelle felt her heart clench, but it was time to reveal

the secret she'd kept for forty years.
"That's just it, Luce.  I did."

## CHAPTER THREE

Mari shivered a little as she passed two runners on the road into town. Her own near-miss with injury while jogging that morning had her spooked. The feeling followed her as she parked her sleek red rental car in the designated Witches Walk staff area. She patted the hood as she got out. She liked it enough that she might buy one like it.

The staff door was locked—Gus was being passive-aggressive and hadn't given her keys yet. So she walked around the block, dodging another, more-cheerful-looking jogger. She thought again about the morning's mishap. She was really glad she'd left Pepper home when she went for her own early morning run. Some asshole in a black SUV had nearly hit her, and she'd had to jump up onto the embankment at the side of the road. Fortunately, it had been in a fairly clear spot, without a lot of the brush and scrubby trees so common around New England.

Unfortunately, she'd turned her ankle just enough that the ankle hurt, along with her hip and back where she'd landed on her rump.

Squaring her shoulders and putting the irritation aside, Mari walked toward the Witches Walk office. She'd been here a week, and other than small annoyances, like her rental car not starting, and getting a flat, she'd been able to get in a lot of important meetings and introductions.

She even had a date for Thursday night, which is the only thing that had kept both her friends, Babs and Cynthia, from coming to Haven Harbor and hauling her out of "that backwoods nowhere you tied yourself to," as Babs had put it. Mari rolled her eyes at the thought of her friends' passionate dislike of a town they'd never been to.

The date, however, had mollified both her friends. Kevin Torsk, the Boston lawyer she'd met at the Salem Chamber of Commerce meeting, had asked if he could come out to Haven Harbor and take her to dinner. Not too shabby for only a week in town.

Cheered by the thought, she pulled open the door to the Witches Walk office with a smile on her face.

"Good morning, Carol," Mari said to the young woman sitting at a desk in the outer office.

"Morning, Ms. Beecham," Carol returned the greeting, jumping up to go to the little beverage area. "Tea, this morning? It's no trouble. Really."

Mari usually made her own tea or coffee, but in the week she'd been there, she'd done everything she could not to dampen the young woman's enthusiasm. Since Gus did everything to put her down, Mari was determined to do the opposite.

"Actually, I think I'll go for coffee today." Putting her hands on her hips, she looked around the office. "So what's on the docket? We're what? Four weeks out?"

"Yeah, well, a little closer to five, thank heavens. But it's looking great," the girl enthused, pouring coffee into a mug. "The last of the twelve bands this year got their forms in. It's going to simply rock." Her rapturous look spoke volumes. "Oh, and the vendors? We've gotten another eight checks. They came into the PO box on Saturday. Last week's batch all cleared too. How do you want your coffee?"

"Just black and sweet, please. And that's great that all the checks are clearing," Mari complimented.

The door chimes sounded again, and a stylishly dressed woman walked in the door, carrying a briefcase and a go-cup. "Good morning."

Her clipped New England accent was warmed by her smile. "I'm Geneva Banks, the auditor from Grayson, Myers, Banks and Greene."

"Oh, good morning," Carol said, looking panicky. "Um, I'm sorry, I thought you were coming on Thursday."

"Originally, I was, but we finished a previous client's project early. I spoke to Mr. Hestworth, told him we could start the project sooner. He agreed. I believe he was going to notify Mr. Wilkerson?"

About that time, Gus walked in. He didn't even look up. He just said, "Carol, coffee."

"Uh, Mr. Gus, the auditor's here."

Gus stopped dead in his tracks, and shot Mari an evil look. "Did you do this?"

"I'm not sure what you're referring to," Mari said, coolly. "I just arrived myself."

He shifted his gaze to the other woman. "Auditor. Sorry. No coffee yet." As if that excused his behavior. "Carol, get her set up in the conference room."

"Actually, I'd like to meet with you first, Mr. Wilkerson," the auditor injected smoothly. "Go over what I need from you, then," she said brightly, "I'll begin delving into the past."

Carol hurried to fill another mug. Like a seasoned waitress, she had the cup poured, cream and sugar added to taste, and in Gus's hand before he could blink.

Mari thought that was a peculiar way for the auditor to

phrase it—the delving part—but kept her thoughts to herself as the auditor followed Gus's curt, *come ahead* hand wave, and went into his office. His door shut with a significant bang. She didn't think he'd actually touched the door.

That was a little freaky.

Carol stood wringing her hands and staring at the office, and Mari repressed a sigh. She'd hoped this wasn't going to be a trial by fire, so to speak, but the more she learned about Gus Wilkerson, she realized it would be. Being in and out of the office, meeting people in Salem and Boston, and around Haven Harbor, had kept her first week busy and productive. The start of week two wasn't looking as good.

"Why don't you bring me up to speed on where the bands will be," Mari said into the tense silence. She moved to the giant map on the wall and motioned Carol over. "You said we had new vendors?"

"Oh, okay," Carol said, turning as if she'd forgotten Mari was there. "Sure. Great."

The oversized map of Haven Harbor was mounted on the wall, and pushpins in varying colors denoted vendors, food establishments, porta-potties, first aid facilities, and so on. Within a few minutes, Carol had regained her enthusiasm and was deep into explaining how they were rearranging a certain street set-up to accommodate one of the larger new vendors when Gus walked back out of his office.

"Oh, hey, Mr. Gus, we've been going over the maps. Ms. Beecham's had some great ideas, you know?" Carol beamed. "Seriously, Mr. Gus, you wouldn't believe, I managed to get two of those new vendors a better spot, thanks to her."

"Great." He looked at Mari and the map, looking for the changes. "Already earning your pay, Ms. Beecham, between that and all those meetings last week," he said, with a slight smile. The condescending tone belied the words, and the once-over look was far too familiar. Gus had grated on her nerves from day one and it looked like that sensation wasn't going away.

The auditor walked out behind Gus. She looked a little flushed.

Uh-oh. He was evidently turning on the charm when it came to the auditor.

He opened the door to Mari's office and ushered the woman in. Since Mari left on Friday, there were taller stacks of boxes packed into the room. The only thing clear now was the desk, and that had acquired stacks of smaller boxes on the corners.

"Oh, Mr. Gus—" Carol began.

"Ms. Beecham, the auditor needs a place to work where the door can be closed and locked." He looked at Mari, and his smile had a nasty edge when he turned to Carol. "I'm sure Ms. Beecham won't mind setting up in the conference room until the audit's done." The nasty edge deepened when he added, "After all, she's not the director until next year's event, and at this point, she's mostly out meeting people."

Geneva looked nonplussed, and Carol looked like she was about to die on the spot. Mari quickly considered the odds on how to play this one. Gus was secretive, annoying, and a bully, when it came down to it. But Mari wanted the audit, badly. She knew something was off. Gus's prevaricating about releasing the records of the event's previous years told her that he was up to something that involved the Walk finances. She'd seen this kind of evasion before—especially when someone was embezzling or cooking the books. Gus's actions spoke volumes about his desire to hide something. What, she didn't know.

Whatever it was, an audit would uncover it.

"Of course," she said, infusing her voice with graciousness, as she turned to Geneva Banks. "I'll be out of the office a lot anyway, as Gus intimated. Improving the lines of communication with all the stakeholders in the Walk is part of why I'm here." Both the auditor and, to her surprise, Carol shot equal looks of interest at Gus—although Carol winced at the hidden barb in her comment about stakeholders. Gus was oblivious, as usual. "So, not to worry, Ms. Banks, I'll be glad to get the few personal things in the desk out of your way today so you can settle in."

Geneva looked both relieved and annoyed, glancing at Gus with a hint of irritation in her gaze now. He'd put her on the spot, and despite whatever charm he'd been turning on in his office, this woman seemed a no-nonsense sort who didn't like being caught in the middle of Gus's power play.

"Thank you," Geneva said warmly. "Please, call me Geneva, and there's no rush. I'm sorry to put you out." Her lips thinned but, when Gus turned his back on them to move some boxes, Mari winked and smiled.

"Not to worry. I'm sure we'll get through this just fine."

Geneva's answering smile told Mari the other woman understood all too well.

"Carol, these belong in my office. How many times do I have to tell you that this vendor goes right to me?" he snapped, picking up five smaller boxes and stomping out to deposit them in his office.

Geneva set her briefcase down on the now-cleared desk. "Thank you, again," she said quietly. "I really do need the office to lock."

"Not a problem," Mari said. "I get it."

"As do I," Geneva said softly, with a glance at the doorway where Gus was returning.

Five weeks and she'd be rid of him, Mari reminded herself as Gus blustered and shifted more boxes off the desk. She'd just wait him out, pour on her own charm. She knew more about event planning and how to run a major program like the Witches Walk than he'd ever learned. However, he had the historical knowledge of the event she needed. He hadn't wanted her—the professional—to steal his thunder, even as he admitted he couldn't manage the Walk getting bigger. But if she could coax that institutional knowledge out of him…priceless. If not? Well, she'd figure it out.

*You'll get through it, Mari,* she reminded herself. *Same as always, work with the good ones, work around the duds.* Gus was definitely one she was going to have to work around on all fronts.

Gus held his cup out to Carol so he could shift another box, with an accompanying grunt, and Carol took it automatically. Then she turned absolutely scarlet as she faced Mari and the auditor.

"Oh, my gosh, Ms. Banks, I didn't even ask if you wanted coffee. I'm so sorry." Carol looked like someone had shot her dog. "I'll get you some right now. How do you take it?"

"Thank you," Geneva said, smiling. "It's Carol, isn't it?" She went on as soon as Carol nodded. "I prefer tea even in the summer. Hot, sweet and black, if you have it. If not, I'll just get some at lunchtime."

In another lightning shift of mood, Carol's smile lit the room and she nearly bounced to the coffee station. "I love tea too! And so does Ms. Beecham. Isn't that great? I have oolong, a bunch of herbals, um, Earl Gray, English Breakfast, and Constant Comment, and—"

Geneva cut off the flow with a raised hand. "Earl Gray is perfect. Thanks."

"No problem. One lump or two?" Carol giggled. "Oh, man, I've always wanted to say that, but it's true, 'cause we got those sugar cubes this time. So, uh, how many for you?"

"Two, I'd say," Geneva managed to comment without laughing over the girl's enthusiasm. "Thank you."

"Get Geneva whatever she wants," Gus ordered as he came back in again, after delivering more of the smaller boxes to his office. He ignored the fact that Carol had already gotten Geneva her tea and handed a fresh cup of coffee to Mari.

"There you go, Geneva," he said, all charm again. "Those are the first two years' records." He pointed to two boxes he'd just pulled from a closet in the corner of the office. "We'll let you get started."

He motioned Mari to follow him as he turned for the door. As usual, every gesture and all of his body language screamed that he was in charge and she was the interloper. He plopped in the worn leather chair behind his desk, leaving her to choose between the stiff guest chairs in front. Gus was making sure she knew, loud and clear, who was in charge.

"So you've met all the players," he said, sipping his fresh coffee. "Boston folks, Salem Chamber types and crazies." He smirked now. "They're interesting, eh?"

"Very," she agreed. He was making fun, of course, but she was serious. The Salem Chamber people had been fabulous, eager, and devoted to the event as had the stakeholders in the towns of Mouldon and Pennyfield where the Walk participants stop overnight.

"You got the pansy stuff out of the way then," he stated, still smirking. "Ready to really learn the ropes?"

Gritting her teeth, Mari bared them in a smile. "Of course. Let's dive right in. I know," she said, adding a sweeter tone to her voice, "that you have every base covered, so you can give me the lowdown on the way things work, and then I'll learn from you as we move forward."

Flattery worked, because he puffed up his chest and began to pontificate. "Well, after so many years of doing this, most of it's just instinct by now," he bragged. "A sense of things, you know. Knowing the community like I do, well, it just works for me."

He extolled the virtues of the festival's benefit to the town, but when he ran out of that, she egged him on by saying, "You know, Gus, I'm going to take some notes, do you mind?"

"Carol?" he hollered, even though the door was closed. "Bring us a couple of pads of paper."

"Right away, Mr. Gus," Carol called out, even as Mari pulled her leather portfolio from her briefcase, unfolded it to a clean page and uncapped her pen.

"Thank you, Carol," she said, when the girl popped in, as if on springs, to offer three different kinds of writing pads. "I'm good, but did you need something Gus?"

It was a cheap shot to make fun of the fact that she was prepared and he wasn't, but a fun one, since it sailed over Gus's head. To her surprise, she saw Carol's gaze snap toward her boss. Interesting. The girl was sharp. Once again, she caught the barb on the comment when Gus didn't.

"Naw, I keep it all up here." He tapped his temple with a pomposity usually reserved for Hollywood's caricatured villains.

"I'm sure it's served you well, but I'd appreciate it, when you have time, if you'd write down some of your thoughts on the mechanics of the event," she prodded him. She needed to know what he knew, if she could get it. She'd come into events where the director or organizer had quit cold, leaving no paperwork, no direction, and often, no money. The mess was massive. No need to instigate that here.

"Of course, of course. Happy to help any way I can," he said heartily. It rang false, but surface agreement was better than nothing.

For another two hours, Gus rambled on about the event and the players. She took judicious notes. All of the meetings she'd had so far about the Walk had been productive and professional. Until this.

The more Gus talked, the more the gaps became apparent.

In fact, Swiss cheese had fewer holes, she decided

when she escaped to the ladies' room just before lunch. Mari freshened her lipstick, mentally girding herself for another session.

She needed to figure out why there were twelve bands paying fees and only nine on the program. Why there were eight paid tarot readers assigned to positions in the Faire, but only five showing as set, including those operating out of Lydia's Besom Shop tent. There were also four freight haulers, but two of them had been paid up front.

You never paid up front.

And the picketing organization, CAWW, had filed a specious lawsuit. Great.

"Oh, hey, Ms. Beecham?" Carol hurried over as Mari came out of the ladies' room, anxious to impart her news. "Mr. Gus had to leave. Something about one of his other businesses, you know, the No Colds Barred Urgent Care Centers? He has a couple, and the U-Store-It and the car wash too. Anyway, he said he'd meet you here tomorrow morning, nine sharp. Um, if that suits you, of course."

The last had been added for her benefit, Mari was sure. She'd lay odds Gus had said no such thing.

"Thank you Carol, and please, call me Mari. Save the Ms. Beecham for when the sponsors show up. Otherwise, we're working this together, right? You've got a lot to teach me, and I'm ready to learn."

Carol straightened, and her nervous hand twisting disappeared. "I thought you'd be mad," she blurted, then blushed. "That he left." She blushed even more. "And then he gave Ms. Geneva your office."

Mari made a snap decision, based on that look in the office. "Power play," she stated and watched Carol's eyes widen.

"Really?"

Mari just smiled, letting the young woman work it out. Gus wanted to give her a thimbleful of information, then deny her any more until *he* was ready to dole it out.

Damned if she'd let that stop her.

"Let's get some lunch," she suggested. They invited Geneva along, but she demurred, waving at two dusty boxes. "If I can get through these first two years today, I'll have made progress."

Still wide-eyed at being invited, Carol walked with her to the nearby deli. They came back to the office to eat. In that short hour, Mari got more information from a bubbling, enthusiastic Carol than she'd gotten in nearly three hours with Gus.

"Time for more meet-n-greet," Mari said when they finished. She slipped her purse out of her briefcase along with her car keys. "I'll be back before you leave at five. I'm going to stop at Lydia Webb's shop, then drive out to MicroMechanics to see the Walk's end point."

"I'll wait till you get back, then," Carol said with a smug look of her own, turning back to her desk, "before I lock up and all."

"Sounds good," Mari said. "I've got meetings in Boston tomorrow with Boston Chamber and with the Massachusetts Chamber of Commerce people. Their promotions committee is having a dinner, and they invited me."

Carol looked shocked. "They've never asked Mr. Gus to come to Boston."

"Gus didn't run an event at the Fogg Museum for four hundred of the country's top CEOs. I made some friends in Boston last time I was here."

"Wow." Carol's grin about split her face. "That is majorly awesome."

"Yeah, it was pretty cool. And on that happy note, I'll head out."

Mari turned to the door and ran right into the solid, sexy form of Peregrine Hestworth.

Visions of smoke, fire and blood assaulted him the minute Marisol Beecham's hands hit his chest. Off balance and obviously startled, Mari's attempt to back away warred with the forward motion of her pivot, leaving them both stumbling, and with her nearly helpless in his arms.

He smelled expensive perfume and lush, powerful woman. It reinforced the echo of the vision's smoky warning.

*What the hell?*

The hint of foresight passed as quickly as it had come, as they all did, leaving him breathless and hyperaware of the woman in his arms. She was a tidy package of femininity and force. His body's instant reaction to her shape and scent could be chalked up to recent celibacy, he was sure. Still, she was attractive with a wealth of dark hair and snapping dark eyes.

"I beg your pardon, Mr. Hestworth," she said, untangling herself and pushing away. It wasn't a shove, but it was a sure warning that she stood on her own two feet. She was fairly petite, and now that she'd backed away, he could see she'd emphasized her gorgeous legs with stylish heels and a slim skirt. He didn't know what the fashion was called, but it made the most of every curve

"No, I should be begging yours, Ms. Beecham," he replied, and enjoyed the confusion that washed over her mobile features. "I brought you these," he dangled a ring of keys, shiny and newly cut, between them.

"And these are?"

"Oh!" Carol, who had come to the door when she saw them collide, interrupted, pointing at the keys. "The office, the four temporary storage spaces over at the U-Store-it, the supply closet, and," she frowned and came forward to tap the last brass key on the rings, "what's this one? Is that to the big closet in Mr. Gus's office?"

"It is," Pere confirmed, resisting the urge to ruffle Carol's hair as he had when she was younger. She'd hate him for treating her like a kid, so he smiled, and nodded his approval. "Keen eye, Carol. Ms. Beecham, you had asked to look at all the financial records, as well as the list of vendors from the past couple of years. Has Gus gotten you those?"

"Yes and no. While I did see the modified version that was used for the Request for Proposal for the position as Walk director, I'd like to see the final you actually used." It surprised him that she turned to Carol with the explanation. "Looking at the financials will tell me where we can maximize profits, and looking at vendor lists can tell me who's come before that we might entice back."

He caught the undercurrent of excitement from Carol. Marisol Beecham had somehow managed to see what few others had, that Carol was brilliant, but it was overshadowed by her need to please and her nervous fear of doing the wrong thing. Pere had tried to hire her at MicroMechanics, thinking some of his staff could encourage her, but Carol had stubbornly clung to her position at the Walk office.

"Ah, that seems…logical." Carol said the last bit almost as a question.

"I think it will prove to be, if the records are good."

"I've asked Gus to be sure you have them before the end of the week." Pere approved her proposed methodology. "The records are a good place to start. How was your morning? Did you find everything you needed?"

Puzzled by the almost fearful look Carol shot Marisol's way, he frowned. "Office not to your liking?"

"The auditor is using the second office at this point. She's in there now with the first two years of the Walk's records. Is that the office you meant?" Marisol inquired with a tilt of her dark head. He could see something in her eyes, but whether it was temper or amusement, he couldn't tell. "I'll get the records when she's done."

"She's using your office?" he said, going around her to open the door to the office behind them after a brief knock.

Obviously her look had been suppressed temper, because his own temper flared in an instant at the sight of the box-filled room and the startled-looking woman who sat at the desk now covered with stacks of paper in manila file folders.

"Good afternoon," he said, modulating his irritation to a smile. No need to antagonize the woman just because he was pissed with Gus.

"Well hello," she said, with a surprised note in her voice. "You must be Mr. Hestworth."

They exchanged introductions and pleasantries, with her assessing him the whole time. Everyone expected him to be older, or weirder, given that he ran a gaming company. It irked him, but he let it pass. He'd had a full plate of that throughout his morning meetings regarding a buyout. He'd escaped as fast as he could, using the keys and the Walk as an excuse.

"I'll let you get back to it then, Geneva," he said, using the given name she'd encouraged him to use. "Thank you for being here."

"Of course, I'm happy to help," she said, smiling as she sat back down. She might be surprised at his age or his lack of gamer vibe, but she was serious about her own work. He was pretty sure she'd already forgotten his presence before the door shut.

"Damn it," he growled as he turned to the two women watching him. "Carol, where's Gus?"

"Uh, he's gone, Mr. Hestworth, had something at No Colds that needed his attention, he said."

"He left while I was in the ladies' room," Marisol added, that same tilt to her head, that same watching gaze. Now, he realized, she was waiting to see if he was on her side, or on Gus's team, since he hadn't voted for her.

"Idiot," he murmured, turning away from the door. He shot a look Carol's way. "Don't repeat that, Carol."

Mutely, she shook her head, shifting her nervous gaze from him to Marisol and back again.

"This is ridiculous." He tapped a finger on his chin, then stopped when he recognized the habit again, one he'd adopted from his father. A solution occurred to him, and he snapped his fingers, making Carol jump. "Perfect. Carol, get Truett Powers on the phone, please."

"The space next door?" Carol said, going on alert. He nodded, appreciating her quick jump to understanding what he'd decided on the spur of the moment.

"Exactly. Then, call Marcus." When Carol looked puzzled, he added, "Tell him he's got a job waiting over here, and to call me for confirmation."

Carol cocked her head to one side for a moment, an imitation of Marisol's waiting pose. It was such an obvious hero-worship move that he had to repress a grin. True to form, Carol got his plan within seconds.

"Oh," she said, glee echoing in her voice. "I get it. Mr. Powers to rent, Marcus to renovate. Should I call your main office or mobile?"

"Mobile. Thanks. Now," he said, turning to Marisol. "I heard you say you say you were headed out to MicroMechanics after visiting Lydia's place. Mind reversing the order? I'll get you back before Lydia closes."

"That would be fine." He could practically see her running possible scenarios in her mind. But all she said was, "Where is Mr. Powers' space?"

Before he answered, Carol piped up. "Over on that side, back of the conference room. It'll make a great office for you for now, and storage, and a second conference room, and then, uh, maybe for an assistant next year." The last bit came out in a rush and Pere caught a glimpse of Carol's ambition. Gus would never have considered an assistant, or given a thought to Carol as a candidate.

Interesting.

"Ah, I see," was all Mari Beecham allowed. He was pretty sure she did see, both the politics and Carol's hopes. He hoped Mari took his immediate action to solve the problem as him being on her side.

He was. Sort of.

"Shall we?" He indicated the door. She hesitated only a moment longer, then took the keys he still held out as she walked past him out the door. The keys were in her purse before he hit the sidewalk and she said nothing more about them. "We'll take my car, if that's all right. I know you got a good sense of the town when you were here before." At her surprised look, he added, "You were very knowledgeable in your presentation. It was obvious you'd driven the streets, assessed the neighborhoods, the business district, everything that might impact both the community and the Walk."

"Thank you." She didn't say anything until he'd started the sleek Mercedes Benz and left the parking lot. "So let's get this out of the way. Why were you against my coming here, taking the director's position?"

He hadn't seen that coming, so he shot one back across the bow.

"Do you believe in witchcraft, Ms. Beecham, or is it all hokum and show for the gullible to you?"

"I believe that there are more things going on in this world than science can account for, to paraphrase the Bard." She smiled at him. "Mr. Hestworth, I grew up all over the world, exposed to every kind of religion and culture, thanks to my father being in the navy. Everyone's beliefs should be respected, and I believe that faith, no matter what name you attach to it, can work literal miracles." She paused, waiting for his reaction, but he said nothing, just let the silence stretch out waiting for her to continue. So she did. "I've not seen witches or witchcraft in action, so to speak, but I guess you'd say I'm inclined to believe. My belief, or lack of it, however, isn't germane to my ability to make this event even more of a success."

"An honest answer," he said, his eyes still on the road, but the tension in his jaw eased a little. "What do you think of our current event director?"

"Gus?" she said, and she seemed surprised. He hadn't

planned to ask that, exactly. Probably shouldn't be doing it. However, Mari Beecham had figured Carol out in record time. Maybe she could help him figure out what Gus was up to, because he was certainly up to something.

"Yes, Gus," he smiled. "Despite this morning's obvious snub, he's devoted to the event. Do you think he's gotten the Witches Walk to a good place, a place where he can hand it off to you? He's obviously reluctant to part with keys or office space."

"The event is very successful, so it's hard to fault anything that's happened to date," she said primly.

"But you think you can make it better." He made it a statement, not a question. "Why?"

"My presentation," she began, but he cut her off.

"Yes, it was thorough and strong. Obviously, you got the job. I want to hear why you *took* the job and why you think this opportunity was better than the position you turned down in Nashville. What do you see in the Witches Walk that you didn't see in their event?"

Mari forcibly kept her mouth from dropping open. How had he known about Nashville? "I'm not sure where you get your information," she said, frowning. "That post wasn't as interesting as this one."

She kept her voice firm. She wouldn't be baited, or let anything slip. Giving anyone information—from her first blush opinion to why she took the job—always got her in trouble. Besides, if she couldn't explain it to her best friend, she sure couldn't tell Peregrine Hestworth. Nor had he given any indication of where he stood on her being hired, so why should she be the one to give? He seemed too arrogant and aloof to be anyone's confidante. As the brand new executive director of the Witches Walk, she couldn't afford to make an enemy out of him either.

And she had to figure out how to get past her visceral reaction to him. The man had some serious animal magnetism. A feminine part of her kept wondering if his lips tasted as good as they looked, and that was just *so* wrong.

"That's a politically correct answer. What interested you about this that the other couldn't provide?" he persisted.

"Pretty much everything," she admitted, since he wasn't going to let it go, and it was better to talk about business and corral her wandering hormones around Pere Hestworth. "The Nashville event was musically based, as you can imagine, and pretty typical. This, however, is anything but typical."

"You can say that again," Pere muttered. He smiled then, and the brilliance and warmth of it hit her in the gut, and warmed her all the way to her toes. "It's pretty insane."

"Nothing like it," she managed, feeling the visceral effect of his smile. "From the concept of following in the footsteps of refugee witches, to the Faire with its herbalists, crystal sellers, Tarot readers, games, amusements, classes with real witches, to the whole town coming together to make it work. That alone, the sheer commitment of the town, is unique. So the learning experience, the option of doing something new and stretching my skills, was a tremendous draw. I've also never been to this part of the country, which appealed to my wandering feet."

"Do you claim a bit of the Romany in your family?"

"That's gypsies, right?" she clarified and continued when he nodded. "And no, not literally. I'm a military brat, as I said," she explained, frowning a bit at the way he'd phrased it. It seemed like the umpteenth time she'd explained. "Although when some of the members of the main Haven Harbor coven came to the house yesterday, I discovered I had some family I didn't know. Both my grandparents are originally from this part of the country. According to Dolores Webb, and her niece Lydia, I have relatives around here."

"Oh, really," he drawled, flicking a glance her way.

"And who might that be?"

She wasn't sure if he meant who told her or if he was asking to whom she was related, so she answered both questions. "Mrs. Webb informs me that I have Hachette cousins around here, from my mother's side."

Pere swerved a little as he tried to both drive and look at her at the same time. "Hachette? Your family's Hachette?" he demanded, as if she hadn't just said that.

"Odd, isn't it?" she asked, trying to not be alarmed by the sudden sense of cold hostility. "I always think of my grandparents as being from Colorado, not Massachusetts. They didn't have the accent, you know? They just sounded like...my grandparents."

"Why didn't you let the council know?" Pere ground out the words. He was angry now, but she had no clue as to why. "It might have made a difference."

"I wouldn't have used any family connection as a basis for my proposal," she answered trying to keep the disdain from her voice. She wasn't sure exactly what he was implying, but she didn't like it. "And, as I said, Mrs. Webb and Mrs. Birkland came by to bless the house, I didn't remember it." Anger prickled along her nerves. What the hell was he so pissy about? She could usually leash her temper, but his attitude made it slip a little. "The picketers were there too. Should I have let them know that I had newly discovered roots in town? Do you think they would have stopped picketing? Or perhaps they'd have grabbed a pitchfork and run me out of town even faster?"

"You had picketers?" Now he was astonished. It was all she could do not to roll her eyes. For a man who was the leader of the town council and a supposed witch, he obviously didn't know much about the gossip in Haven Harbor. To hear Lydia tell it, the fact that she was a near-local had made the gossip rounds in two days.

"Picketers and witches, a fine welcoming committee," she said, with some sarcasm. "It's a first for me, actually."

In a surprising move, he reached over, his hand closing

unerringly over hers to give a slight squeeze. All of her resolve about keeping any salacious thoughts of him flew right out of her head. She went hot at the touch. "I'm sorry about the picketers. I didn't think they'd do that."

Nonplussed, she looked down at his hand. How could he be so hot? It was August, sure, but the temperature was in the low eighties with a breeze. As easily as he'd reached out, he slid his hand away.

"I'm not afraid of picketers," she snapped, struggling to order her thoughts and stay on topic.

The look he gave her sizzled with his own temper, and something else too. Something darker. Hotter.

"What about the witches?"

####

"It's a disgrace," Calvin muttered, as he fired off email after email, hoping to build support for his God-given mission in Haven Harbor. Somehow, this enclave of witchcraft, this wormhole to the very gates of Hell, must be nullified. No one seemed to realize that these people, these seemingly innocent witches were spawns of Satan. Their normalcy was a lie, they were heathen demons and he knew what he had to do.

He'd been initiated in secret, given his mission.

That he had grown up among them just magnified the sin.

"To kill the snake, you cut off its head," he muttered.

A part of him remembered when he didn't feel that way, when he'd felt comfortable with Haven Harbor and its residents.

The latest addition to the legion was the new woman, the one who had come to use her wicked ways to bring yet more power and funding to promote evil. She was going to help the witches spread the taint by making the Witches Walk a national event. She had to go. She was duped, but powerful, and she would lead too many astray.

She had to die to this terrible existence, be reborn in the knowledge of righteousness.

"Calvin, why are you still here, so late?" Pastor Leroy Walthers, the senior pastor, and a man stooped with grief and old age, stepped into Calvin's office, clutching an umbrella and his worn Bible.

"I'd ask the same of you, Brother Walthers. Here, come sit." Calvin cleared a pile of papers off the chair. "I'm just scheduling some Walk efforts."

"More picketing? You haven't given that up?"

"No," Calvin said firmly, then more meekly, "Do you want me to?" Walthers was, after all, his senior.

"Not if you feel called to it," Leroy said, laying the Bible on the desk as he made himself more comfortable. "But these late nights, Calvin, they'll steal your health. You need your rest. After all," he said with a grimace, "you're taking the hospital pastoral care efforts because you said I needed to rest. I'll thank you to take your own medicine."

Calvin returned the old man's smile, appreciating the fatherly chiding. He was right, of course. Brother Walthers was a wise man. And a strong one. Even in his grief for his late wife, he'd kept to the pulpit, led the flock. He'd helped Calvin secure the post.

Calvin's initiation into the real mysteries had taken him in a different way, however, but that wasn't Brother Walthers fault. Citizens Against the Witches Walk— CAWW—was, despite its unfortunate acronym, fully invested in shutting down the event and making sure that the town returned to a more stable and godly path.

"Of course, Brother Walthers. I'll go now. In fact, if you don't mind waiting, we can walk out together."

"What about a bit of dinner?" the older man said, gathering his things as Calvin shut down his laptop and put it in his briefcase. "Unless you've got a date?"

"No." Calvin smiled. "I have a CAWW meeting tonight, but no date, so we bachelor types should stick together, get dinner. The meeting's not till eight."

Brother Walthers and he had had this same type of

conversation at least two nights every week since Calvin had arrived. After each boring dinner, however, Walthers relinquished more of the duties of the pastorate to him, so Calvin decided they were well worth his time. Hospital ministry was incredibly rewarding, even if it was attending a death. Maybe especially then, as you knew you'd been a part of sending a good Christian to his or her just reward.

Calvin slipped his own Bible into his briefcase as well, patting its well-worn cover and thinking how well it served him, even now.

## CHAPTER FOUR

"This is MicroMechanics," Peregrine said, changing the subject briskly. Mari wondered what was going on with him. He'd seemed to thaw toward her, until he found out she had local relatives. Really, what the hell? Like she'd known and planned to keep it from him?

She forced her temper back into its box. Whatever he was thinking, it wasn't her problem. She had a contract and an event to learn. If she had to work with Peregrine Hestworth, she'd work with him. Obviously he had some issue with her that he wasn't willing to tell her about. First Gus, now him. If she hadn't liked the idea of the Witches Walk so much...

"The field, there." She pointed. "That's where the Walk ends, correct?" She'd driven by it, but hadn't wanted to go through the secured gates to walk it.

"Yes. It's where we have tents for all the walkers to sleep, aid stations, restrooms and showers, and so on. There are regular shuttles between here and the town center and the Faire field next to the high school."

"Did you buy this parcel for expansion?" she asked, noting that the parking lot around the ugly, industrial-looking building was full and some cars were parked on the grass in "creative" spaces. That meant he had more workforce than the building was originally designed to hold. That meant it was growing. Good. Strong businesses meant a strong event.

"Yes," he said, shooting her a thoughtful look. "But now it's become vital to the success of the Walk, so I won't be using it for that. I've purchased that parcel," he added, pointing to a heavily wooded lot behind the building. "Its seven acres, so it'll be easy to build that way, add parking as we grow."

"Too bad about the trees," she murmured, thinking how it would be sad to see all that lush vegetation—dark green leaves fluttering in the late summer breeze—cut down.

"The plan is to keep as much as possible," he said, sounding defensive. She kept her face bland, but it took effort not to smile. She'd hit a nerve, evidently.

"That's good. The parcel across the street?"

"Part of an estate, but I've put in a bid," he said.

They pulled into the sole empty space in the lot, marked with his name and a reserved sign. "You've met our company team, those in charge of our part of the Walk. They'll join us on the roof and you can get a bird's eye view of the event ground."

"Great." She didn't wait for him to open her door, though he appeared to be coming to do just that. She met him on the sidewalk and they headed into the building, under a colorful banner which read *Welcome Halliday Enterprises Team*.

When she looked at the sign, he nodded. "A company we're buying out. We finalized the deal this morning. We'll double the workforce with this acquisition."

"That's amazing," she said, genuinely delighted for him. His success meant success for the town and the Walk, so it was good for her too.

He held the door there and stepping in, she got another surprise. The interior was as different from the exterior as chalk to cheese. Where the outside had a blank, almost foreboding, industrial aesthetic despite the cheery banner, the interior was light-filled, with trees in big pots, greenery and a fountain in the small lobby. Comfortable seating and a reception desk took up the rest of the tidy space.

"We don't get much walk-in," Pere said, waving at the receptionist, then introduced Mari to the young man. "We took every scrap of space for offices."

"You're growing, significantly," Mari said as they moved through another set of doors, interested to see how he answered. MicroMechanics was a privately held company, but if the news stories and the parking lot were to be believed, inventing new games had it going gangbusters.

"Too fast," he said, giving her another of those appraising looks. The hostility still simmered under the surface, but he was making an effort. "We've doubled in the last five years and finalized a buyout of Halliday Gaming Inc. this morning. If I could figure out where to put people, I'd double my employment base in Haven Harbor. As it is, a few will come here, some will stay in Boston, and I'll figure out a space in the middle for now."

Mari tucked that away as they wound their way through the building. Pere was hailed as they passed, giving Mari the impression of a warm, friendly work environment. That was still evident as they met the team leaders for MicroMechanics on the roof.

"Great to see you, Mari," Jennifer, one of the team leaders, said with a smile. "I'm really excited about what you bring to the Witches Walk."

"Gus and the volunteers have done a great job," Curren, the other team leader added, diplomatically. "And I know it's been their work that's let us bring you in. As I said when we met last week, I really look forward to your ideas and how the Walk grows."

"Thank you," Mari said warmly. "I'll do my best to build on the great foundations that have been laid."

"We have a security team during the Walk," Pere said, his hand resting lightly at the small of her back as they all moved across the roof. "If it's as hot as it is this week, we set up canopies too. The pathways laid out on the roof are reinforced, but I can't guarantee the rest of the area."

Obvious pavers led in a square around the edge of the building's roof with a crisscross path of tiles from the central stair tower to the corners. At the edge of the roof, Mari shaded her eyes so she could see the field beyond. The grass was neatly cut and several areas were covered with large graveled rectangles.

"The graveled areas are where the bathrooms are set up. We get the large, corporate-style mobile bathrooms. The walkers are doing this for charity, so they deserve the best," Curran said.

"Pere and MicroMechanics sponsor those, at no cost to the Walk," Jennifer added.

"Excellent plan. And thank you," she said to Pere, knowing that the expense for those was significant.

"Of course." The haughty, suspicious tone was back.

Jennifer and Curran walked the roof with them, giving more details and she could easily see how much the company was committed to the Walk. They excused themselves after ten minutes, leaving her alone with Pere.

"So, have seen what you need to see?" He was still acting like the remote king-of-the-ice-mountain, like he had in the car. It was incredibly annoying. She huffed out a breath. Did she confront this now, or let it lie?

Before she could decide, his cell phone rang and he excused himself to answer it.

"Yes? Excellent," he said, smiling at her. There was a wicked, darkly amused glint in his eye. It changed his dark, brooding looks to something out of GQ. "I'll authorize it as part of the council's expenses for the Walk. Tell him to get started right away." When he'd hung up, he turned back to her, a satisfied expression on his patrician features.

"The office?"

"Tomorrow afternoon, or the next morning at the latest, you'll have additional space and furniture. I'll sign the paperwork when I drop you off, if it's ready. If it's not, I'll go in when it is."

"Handshake and a phone call," she murmured, nodding. Small towns did business that way. Stuff got done. Committees were great, but sometimes the "who you know" of a small town really worked well, and in this case, in her favor.

"Of course," Pere said, looking at her quizzically. "We know one another."

"Yes. My last event in Las Vegas was the size of Coachella or one of the AmberWorld events. Lots and lots of important committees, celebrity sized tantrums, and paperwork by the truckload." It had also featured a married promoter who had refused to take "no" for an answer. After the last incident with him, she'd pressed charges. The event organizers and sponsors took it seriously, but in the end, she'd essentially been paid to leave town.

She never wanted to work in Vegas again.

"You like a more streamlined working process?" he asked, his tone neutral. She shook off the memories and answered.

"When it works," she said with a smile. There were times when it did and times when it didn't. She was still thinking Gus might make sure that, for her, it didn't.

"Don't worry about Gus," he said, shocking her into staring. He laughed, the ice fading. "Not witchcraft or mind reading, I assure you. Just that I know Gus, and he's always being obstructive."

"Yes," she kept her voice neutral. She wasn't sure about the witchcraft, but he'd read her mind pretty accurately. She'd need to be very careful with Pere

Hestworth. He saw too much, and was too volatile for her peace of mind. Hell, he was too attractive for her peace of mind.

Pere sighed as they moved back across the roof. "Gus is too fond of the power of it. He'll be relieved when it's no longer his responsibility, though. It gave him ulcers two years ago, and he broke his leg during the event three years ago, which hurt all his businesses. He agreed it was time to pass the baton, which is why we began our search."

Interesting. "Events can be stressful on all concerned, even when they're exceptionally successful. Maybe even more so when they're successful. Running a volunteer event can make you nuts."

"Perhaps that's it. I believe Gus will be easier to manage when this year's event is over and he's stepped back into his businesses with more freedom."

"I'm sure you're right," she offered diplomatically. She didn't believe it, but she'd worked with worse, and still managed to turn out a brilliant event. This would be no exception.

She asked him questions all throughout the return to the office, but all were event related and nothing personal. Part of her mind was still working on the issue of his expansion. She liked to solve problems, and solving Pere's space issues would benefit the Walk.

"Every company in town supports the Walk, Faire and the gala, of course," he said in answer to one of her questions. "MicroMechanics just happens to be one of the biggest sponsors due to our size."

"Of course. Who's the next largest sponsor?"

"Maginot Properties, the boutique lodging company that owns Haven Harbor Inn, where the end-of-walk gala is held. After that, Aspen Aire Handling Systems, a growing HVAC/plumbing contractor based in Mouldon, the second overnighting town on the Walk. We picked up another large sponsorship from Harris-Perkins

Pharmaceuticals last year. They located a small biotech production facility in Pennyfield, the first town where the Walkers stay the night."

"Yes, that's an excellent sponsor. Who managed to corral them?"

Now his grin was genuine. "Carol and Lydia Webb pulled that one off." He slanted a glance her way. "But Gus got the credit."

"Hmmm."

If Carol could do that sort of thing, her not-so-subtle angling for becoming an assistant Walk director wasn't that far-fetched.

Mari jumped when her phone rang. "Excuse me," she said to Pere, and took the call. "Mari Beecham, how may I help you?"

"Hi Mari, its Kevin, Kevin Torsk."

"Yes, hello, Kevin." She was supremely conscious of Pere listening to every word.

"Are we still on for Thursday? I made reservations for seven at the Judge's Chambers. Does that suit you?"

"That would be lovely, thank you. I'll see you there."

"I'm very much looking forward to it," he said warmly. "I sense you're either in a meeting or with someone, so I'll let you go. But thanks for agreeing to dinner."

"I appreciate your understanding," she said, answering his question about being with someone even as she meant the words. "And I'll see you Thursday."

"Great. See you then."

She ended the call and slipped her phone back into her purse. Pere shot her a suspicious look, but said nothing. He was back to his remote, artic, self.

He pulled up in front of the Walk office, letting the powerful car idle at the curb. "Thank you for coming out to MicroMechanics. I'll look forward to any improvements in our Walk process you may suggest."

"Really?" The word was out of her mouth, and in a decidedly skeptical tone, before she censored it.

"Really," he said, curtly. "Have a good afternoon, Ms. Beecham."

Well, that was a dismissal.

She inclined her head. "You as well, Mr. Hestworth. Thank you in advance for my new office. I'm grateful."

He looked surprised, but she was out of the car before he could speak.

She walked into chaos. Carol was grinning like a loon and the sound of hammering, and a sudden blistering curse, floated out of the conference room.

"Already?"

"People jump when Pere says *Go!*" she said, then looked stricken at being so baldly honest.

Mari laughed. "I guess so." She peeked into the room and quickly ducked back out. There was plastic over the far end of the long conference table and more billowing plastic taped to the ceiling. Through it, she could see two men working. They had already opened up the wall and were wheeling debris out through the other room. "Did that room used to be part of this set of offices?"

Carol nodded, explaining, "Few years before the Walk started, this was a law office. They didn't want to pay for all the space, or sublet it or whatever. The former owner was a real New England skinflint. He walled it off 'cause the lawyers were using the space and not paying for it. He cut a door at the street and rented the whole long kinda shovel-shaped space to some guy who had a multi-level marketing business."

"It didn't work out?"

"Oh, no, it did great. He outgrew the office real quick and moved to Boston. Now there it's sat for eight years, empty. Mr. Powers inherited it three or four years ago, but he's so busy he hasn't worried with it much. It's too small for retail, and no room to expand, so most people aren't interested in it." Carol poked her head around the corner to look. "They're going to open the whole space. Cool."

"Hey, Carol!" came a muffled call from behind the

plastic.

"Yeah?"

"There's some boxes in here. You wanna look at them? They got Gus's name on 'em."

Carol's pretty features slid into a worried frown. "Wonder how that happened?"

"Carol?" A lanky, lean man with tanned, surfer-dude kind of look ducked under the edge of the taped plastic. "Hey, somebody cut the drywall into the back of the closet in Gus's office. There's some boxes stacked back here in this part, from that closet. Pretty dusty now. We didn't know it was there so we didn't put up plastic up when we started cutting this door in and takin' down that temp wall."

"Uh, that's okay. I'll let Mr. Gus know. Just put some plastic over them now, I guess?"

"Okay." The lanky man turned to Mari, held out a hand. "Marcus Jenkinson. Builder, and at the moment, handyman."

"Mari Beecham," she said, liking his no-nonsense handshake.

"Pleased to meet you." Then he nodded and ducked back behind the plastic.

Carol was wringing her hands again. "He's gonna be mad. He's gonna be really, really mad."

"I'm betting Gus doesn't like it when Mr. Hestworth orders a change."

Carol focused on her, and the change of subject, pausing in her hand-wringing. "Oh, no, he really doesn't. They get along, but, um..."

"You know, if you called Gus and let him know that the boxes were covered so they didn't get damaged, you know your call will go to voicemail, right?" When the young woman nodded, Mari smiled. Gus would never answer a call from a subordinate, even if it might be important. "Then he'd know about all this. You're covered because Mr. Hestworth okayed it, and you're covering Gus because whatever he stashed is being protected. Leave him a message. I'll get out of here, and so can you, right?" It was nearly four-thirty, and Carol had said she'd leave at five. Mari had keys now, so she could leave her things here and go see Lydia, then come back and take a look at whatever Geneva had finished. "Then he can come back and deal with it without either of us being here to shout at."

Looking relieved beyond all measure, Carol nodded like a bobblehead doll. "That's right. That's great. Thanks. I'll do that. And," she grabbed her sweater and picked up her purse. "I'll do it as I go to my car."

"Great. I'll get my things and we'll walk out together." Mari went toward the conference room where she'd left her briefcase. "Wait." Mari stopped in the middle of the room. "What about the auditor? Is Geneva still here?"

"Oh, no, she left about twenty minutes ago. Said she wanted to check into her hotel room and all that. Said she'd be back in the morning. She got through year one already."

"That's great! If you see her before I do, have her put that year in the conference room. I can look at it in the morning now that she's done with it." Year one wouldn't tell her much about what Gus was up to, as he hadn't been director back then, but she still needed the facts of how the Walk got it's start. "Ready to go, then?"

"Yeah." Carol seemed to bounce back to her usual ebullient self. "That's great then, on you being able to see the year one stuff. Would you, um, tell me if there's anything you learn from it?"

"Of course," Mari said, smiling. "We're in this together."

Carol lit up like the sun. "Okay, that's great. I'll call Mr. Gus from the car," she blurted. "I'm ready to go." She snatched her things up and almost ran to the conference room door. "Hey Marcus, you and Jeremy can go out the other way, right? Lock that up? I'm gonna go."

"Sure." Another shouted reply accompanied by the sound of something heavy hitting the floor. "Shit. Didn't know that was there." A pause. "Hey Carol, does Hestworth want this painted?"

Carol turned to Mari, panic in her eyes. Mari answered, raising her voice so the contractor could hear her. "Yes, Duricon Paint number 4439." She loved that color, and if she got the chance, every office she had, she painted it the warm, toasty cream.

There was a full minute of silence, then, "Great. I'll have it done late tomorrow."

"Thank you," Mari called out.

"No problem. We didn't have anything else right now 'cept Walk stuff."

Carol grinned at her, and they locked up, leaving by the staff door, with Mari using her new keys to lock up behind them.

"See you tomorrow," Mari returned the grin.

Carol waved and put the phone to her ear. Mari pulled her briefcase over her shoulder, then turned the other way, walking down toward Lydia's store, The Besom Shop.

"Hey! You came by," Lydia said, hurrying to give Mari a hug before she'd barely gotten in the door. "This is great. Let's put your stuff back here so I can show you around."

Mari grinned at her enthusiasm. It had been a long time—college really—since she'd hit it off so quickly with someone. It was a great feeling to have a new friend.

"I'm looking forward to it."

"Super." Lydia put Mari's things behind the counter. "Oh, and I have that book for you. Don't let me forget to give it to you."

"Okay." Book? What book...Mari remembered Lydia had promised a book on witchcraft, magick, the town's history, and as she'd put it, *how all this woo-woo stuff works.*

"It's been busy today," Lydia said, coming out from behind the counter. "I've got to straighten stock, do you mind if we talk while I do it?"

"Not at all." Mari was content to listen, and Lydia's chatter was full of information she needed.

"We always have a big rush at the end of summer, especially at Lughnasadh." Mari's poker face failed her for once, because Lydia laughed and said, "That would be August first, the first of the big harvest festivals. They call it Lammas Night in England."

"Oh, I remember that," Mari said, relieved to have a connection. "Dad was stationed in England for a couple of years, and the church we attended had Lammastide blessings for the crops and farmers. I never really understood it, but it was fun."

"Always is," Lydia said cheerfully. "It's a harvest festival, blessing of the first fruits. Anyway, we get a rush around then, but that's calmed down now, mostly." She frowned a little. "From here though, we're on a steady build-up to the Walk. In the next two weeks I've got to get inventory ramped up, then it's full-out-crazy through the Faire, the Walk and the Gala. We all collapse in a heap for a couple of weeks, then it's Samhain—" Mari must have looked blank again because Lydia's rich, bawdy laugh rang out again. "Halloween, including full on Trick-or-Treat, a fabulous Witches Ball and a huge, town come-together, kumbyah-kind-of-month in October."

"Really?" Mari laughed with her. "That sounds great. I'm betting it's a fun time around here."

"It is indeed," Lydia said with a huge grin. "Everything's decorated, even more than at Yule. Everyone has decorations at Halloween. Even the non-witches get into it. At least, most do." A little frown there, which gave Mari the opening to ask a question.

"I'm guessing the ones who picketed me do the 'fun at church' instead of trick-or-treat?"

Lydia rolled her eyes. "Yeah, some of them. You'd think they hadn't lived in Haven Harbor their whole lives. If you don't like it, live somewhere else, I say."

"Jobs prohibit that, sometimes."

"Yeah, I know. But most people are like my mom, who just couldn't get next to the whole witchcraft thing, they move on, move out, find a place where they fit." She shrugged. "Mom was way happier that way. I'm not sure why people don't want to be happier. But hey." Another shrug and a return of the grin. "Their loss."

"So true. So what are these lovely things for?"

"Oh, those are dowsing crystals. They're used for finding things."

"They're like little plumb-bobs," Mari said, remembering her father using something like that to set straight lines. "Like you'd use in construction."

"Oh, yeah. Exactly."

"Very cool. So many colors and shapes." Mari kept looking at one that was a warm brown and gold stone, labeled tigers eye. It was paired with a glorious swirl of copper wire and yellow crystals. "That one's beautiful," she finally said.

"Oh, you like it?" Lydia's happy demeanor sharpened to interest. "It draws you?"

"Draws me?"

"You like it better than the other ones in the case? Your eye keeps coming back to it?"

Not willing to ascribe anything odd to it, Mari shrugged. "I guess. Those are some of my favorite colors. The stone seems very warm and inviting."

"Here, hold it in your hand." She laid the stone in Mari's palm and, to Mari, it actually did feel warm. "Do you feel warmth from it?"

A little startled, Mari nodded. "Yes, how did you know?"

"I'm a witch, remember?" Lydia said, with a sassy grin.

"Right," Mari drawled, realizing Lydia was teasing about all the witchy warmth and stones and such.

"No, keep it," Lydia said when Mari handed it back. "If it called to you that strongly, it's meant to be yours."

When Mari started to protest, Lydia added, "Consider it a housewarming present, then. And a thank you for coming to town and all that." Again she rolled her expressive brown eyes. "So great to have another single woman around my age that I didn't grow up with, who doesn't remember my every crazy stunt from the summers I was here."

"But you already gave me the broom," Mari began, gesturing toward the full wall display of brooms of every shape and size, from tiny ones on keychains to full-sized, house and yard brooms.

"Yeah, that was from the shop, so to speak. This is from me."

Moved by her generosity, but grateful for the distraction to another, less emotional topic than being single and in the dating market, Mari laughed. "Yeah, that sense of belonging has a price too."

"Exactly. Like that one really bad haircolor choice. They never let you forget it."

"Oh, Lord, yes. Once, when we were back in Hawaii, I dyed my hair blonde. I wanted to look like my mom, and like all the California beach bunnies who came to the island."

"Disaster?" Lydia asked, eyeing Mari's thick, dark hair.

"Totally. My hair went this odd greenish bronzy shade. It would have been great for Halloween," Mari said, remembering her embarrassment. "But not for my proposed summer job at a law office."

"Oh, crap," Lydia sympathized.

"Yeah, but it turned out all right," Mari said, remembering with a smile. "The lawyers let me go, so I ended up working for this guy who booked summer acts for a theatre that catered to the tourists. It was my first job working with events. So maybe the hair thing was meant to be."

"Probably so."

They continued to move around the shop as they

talked, with Lydia straightening stock and Mari asking questions, until a little chime broke off the conversation.

"Oh, hello Mrs. Hestworth," Lydia said with a huge smile. "Great to see you. Have you met Mari Beecham, the new executive director of the Witches Walk?"

Mari found herself face to face with Pere Hestworth's mother.

The elegant, silver-haired woman was smaller than Mari would have imagined, given Pere's impressive height. She was taller than Mari, but not by much. She was very trim, and looked sharp in a gorgeous, light blue linen blazer over white pants and shirt. The blue lit up her lovely blue eyes, which were sparkling with interest.

"How lovely to meet you, Ms. Beecham. We're all excited to see what you do with the Walk in the coming year."

"Thank you for the welcome, Mrs. Hestworth. I'm happy to be here and to get started."

The older woman nodded and asked after Lydia's aunt, and then said, "Are you settling into your house all right, Ms. Beecham? I wasn't able to come to the blessing the other day. I'm so sorry to have missed meeting you then."

A witch. This elegant little lady, like the formidable Lucille Birkland, was a witch. That was just freaky.

"Thank you." Mari managed to keep her composure and smoothly segue into another topic. "Carol tells me you're in charge of the Walk gala that wraps up the event. I hope we can have coffee or lunch sometime soon and you can fill me in on how you and your team make that such a sought-after ticket."

Pere's mother glowed with sudden enthusiasm. "Oh, that would be lovely. I'm always happy to talk about the Gala, aren't I, Lydia?" She crinkled a mischievous smile toward Lydia. "I drive them all insane," she said behind her hand, her tone conspiratorial. "By the time the Gala's over, they all hate me."

"We do not," Lydia defended. "We all know you make

it the biggest, most elegant, and most happening event in town, bar none. You slave driver, you."

The last was said with a dramatic hand flung to Lydia's brow, then a genuinely affectionate laugh as she hugged the older woman. "I swear, Mari, a five-star general has nothing on Mrs. Hestworth when it comes to the Gala."

A gleam of pride lit the older woman's blue eyes. "Why thank you, Lydia. I like to think even a general would feel right at home. In fact, dress whites would look wonderful at the Gala. Hmmm, maybe I'll see if the Coast Guard chorus wants to perform next year."

She hunted in her neat leather handbag, pulling out a notebook and pen. "Have to write everything down these days. Let's see," she flipped a page covered in neat writing. "Coast Guard band/chorus?" She made it a question, just as she added a question mark in her notes.

"Never know where inspiration may strike," Mari said, delighted in the older woman's dedication and interest. She'd heard about the Gala before she'd heard about the Walk. It was indeed one of the most sought-after invitations in New England. The Halloween Ball wasn't as open to the public, and kept mostly to townsfolk and invited guests, she'd learned, so tickets to the public Gala at the end of the Walk were sought after.

"Exactly," Mrs. Hestworth pointed the silver pen at Mari in emphasis as she slipped the notebook back into her bag. "That's the spirit. Now, I need to get several things from young Lydia here, and then I'll be off and let you two enjoy your time together."

She turned to pick up several candles and tidily arranged them on the counter by the cash register. "Lydia, I need some of your soothing bath salts, the special ones."

"Coming right up." Lydia stepped through a curtain and was back within a moment with a lovely apothecary jar which had a small scoop tied to it with pretty, colored twine. "Here you are. And that'll be $44.50."

They made the transaction and Mrs. Hestworth picked

up the pretty package Lydia had put together with tissue and her brightly colored bags with the shop's name on it.

"Now, you call me tomorrow, Ms. Beecham," she said, handing Mari a crisp square of paper which had her name and a number on it. "We'll set up that lunch and talk about the Gala."

"Thank you, ma'am."

A tinkling laugh, and a flash of something in her eyes—speculation?—and Pere's mother swept out of the store.

"Is she like a force of nature, or what?" Mari said, fingering the card as she watched Mrs. Hestworth walk down the street in the late afternoon light.

"How did you know?" Lydia said, a strange note in her voice.

Mari turned, surprised. "Know what?"

"She's a weather witch."

"Oh," Mari frowned, wondering what prompted the question. "Oh, I didn't mean anything. Just a turn of phrase. She's a strong personality. You sure wouldn't mistake her as being anything but a prominent citizen, would you?"

Lydia nodded, but looked unconvinced.

Mari had to laugh. "Seriously, Lydia," she said, dropping her voice to the lower ranges to say, "I have no hidden, unbidden talents." As Lydia laughed, she added, "I just think she's a strong personality."

Lydia smiled, but despite the banter, she didn't seem entirely convinced. "She is, but thankfully, she uses her powers for good."

"I'm glad to know it. She'd make a serious opponent."

The door chime sounded again and a harried looking woman bustled in. "Hey, Lydia. Oh, you're with a customer," she said, as if seeing Mari all of a sudden.

"It's okay, Sharon. This is Mari Beecham, the new Walk director." Sharon shook her hand briskly, and turned back to Lydia when she asked, "What can I do for you?"

The woman's face blushed pink under her warm tanned skin. "I need a charm for the charter boat. Madame Sabina's out of town. Do you think your aunt would have time?"

"Of course. When do you need it?"

"Any chance I can pick it up in the morning?"

"Sure. For the lobster traps again, or the fishing lines?"

"Lines. We've got important clients, so I'd love it if they could catch something good, make their trip as fun as they're hoping for."

"Got it. You pick the waters, the charm will call the fish. See you in the morning."

"Usual price?"

"Usual price."

The other woman gave Mari a friendly wave and hurried on her way, obviously thinking of a million different things.

"Charm?"

"Charter fishing. Sharon has a company that works out of Haven Harbor. Her business is growing and fishing's good, but you know," she paused. "Or maybe you don't. Charters sometimes go out and never catch a thing. It's the facts of fishing, but for a charter company, that can be disaster. There are always fish that are ready to be food," she continued. "It's just having them be in the right place at the right time. Aunty D's charms helps that along."

"She pays you for it," Mari said, wondering how that worked.

Lydia smiled. "Of course. She's not feeding us with the fish she's catching, and she's using Aunty D's magick to improve her business. So, yes, she pays for the charm. Madame Sabina likes to be paid in fish, so she often goes there first. Aunty D doesn't really eat fish."

"Okay." Mari thought about it for a minute. "That makes sense, except not liking fish." She grinned and Lydia returned it. "Thank you for helping me navigate this, Lydia."

Lydia moved forward and gave her a spontaneous hug. "Totally. Hey, I had my aunt here when it was all new to me. Least I can do is pass that on."

"Thanks."

"Hey, want to get a beer at the Judge's Chambers?" Lydia said as she turned the CLOSED sign on the door. "I'm done for the day and could use one."

"Sure, I can't stay long, though. I'll need to get home and let Pepper out."

"Cool. I can't stay long either. Working on more product tonight."

Mari decided their timing sucked when they managed to walk into the restaurant, situated in an architecturally amazing old house, right behind Pere Hestworth and a date. She wasn't ready to run into him again, after their chilly parting earlier in the afternoon. It was even more awkward as his date looked at Mari and Lydia like they were dirt on her shoes. The woman was dressed to kill in siren red, her sparkling black stilettos betraying their expense with their red soles.

When Pere greeted them both, and introduced the woman as Lissa Halliday, of Halliday Gaming, the company he'd bought out, the woman's glare went from dagger glances to murderous dismissal of a mere Walk director and shop owner.

This Lissa chick apparently thought Pere shouldn't greet other humans when she was present.

Oddly enough, a man at a booth in the restaurant, ten feet beyond them was giving them the same hateful glare.

# CHAPTER FIVE

"So who was the guy?" Mari asked as she and Lydia split away from Pere and his date into the cool confines of the bar.

"Pere?"

"No," she scolded, rolling her eyes at Lydia. "The one over in that booth," Mari said, trying not to be obvious as she pointed out the man who was still glaring.

"Oh, him. I'll tell you in a sec. Better question though," Lydia said, giggling a little, "is who's the blonde?"

"The blonde?"

"Ouch," Lydia was giggling in earnest. "She looked like she'd like to kill you for some reason. I, on the other hand got the glacial dismissal. You played it cool," Lydia said with admiration in her tone. "Didn't get ruffled at all."

"The one with Pere? Why would she care who I am? She's with Pere, so hey, man candy." And Mari was so not going to admit that she'd seen a tinge of jealous green in her own vision when she'd been introduced to the blonde. She reminded herself that hotly sexy, intense, hungry-looking men who treated her with utter disdain were definitely NOT her type.

Now Lydia laughed full and strong. "Oh my God, I've never heard him called that. Intimidating, ruthless, serious, but never man candy."

"That's how she was looking at him, and wow, possessive much?" Mari laughed as well. "I'm not surprised he attracts the barracuda-type. Wonder why she decided I was a rival?"

"Maybe because he spoke to you first? Or maybe he was talking about you."

"Huh. Maybe, but hey," she held up her hands. "I got no claims, don't want any."

"Really?" Lydia said. "I'd have thought our sophisticated Pere would have been your type. There are already bets around town."

"Seriously? Oh, my God, why?"

Drinks appeared at their table as if by magic, and Mari looked up in surprise at the waitress. "I remember you from when you were here before," the young woman said, smiling. "And Lyds is a regular. I'm Sarah, by the way, and I work the info booth at the Faire, come Walk time."

"Great," Mari said, nonplussed, but always happy to meet people. "Thanks."

Lydia waited until the girl left to answer Mari's questions about her being Pere's type. "Why? Because Pere won't have anything to do with anyone who's local, and besides, he knows all of us. You? You're new. Attractive as hell, if you're into women," Lydia said with a growing smile, marking points on the table as if keeping score. "And only here, supposedly, for two years. Prime target for Pere."

"Lord," Mari gusted the word on a breath. "I'm here to do a job, not seduce anyone, much less be the subject of a bet," she said with a frown. Of course, that didn't count the fact that she was dreaming about Pere more and more. And the sense of danger around him only added fuel to the fire.

"Ha. Some folks will bet on anything. My second cousin, who, by the way is married to a Hachette, will take a bet on anything. Not like a serious gambling thing, just 'betcha a dollar' kind of thing."

It was Mari's turn to roll her eyes. "Great."

"You bet," Lydia said drily and they both laughed. "As to your other question, the angry man in the restaurant is Calvin Parris, Christian Reformers minister and firebrand, anti-Witches-Walk preacher. He's the instigator of most of the picketing you saw, and the lawsuit. He's the chairman of CAWW, Citizens Against the Witches Walk."

"Wow, I thought preachers were supposed to be about acceptance and gathering the flock. And not hanging out in restaurants with bars or lawsuits."

"Not this one. Exclusion all the way," Lydia said, munching on nuts. "He's an 'us versus them' kind of guy. He's been around about a year. Started out really nice and seemed too good to be true. Aunty D even tried a little matchmaking." This time Lydia's expression seemed a little disappointed. "Which would have been great, but suddenly he did a one-eighty and became a real Bible thumping rabble rouser." She made a disgusted noise. "He's been talking to the national Bible-thumper press types about what a hotbed of Satanism we are." She shuddered delicately. "As if. We're all Light-workers here. Nobody messes with the dark stuff."

"Does he pick on Salem too?" Mari was thinking about how many allies she could muster to combat that kind of press.

"Oh, no," Lydia drawled the word as if it were distasteful. "You see, he believes that the Christians won the battle at Salem. The witches hanged, didn't they?" She shuddered. "So he sees Salem kinda like some people see

Jerusalem. Somebody died, sure, but the Christians got all the goodies in the end."

"Nice. How does he even have time to do all this?" Mari wondered.

"Yeah, that's the thing. He's not the main minister. That's Pastor Walthers. But Calvin's the heir apparent. Evidently the stricter Christian Reformers practitioners in the group wanted a more dynamic speaker than Pastor Walthers, who's a year or so from retirement. So they got the new guy, so Walthers could show him the ropes, I guess.

"Somebody told me that when Walthers lost his wife to cancer, he lost his drive for the sermon," Lydia added, a sad note in her voice. "But some of the older folks are really upset that one of our churches hired somebody like Calvin. In fact, some of the people in his own church are upset at how he turned on the hellfire and brimstone all of a sudden. They claim that wasn't what they thought they were getting, and that certainly wasn't how he seemed at first."

"Most are more tolerant? Even the Reformers?"

"Oh, totally. Even the Baptists are completely respectful, and they headed off a major picket by that whacko Baptist group that likes to tell people they're going to hell because they breathe wrong."

"Brethren Holy Baptist." Mari's disgust rang in her voice, she couldn't help it. "The least Christian of all Christians."

"Yeah. Them. They came to picket the Walk a couple of years ago. All the local churches set up a perimeter, even some from Newburyport and Salisbury. It was awesome."

"I remember reading about it," Mari said, and that sense of unity and community had been one of the reasons she'd been drawn to the event. "I guess Preacher Parris would have sided with the Holy Brethren?"

"Seems like it, yeah. He'd probably have joined them

in shouting nasty things. Pastor Walthers isn't like that at all."

"Why? Why would someone like Calvin Parris even come here?"

Lydia looked sad, then angry. "He grew up here."

Before Mari could question that, the waitress returned with a second bowl of nuts along with a basket of crusty brown bread and butter.

As she set it down, Sarah asked, "Hey, did you hear Gus Wilkerson had a break-in over at No Colds Barred?"

####

"Who is she?" Lissa demanded.

"The new director of the Witches Walk," Pere answered easily, leashing his annoyance with Lissa's attitude. He'd bought her gaming company and he'd hoped that was the end of it. The attorneys had finalized everything this morning, just before he picked Mari Beecham up at the Walk office. Lissa showed up in his office at six with champagne and a red dress. He'd managed to redirect that to dinner out.

He'd already told Lissa that the first thing he was going to do was get rid of her. It was in all the paperwork. She'd signed it, but didn't believe it. He shrugged inwardly. It wasn't his problem, not anymore. The deal was done. Permanently inked and legally binding.

He should never have slept with her. In his defense, he'd done it long before he knew she was the founder and CEO of the business he was buying, but...

"Oh, an employee," Lissa said, dismissing Mari Beecham with a wave of a wickedly manicured hand.

"No," he corrected. "The executive director of a major community event." The more he dealt with Lissa, the more he couldn't believe she'd built a multi-million dollar gaming business. Perhaps her single-minded focus accounted for her initial success, he mused. But, ignoring good business practices, like knowing your community, was why her company, Halliday Gaming Inc., had been ripe for a buyout. All to the good, in this case.

"Pere," she said sharply. "I'm speaking to you." Her clipped New York accent made the words a staccato snap.

"My apologies." Unfortunately, she thought this business deal was a merger—both personal and professional. Pere had told her it wasn't. Even her lawyers and his had told her differently. She didn't want to hear it and had dismissed all the lawyers immediately when the paperwork was done.

He asked for a table, but she'd demanded a booth. She slid sinuously onto the seat, sliding back toward him when he too sat, so that she was pressed into his side.

"Lissa," he said, firmly, moving away. "This is business. It's important you understand–"

"Exactly," she purred. "We're important. And I do understand. Business is boring. We have so many other interesting things to talk about."

"Do we?" he said, injecting a cold note into his tone. Her desire for him had given him an advantage over other buyers. He'd used it, but he had no interest in her beyond the buyout.

*So sue me.*

"Yes, of course we have things to discuss," she said, snapping open a menu. "Why else would I come here, to your silly little town. To talk more boring business? I don't think so," she scoffed. "We need to celebrate the merger. To talk about us, about where we want to take our new joint venture." She gave him a heated look. "Our personal joint venture."

"Lissa, you don't ever listen, do you?" Even as irritation slid into his tone, she still ignored his words. "You don't make any points with me by insulting my hometown, or the people who live here. You are brilliant at design and built a good system, but we are not business partners. We're not partners in any sense. At all."

Lissa pouted, but was so sure of her hold on him, so sure of herself, that once again, she didn't listen.

A flash of memory blinked into his mind. Marisol Beecham, her eyes flashing as she acerbically told him, without ever saying a word, that Gus was being an ass. Brilliant.

The sense of smoke, blood and danger he had when he was around Mari hadn't lessened, but his desire for her had grown exponentially. It was almost enough to make him want to test the vision, ask her out, kiss her.

The thought turned his blood molten in a heartbeat and he jerked in reaction. *What the hell?* His intellect said Mari was trouble. His libido said she was his.

"I'm talking about *us,*" Lissa hissed, breaking his hot reverie about Mari.

"Lissa," he said, making sure they had eye contact. "There. Is. No. Us."

She jerked away from him and snapped the menu again. "I don't believe you. I don't know why you're upset or whatever." She waved a hand his way. "You'll get over it. Let's order."

This was the second dinner of this sort. She dressed to kill, and flirted. He talked business. She insisted they were a couple. He pointedly, bluntly, told her they weren't. He'd put up with it the first time since the deal was in the works. This was too much.

The grim certainty that his mother had tampered surfaced again. Just because she'd sworn—and he believed her—that she hadn't bespelled *him*, that didn't mean she hadn't bespelled the women he met and dated.

They ordered dinner, and as the waiter set down bread and brought wine, Lissa nattered on about how they should go to the Hamptons in October for a fall regatta.

"Lissa, I have family and business obligations throughout October." Despite his mother's meddling, he'd do his duty to Haven Harbor, the Walk, and the annual Samhain Ball.

"You always say that, Pere. You need to pay more attention to me if you don't want to lose me," she said archly, deliberately licking her lips as if she was licking him. It left him unmoved. The initial attraction between them had flashed, then cooled to ash, at least for him. All her attempts to arouse him, instead, had the opposite effect.

A husky laugh mixed with a familiar, bawdy one rang through an odd moment of silence in the restaurant. Pere looked at the bar where Mari Beecham and Lydia Webb sat together. That awareness inside him, the one focused only on her, raised its head, listened to that low laugh and heated, lasered in on the sound of her voice.

*No.*

He cut it off. He wouldn't be trapped that way again.

"Pere, I *asked* if you wanted more wine."

Sighing, Pere declined the wine. Lissa indulged, heavily. This could be more difficult than he'd imagined. He noted it when Mari and Lydia left after thirty minutes.

"Once again, Lissa, let me emphasize that there is no *us.*"

#### 

*How DARE he?* Lissa stalked around the elegant room at the Old Haven Mill Inn. She ignored the beauty of the period details, dismissed all of the luxury in the gorgeous suite at the top of the building. She turned her back on the balcony that beckoned with a river view and the glitter of stars over the nearby ocean. *How dare Pere Hestworth turn her down. She was irresistible to men. She was flawless, sexy, and he'd been her slave in bed. What had happened?*

She took off one of her shoes and threw it at the long French doors. Thankfully, it bounced off the glass, but that didn't stop her from throwing the other one as well.

"Haven Harbor," she sneered. "Stupid, idiotic wannabe town. A town, for God's sake. Pitiful." She thought about the Hamptons, and how stupendous she'd look with Pere on her arm at some of the most sophisticated parties. Why the hell would such a great-looking, brilliant gamer like Pere Hestworth hole up in some dinky, backward *town*? She cursed again, stalking around the suite in frustrated bafflement. She kicked the shoes as she passed, cursing when that hurt her foot.

Her cellphone rang, and it was a special tone she'd assigned to unknowns. "Screw it," she cursed, but when it stopped, then started ringing again, she dived for her sleek evening bag. "Whoever it is, I'm going to make them wish they'd died."

She needed to ream someone out, and the unknown caller was it.

Before she could start, the caller hung up.

"I am going to kill him," she snarled tossing the phone, thinking about Pere again.

But the call made her realize she should be proactive. She was going to confront him. Nobody told her it was over. *She* did the telling. She grabbed the sexy shoes and slipped them back on. She called the desk for her car to be brought around.

"Asshole's at the office, I just know it. Freakin' workaholic," she hissed, as if she weren't one too. She tapped her foot. "Slow freaking elevators. Damn old hotels," she cursed the whole place, hating the delay, wishing for the fresh, shiny and new, something she insisted on in her home and office.

Thinking of her office, she smiled. They'd made love on her desk. Maybe they'd repeat the event on his desk. The thought of that made her smile. After he groveled, she'd agree. She adjusted her dress to show more cleavage.

When the creaky old elevator car finally got to the lobby, she stalked across the beautifully carpeted expanse to the big glass exit doors. Her car idled at the curb. The tinted windows looked ominous in the early evening light. She slid in as the doorman opened the door for her. In the rearview mirror, she checked her makeup and smiled in satisfaction before heading out.

The smile widened as she drove, thinking of the confrontation. It was going to feel so good to yell at Pere, then do him, right there on his desk.

The smile fell away when the car behind her bumped her.

"Asshole!" she hissed, fumbling in her bag for her phone. Even in some two-bit town, they didn't stand for that kind of thing. The hokey-pokey cops would get to be champions.

She'd barely dialed 911 when the car hit her the second time.

The call connected just as the car behind her hit her the third time, hard enough to spin her car out of control on the curve just before MicroMechanics.

#### 

Pere was waiting at the Walk office the next day when Mari and Carol both arrived. Carol was obviously nervous and excited when they all walked in.

"Can I get you coffee, Mr. H? And coffee or tea for you, Ms. Mari?"

"Coffee would be great," Mari said, having already figured out that Carol worked better with a task to complete. "I take mine…"

"Black, two sugars," Carol said. "I remember. The usual for you, Mr. H?"

"Yes, please. And thanks, Carol."

"Of course." She bustled off to get the pot started.

"He's been here," Pere remarked, pointing at the dust on the carpet going from Gus's office to the back stairs. "After hours."

"I'm sure he wanted to see what work you'd authorized," Mari murmured. She felt oddly distracted by Pere. The way he was looking at her was different, interested-male different.

The front door opened and they turned as one to greet Gus as he came in.

Pere held out a hand for a handshake, immediately distracting Gus from the words he was about to speak. Mari admired the redirect.

"Morning Gus," Pere said, his deep resonant voice

tinged with amusement.

"I can't believe you authorized this fiasco, Pere." Gus shook his hand briefly, then recovered and started in on his complaint. "We're only four weeks out from the Walk, and you initiated construction without my okay?"

Pere shrugged and smiled. Somehow, he managed to look both supremely confident and give the impression of "Aw, gee shucks" at the same time, disarming his opponent.

"I didn't want to disrupt your arranging of things, Gus, you know that. This was just something we were going to have to do soon anyway. Things have been too cramped in here for a couple of years now, and with the auditor arriving early, it was a good excuse."

"Yes, but you should have waited," Gus insisted, his jaw jutting out and temper in his eyes. "I'm in charge of this, Pere, not you."

Four people came in the door at that moment, two men, two women, all with folders or bags or notebooks, obviously ready for a meeting. They stopped dead at the tableau of the confrontation of Gus and Pere.

Pere held up his hands in mock-surrender. "You're absolutely right, Gus. I overstepped. My apologies."

*Oh, neatly done.* Pere had gotten his way, and now, by apologizing in front of witnesses, Gus couldn't be anything less than gracious about it or lose face.

"Good. Thanks," Gus said, with a brisk nod of his head. "Now that we've got that handled, I'll let you get back to things, Pere. Thanks for showing Mari around yesterday."

"*Ms. Beecham,*" Pere stated, reminding Gus that she was due respect, "was a pleasure to work with." Mari heard the unspoken *unlike you,* even if no one else did. From th quickly smothered grin on one of the newcomers' f she'd caught that undertone as well.

*What happened to the chill of distrust from Pe And where had her own objectivity gone?*

"Sure, sure. Good morning, everyone." Gus turned to the group, as if he'd just now become aware of them. Carol bustled in handing Pere and Mari mugs with the Witches Walk logo before dashing back to get a cup for Gus.

"Mrs. Scarboro, you want tea this morning?" she asked, handing a mug to Gus then turned to take orders from the others, just like a seasoned waitress. "And Mr. Leech, Ms. Hamm? Something for you? Mr. Turner?"

The other two wanted water and a Coke, so Carol popped back out of sight as the group moved toward the conference room.

Mari and Pere followed them in, but Gus turned to his office and left them to the introductions.

"Nicely done," Mari murmured as she and Pere waited for the others to go into the room.

"Since Gus had a call to make," Pere improvised, covering Gus's rudeness, "I'll make the introductions."

The taller woman, Ms. Hamm, snorted a laugh. The others grinned, but they dutifully turned to Mari and were all very welcoming.

"We're the traffic committee," Leech explained. "Getting down to the last details on the coordinating with the safety committee on guards, medical teams, and from there, putting up the notices on which roads will be closed and blocked for the Faire, all that. We," he acknowledged the whole group with an encompassing wave of his hand, "have done this for a couple of years now. Since Hamm here is deputy chief of the fire and rescue department, she's our go-to for most everything. Turner's a retired cop. He helps the sheriff and Chief Strongbow out now and again too, if they need an extra hand."

The older, greyer man nodded to her as he poured the Coke Carol placed in front of him.

"I'm a city planner," Leech continued, "so I got in on the act what, five years ago?" He checked with his compatriots, and they nodded or agreed. "Mrs. Scarboro is with the Ecumenical Council, and she's got a handle on all our first aid stations."

"I'm so pleased to meet all of you," Mari said warmly. Great volunteers were the heart of any event. Volunteers that came back year after year? Priceless. "Thank you for all you've done and are doing. I'll look forward to learning from each of you."

"Would you like to sit in on the meeting?"

"I'd be glad to," Mari began, but Pere put a hand on her arm.

"I'm afraid I'm going to need to speak with Ms. Beecham about the new space next door. You go on and get started."

"Sure thing," Leech said, turning away and beginning to set up his notes. Mari noted that the table was clean of any dust or debris and all the plastic had been cleared away. A tiny bit of blue painters' tape was the only evidence that there'd been work going on less than twelve hours before. She'd bet Carol had come in early.

A raw, unfinished, wooden door with a brass knob led to what she presumed was her new office.

"We'll go through the front," Pere said, curtly.

"Sure," she said, and they stepped back into the lobby, then out the door to go in the street entrance. Sipping coffee, Mari waited as Pere unlocked the scruffy-looking exterior door and turned on the pendant lights that hung in rows from the ceiling. What she stepped into was amazing.

"Whoa, he does great work!" The ceilings were higher in this space, a good ten to twelve feet. The obvious, new areas of drywall were smooth, and if she hadn't known to look for it, she'd have never seen the last evidence of drying on the seams. There were new sections of crown molding up, although it was unpainted. The original tin ceiling was clean and ready to be painted. It was obvious that several layers of paint had been scraped off the tin. It was rusty maroon in several places, black in others and a faint minty green in still other sectors. A wall dividing the spaces was up, and it, too, was neatly dry walled, but with gaping holes at the top. "Windows up there?"

"Yes, he said you'd need more light coming into the front from this back space, so you'll get that. He'll be back to paint in about an hour, and the carpet guys will be here at noon. Furniture catalog's on Carol's desk, so pick whatever you want. It's the MicroMechanics account, so we'll get a good price, then we'll bill the Walk."

"Neatly done," she complimented again, feeling in accord with him for the very first time. Smiling into her mug, she had a renewed appreciation of just how neatly he'd maneuvered Gus without breaking a sweat. They stepped into the second area, which was a more spacious, square-ish space, unlike the long narrow front space, and she nearly dropped her mug. "Wow."

There were two spaces, a front, open office and a second, back office with a door. Right at the edge of the first space was a cut in the drywall. A crude door, complete with hinges.

"I guess that's what led to the closet in Gus's office," she said, noticing the drag marks in the dust on the floor.

"What?" Pere stepped over to look at the cuts in the wall.

"Evidently Gus was storing some materials here. Carol called him as she left last night, and your handyman threw plastic over the boxes until Gus could come move them."

Pere's frown turned his handsome face forbidding and ferocious. "That idiot. I've asked him more than once if the Walk needed more space. We kept talking about this space and he—" Pere cut himself off mid-word. "Old news," he said, with obvious effort. "We'll get Marcus to patch that up too before he paints."

"I take it Marcus is the consummate handyman?"

"He's actually a fine homebuilder, but he can build or fix anything, so he has a standing contract with MicroMechanics and with the Walk."

"No wonder the seams on the drywall are so perfect," she murmured, then offered, when he shot her a questioning look. "And he did mention building. My father was with the SeaBees. Construction. He was like that." She gestured with the mug. "Could make anything work, build anything."

The thought made her so homesick that she had to move, had to shift or get lost in the remembered pain of losing her best guy. She moved across the space to the sliding doors and big windows that looked over the alleyway and beyond, between the buildings to an ancient-looking cemetery. The double door, obviously new, led to an iron balcony that overlooked the alley.

"This is unusual," she said, opening the door to let in the faint breeze. She closed it again and tried to figure out the spacing. "This must be behind another business."

"Yes, the Walk will go for that space too if the Herald ever moves."

"Is that likely?" The newspaper office had seemed very established. She'd been in on her first visit to town, prior to her presentation. There were posters from various events on every wall and the desks were set in what seemed to be time-honored spots. She'd loved the sense of the hometown-ness of the weekly *Haven Harbor Herald*.

"You never know. The owner is heading toward retirement, and if his daughter does take over, which looks likely, she's got plans." Pere sounded indifferent, but he, too, wandered to the large windows and looked out. "That's the original cemetery for the town." He gestured to the view across the street with his own mug then he, too, took a sip.

"It looks peaceful," she said. On the warm August morning, the huge oaks and beeches overshadowed the gravestones, making it look like a glorious place for a cool walk on a hot day.

"It is, most days."

They both turned at the same time, and an instant of

physical awareness hummed between them. There was the faintest murmur of voices from the committee in the other room, but otherwise no sound echoed in the empty space. Just their quickened breathing.

Mari couldn't stop staring, couldn't break the visceral need for eye contact. The need to touch him, to make contact was a near-pain in her chest. When his lips parted, and his hand rose to her cheek, she nearly stopped breathing.

Pere lowered his head, his lips just barely brushing hers, but it was as if she'd been hit by a live wire. Electricity ran through her, and he shuddered under her hand, where she rested it on his chest.

She wanted more, and when his hand slid to the back of her neck, she was hoping to get it.

"Mr. H?"

Carol's voice echoed like a shout in the emptiness, and Mari dropped her mug, shattering the mug on the concrete floor.

"Dammit!" she exclaimed, probably with more force than warranted by just dropping a mug. *What the hell?* Mari sucked in a shocked breath. Her reaction to him had her so agitated, she almost choked.

Pere seemed to be equally agitated, but somehow was able to shut it down before Carol arrived.

"Hey," Carol said, rushing back to where they stood. To Mari, she said, "Ohmigosh, I'll get something to clean that up. Don't worry. Mr. Gus is ready to get started with the second committee meeting, the Faire committee? He wanted to know if you were coming?" To Pere, she added, "And Chief Strongbow needs to talk with you, Mr. H."

"Absolutely," Mari said, quickly. "I'm so sorry to make any work for you."

"Oh, no worries," Carol said, already mopping at the spill using paper towels from a roll that had been left by the workmen.

Mari needed to get out of any intimate space that Pere

Hestworth occupied. The fact that they didn't like one another couldn't explain away that humming awareness. Nor did it help that she was still painfully aware of him.

"This space is so great," Carol said, even as she looked around and found the contractor's trash bag for the wet towels. "Wow, Marcus can sure work miracles, can't he?"

"It's why we pay him the big bucks," Pere said, his tone as dry as dust. "Any idea why the chief needs me?"

Carol laughed. "Yeah, Marcus really doesn't charge us enough for how good he is, does he? And the chief said something about a wreck from last night, out near your place. A red rental car with New York plates?"

"That's weird." Mari frowned, pulling off a paper towel as well. Her hand was bleeding from a flying fragment of the broken mug. "My rental's red, and has New York plates. And so does Geneva's. We were laughing about the coincidence just yesterday."

"Um, that's pretty common up here, the New York plates," Carol said. "And the same type of car too. I worked for a rental car place for a while. Something about tax rates for cars in New York. They're better than Massachusetts."

"I'll bet that was an interesting job," Mari commented, wondering how many Carol had had prior to the Walk. The two women moved back toward the doors, but Pere was pulling out his phone.

"I'll call the chief. You two have fun." Pere's parting shot, said with some sarcasm, made them both laugh. "Carol, thanks for the coffee."

"Not at all, Mr. H. Thanks. See you." The words all rushed out together as she took his mug. Pere nodded to her, then to Mari.

Mari looked around the room, then met his eyes again. There were sparks there that she didn't want to touch with a ten-foot pole. He seemed just as reluctant to face up to whatever had happened between them. "Thank you."

"Of course," he said, and despite the sparks, there was

frost in his tone. "I'll be in touch."

"Of course," she said, not knowing why she echoed his phrase, but he seemed to find it funny.

She followed Carol out the door, glancing back only to see Pere with his back to her, phone to his ear. Mari did notice that he had one hell of a nice ass.

*He's the enemy. Sort of.* She reminded herself. *He doesn't like you. Or doesn't want to like you. Do NOT notice his ass. And could that have been* more *freaky?*

*Oh, my God, I kissed Pere Hestworth.*

"Oh, you're bleeding," Carol said, her voice going high in shock.

"Not badly," Mari reassured. "It's about stopped now. I cut it on the handle of the mug when it broke."

"There's bandages and antiseptic in the bathroom cabinet, do you want me to get them for you?"

She got them herself, of course, then, with a newly bandaged finger, she came back out with a smile for Carol. "All set. Let's get started," she said to Carol as they joined the new committee forming up in the conference room.

#### 

He couldn't walk off the anger. It just wouldn't dissipate. Everything he'd done, everything he'd built was jeopardized. Nothing was going according to plan. They should have waited, trusted him. But if he asked for help, people would find out.

No. He just had to deal with this himself.

As usual.

He unlocked the doors to the office, then turned at the sound of someone calling his name.

"Hey, Gus."

"What are you doing here? You can't be here," Gus said, feeling a slice of panic in his gut as his brother Carl strode up.

"Just going to help you with the shipment. I can take it south tonight, get it out of here."

"Okay, but then you have to disappear again. Don't let

yourself be seen. What were you thinking, coming here?"

"What, you don't appreciate my help?"

Gus snorted in disgust. "I wouldn't be in this mess if it weren't for your *help*, so don't give me that shit."

The turned on no lights as they moved through the space. Carol always left on a low-wattage lamp on the credenza, so there was enough ambient light to get to Gus's office. He shut the door before he turned on the lights, then opened the closet and the wallboard door he'd cut into the vacant space. Together, the two men loaded the boxes onto a hand truck.

"Hang on, I'm gonna take a piss, then we'll go."

In the bathroom, Carl looked at the trash and saw the bloody paper towels. "What have we here?"

"Carol said the new woman cut her hand."

"Well, well, well. Now Gus, my brother, I can use this, for sure."

Gus choked back the immediate protest that sprang to his lips as the bloody towels were tucked into an empty Witches Walk envelope. Gus was in too deep to complain about any method Carl used, even if it was a dark one.

He knew Carl had turned to dark magic. He knew he'd just allowed Marisol Beecham to be put in grave danger. His gut twisted, but he told his gut and his conscience to shut up.

When it came to surviving this stupid transition, he'd be lucky to get out without jail time.

He would be so glad when he was free.

#### 

For the second time since she'd come to town, Mari opened the door to a porch full of women. This time, however, she knew several, and they knew her. Lydia was the first to smile and speak.

"Hey, Mari, you said Friday at 6, is it still okay?"

"Of course, come in, please," she held the door open. Upstairs, where she'd shut him in the bedroom, Pepper barked furiously. After a long week of meetings, dinners and frustration with Gus over the Witches Walk, and the lukewarm—at least on her part—date, Mari worried she hadn't spent enough time with her pup. Now, he was incensed at being left out of the festivities yet again.

"Oh, you have the Hachette look about you," a tiny, very frail-looking woman said, stopping in front of Mari and looking up into her face. She was under five feet tall, certainly, because Mari herself wasn't much over that. "I'm Lavinia Baines Hachette Webster, and I would be your great aunt."

Mari's mouth dropped open in shock. "Granddaddy had a sister?"

The little woman smiled, and patted her hand. "We weren't close, unfortunately. You can call me Vinnia, or Aunt Vinnia if you'd like." Another woman moved past Vinnia, setting a gift bag on the hall table, then turned back with a smile.

"And I'm her daughter Caroline Hachette Webster. And yes, I married a cousin, but he's several times removed." Caroline extended a hand and Mari shook it, not knowing exactly what to feel.

"Welcome," was all she could muster. It was one thing for Lydia and her aunt to claim Mari had cousins here, and to have met a few over the week during Walk business, but these were *real* cousins, not just distant, "oh we're from the same lineage" cousins. "Please, come in."

Mari heard the faint ping of her cell phone message notice several times. The cheerful tones were drowned out by the laughing, chattering voices, and she kept getting distracted each time she meant to go check it.

She remembered it again when she went upstairs to get Pepper so the ladies could meet him. He was a big hit, bouncing politely to each of the women, who professed to be delighted with his personality and antics.

"Oh, isn't he the cutest thing," her great aunt, Vinnia cooed, petting the ecstatic dog. "A Corgi, you said?" When Mari nodded, Vinnia smiled. "Caroline, you need to remember that. I may want to get a Corgi to keep me company." She patted her lap with a frail, veined hand. "Hop up here pup where I can pet you better."

Laughing, Caroline boosted Pepper onto the couch after receiving Mari's okay. "Gran, if you want a Corgi, we'll find a breeder."

All the women laughed and Mari enjoyed the lightning-fast repartee going around the group about dogs and single women, and any number of other topics. By the time everyone left, it was late.

By the time Mari thought to check her phone, it was after midnight.

The calls, from Carol, had continued until after eleven, all of the messages were marked *Urgent*.

# CHAPTER SIX

"I've got things back on track," Gus hissed into the phone. "Now if I can get Carl to leave it alone."

There was a long pause and he felt a bead of sweat gather at his temple. She had that effect on him, even when the air conditioning was going full blast to combat the return of August's heat.

"What do you plan to do?" The voice was sultry, ultimately female. He shuddered. God, she was addicting. And the best thing was, no one knew her, or about her, except his dumbshit brother.

"Got her doing all the committees, meet-'n-greets, and paperwork. She'll be buried in that right up until the event."

"Good plan," the woman purred. "What about the auditor?"

"I'm gonna get rid of the records. No records, nothing to find in them."

"And the shipment?" she insisted.

"Already on its way south."

"Will I see you this Sunday?" she purred again.

"I wouldn't miss it, sweetheart," Gus said.

When he'd hung up, the woman turned to her associate. "I will have another job for you in Haven Harbor. Very soon."

For now, she had to report in to her other contact in Haven Harbor. The one she was actually afraid of.

He needed to know Gus was getting cold feet.

#### 

Pere's black mood followed him into the Witches Walk office on the Saturday of Labor Day Weekend. He knew the incident in the new space with Mari had been due to his mother and her tampering. Nothing else could explain the intensity of his attraction to her.

The fact that she'd had a date on Thursday night hadn't improved his mood either.

"Turning the paperwork over to the auditor means Marisol Beecham can look at it too, Gus," Pere said as he and Gus finalized the paperwork for the new office space. He hated giving up his Saturday morning workout to meet Gus, and hated that Gus was being an ass. "And don't give her grief about it. That's from the council. She's to have access to all the data."

"I know it," Gus said, a growl of temper in his voice. "You and I have had this conversation a dozen times. You stick to your business, I'll stick to mine. I've been running this Walk for five of the ten years now, and we've made a profit every year. The town's profited and grown, and the Walk's done good, so lay off. It's like saying right out loud that you don't trust me."

"I know. And yet, we do and we have trusted you. We all agreed, including you, that it was time to get a professional," Pere reminded his one-time teammate. "She's who the council chose, Gus, whether you and I like it or not." Pere desperately needed a strong hit of coffee.

He wasn't about to stop this discussion to brew it. "Speaking of trust, what the hell were you thinking, storing Walk material in Truett Power's space? When the hell did you cut a freakin' hole in the wall, Gus? It's a good damn thing Marcus Jenkinsen keeps his mouth shut, or Truett Powers would be all over that."

"Get the hell off my back, Pere." Gus stood up from behind the desk and came around to stand toe-to-toe with him. "You don't run this event. I do. You just throw your weight around. Let me tell you, this is no picnic and I'm here, working for the town. Don't you tell me what to do."

It was an evasive and annoying argument, and just like Gus to ignore the consequences if Tru Powers had found out. The fury Pere felt, and the power that pushed at him from within—power with a strength to seriously hurt Gus—made him almost as crazy as fighting with his mother. His mother warned him that he should join in the coven workings and disperse some of the power he held. He knew she was right, but at the moment, he just wanted to blast something.

He was glad they were alone to hash this out. Mari Beecham was working on Saturday too, at the main fire station with the safety committee. The other committees were meeting in other places this morning.

They were three and a half weeks away from the Walk. Everyone was working.

He couldn't keep his mind off Mari.

Thinking about their encounter made him think about the follow up from Chief Strongbow. What the hell had Lissa being doing out on the road to Newburyport? That she had nearly died there, still wearing the same dress she'd had on when they had dinner, continued to weigh on him.

"Exactly the point, Gus," Pere said through gritted teeth, returning to the matter at hand, and still trying for diplomacy. "You have businesses to run. They depend on the Walk. They depend on you. You're the one who said it was getting to be too much, so suck it up and deal with the fact that you have to give up the power too."

"Get out of my office," Gus snarled.

Given the red haze of fury trying to overwhelm him, Pere decided he'd better do just that. He knew that his sense of remorse over Lissa was fueling the anger. He'd sent flowers but not gone to see her. She'd already pushed her plans for "their relationship" too far toward crazytown. Going to see her would only fuel that. He suspected his mother's hand there, too.

He still struggled to believe she wasn't meddling. She'd admitted to doing so with his father, and with a woman he'd dated after college, but she said she'd learned her lesson with that one. He wished he could be sure. This feeling, this intense draw to Mari Beecham, worried him. The fact that he saw danger when he touched her, and yet was still drawn? Strange.

Not that there weren't stranger things in Haven Harbor.

Could his mother have unconsciously influenced his desire for Mari? That was the thing that troubled him most. His mother was a consummate witch, in charge of her power. But she was also a mother who longed for her son to be happy. A heady combination.

Guilt and anger made for a furious and potent brew, and it was stirring inside him. Every witch, every businessman, knew you didn't take fury to the bargaining table or circle with you. It would win every time, and you would lose.

"I mean it, Pere," Gus stepped forward, chest thrust out, jaw set. "Get out."

He and Gus had never gotten along, not since high school. Gus had been a senior when Pere was a freshman. They'd both played football, and the hazing Gus and his brother had initiated...well, they would never be friends.

Pere nodded, not trusting himself to speak. While he had the power as a witch and as council chair to demand answers from Gus, he needed the man to do the work. Despite their differences he respected what Gus had done to grow the Walk. It didn't tamp down the anger that rose when he considered what games Gus might be playing, and whether he was endangering the Walk. Or Mari.

That thought occurred to Pere, and he realized he needed to back down, and get out. Losing his temper would get them answers. Time to go.

"It's not about power, you rich idiot. It's about doing it right," Gus shouted after him as he strode toward the door.

*Doing it right, my ass.* Pere pivoted at the door. It took every bit of his iron will to not knock Gus down and curse him with donkey ears at the same time.

"Good," he snarled. "Have the rest of the account books ready. The auditor said she needed the next three years. I expect you to give her all of them."

Furious, Pere shoved out the door, and barely caught it before it slammed into Mari and Carol.

#### 

"Well, I just think that—" The words stopped cold as Pere Hestworth flung the door open and strode out.

"Ladies," he said, his voice artic with the temper boiling in his eyes. "My apologies. Carol, you may want to head home. Ms. Beecham, walk with me."

Carol nodded and without a word headed around the block to where her car was parked. Turning to Pere, Mari fell into step with him, and they moved down the sidewalk.

After a quick-paced turn around the block, she finally spoke. "Are we walking to MicroMechanics?"

Pere slowed his pace, then stopped. He frowned down at her from his superior height, then shook his head. "I'm sorry. I shouldn't have let him get to me."

"Gus?"

"Of course," Pere said, rubbing a hand over his face. "Here, let's go in where it's cool."

She hadn't realized they were at the diner until he held

open the door. Mike's was as cool as a cave after the day's building heat outside. It might be the first weekend in September, but it was still hot. "You want something to drink?"

"Yes, please," she said, asking for an iced tea. They sat at a corner table. They were the only patrons in the diner now that it was well after the lunch hour on a Saturday.

"So," she said, when he sat. "What was that about?"

He met her gaze with his piercing blue one. "We told Gus before we hired you, before we even started looking for someone, that we wanted an audit. He agreed."

"Hmmm," Mari hummed the sound. She was glad the board had done it, and glad Geneva the silent was on it. Mari hoped the result wasn't what she suspected. The kind of evasiveness Gus showed about turning over the books wasn't good. It smacked of money issues. Having checks bounce before she took over, much less after, pretty much sucked.

"That's a noncommittal noise."

"Yes. It's tough to audit just before the event. It distracts everyone and puts the staff on edge. That said, an audit's a good thing, especially with a volunteer event. And it should be repeated every two or three years, just to be sure everything's on the up and up."

"Yes." He was watching her again. "I agree with you on all counts. But it can't wait till after the Walk. It needs to be done now."

"Mr. Hestworth, I'm not arguing with you. The auditor's working." She kept her tone soft, and frankly, she was wary. Something was seriously wrong, and everything about their interactions was now colored by what had happened in the new office space.

Pere nodded sharply, then said nothing more, brooding into his iced coffee. The silence stretched out. She finally broke it, because she had to get back to Pepper and the work she'd brought home. She couldn't get her brain to stop replaying the instant their lips had met, and her body heated at the thought of it. As much as Pere made her blood hum with awareness, she wasn't going to act on it.

Since she wasn't going to give in, she didn't want to sit here with a broody, sexy man who had no interest in her. Or, he did, but he didn't want to.

*Understatement of the century.*

"Is there something else I should know about it?" she finally asked.

He looked at her, and she froze. The intensity, the sheer power of his gaze, momentarily blanked her brain. She heard the crackle of flames, smelled smoke, felt the kiss of a cinder hitting her cheek.

She shuddered and the sensation was gone, but his intensity wasn't.

He looked at her as a man looked at a woman he wanted. Possessive. Powerful. Pere's gaze said she was something he didn't want to touch, and yet he wanted to devour her on the spot. His gaze said she was a drug so addictive he dared not touch, lest it become vital to his very existence.

*Where the hell did* that *thought come from?*

"Sorry," he said, shifting to look at the counter beyond her shoulder. When he looked back at her, the heat was gone and the cool, Hestworth mask was once again in place. "You heard there was an accident?"

"Yes."

"That was what Chief Strongbow called me about." He brooded a moment more, then said, "And there's something else."

"I'm sorry," she said, then a thought occurred, and she reached over to lay her hand on his arm. The sense of fire and smoke returned. "Not your mother?"

The muscles under her hand tensed. "No." He looked at her hand and she quickly removed it. He looked up at her, and the intensity was back. More smoke and fire licked at the edges of her senses.

*What the hell?*

"Pere?"

"Lissa Halliday, the business colleague you met the other night at The Judge's Chambers. She was the one who crashed on the road by MicroMechanics." His face was a mask of fury. "She shouldn't have even been on the road. I have no idea why she left the hotel." He looked at her. "She had a red rental car with New York plates."

"What the heck is up with that? So do I. So does Geneva Banks, the auditor," she said, but it shook her. She frowned, thinking about the calls from Carol. The ones which had turned out *not* to be from Carol, whom she'd woken up at midnight the previous night after all the Hachette ladies left. Those calls worried her, and she wondered if she should tell Pere. "It's a crazy coincidence that all three of us have red rental cars."

That was so weird.

Mari decided to leave the calls alone. Like the rental cars, and their colors, it was probably just a coincidence. And hey, Carol had told her that CAWW had been trying to figure out how to oust her. She leaned back, trying to create distance from Pere, both emotionally and physically. "I'm sorry about your friend."

"She's a colleague, not a friend." He dismissed that, but she could tell it was eating at him. Before she could say anything, he went on. "Gus is in trouble. I don't know how or why. I've known him since we were kids. He has 'tells.' Something's going on." He said it quietly, evenly. "The audit scares him, even though he's pretending everything is fine." Once again he looked her in the eye. "But he's bluffing, and not well. I don't know if it's the Walk, or personally."

*Great. Just great.* Not that she hadn't pulled events out of the proverbial fire before, but, with that earlier glimpse of conflagration and pain, she was feeling distinctly unsettled.

*Unsettled? Try freaked out.* The Hachette ladies had kept asking her about fire too, because evidently the Hachette lines had an affinity with fires. Lots of blacksmiths in the line, they'd said. And firemen and women. Arson investigators. Then they'd asked how she felt about being able to sense things or know things before they happened, if she did, because that came from the Prescotts. Or if she'd ever had prophetic dreams because that came from the Aldens.

They'd read cards for her and runes and even her palm. One and all agreed that there were exciting things in her future. But she'd caught the worried looks as well, the sideways glances. When she'd asked about it, her frail great aunt, Vinnia, had patted her hand and reassured her that the troubles they each saw in the near future could be attributed to the turmoil of taking over the Walk. Or it could be bad weather, though several of the ladies said Mrs. Hestworth assured them that the week of the Walk would be clear right up to the Gala, when it would rain buckets.

*Really. Totally. Out there.*

She didn't let her inner monologue color her voice as she responded. "If things don't come right in the audit, I can take over sooner. However, we'll hope it's a hiccup."

Pere raised his glass, touched it ever so briefly to hers. What should have been a faint chink of the glasses sounded like a cannon shot.

He grimaced. "Sorry. I'm not as optimistic."

*She had to get her hearing checked.* Had it not sounded horribly loud to him? What in the hell was going on? They each drank, and he avoided looking at her.

"I'll walk you to your car." He tossed a five on the table, and rose.

"No need. I was going to stop in at Lydia's, then at the florist's as well."

"All right." They moved to the door, and he reached to open it for her. "I'm sorry this is proving to be more difficult than we'd anticipated."

She shrugged. "Things happen. We'll roll with it. You

and the board can rest assured that I'll do whatever's necessary to help or to pick up the slack if that's what's needed."

He looked at her again, that sense of something sharp, hot, deeply necessary hit her again, then slid away. He shifted, and the moment was gone again.

Disquieted, she stepped out into the mid-afternoon heat, slipping on her sunglasses. "Thank you for the drink."

"Anytime," he said, off-handedly, turning away. Then he turned back, and the intensity was back. "Just so you know, I'm not interested in anything personal."

Shocked at the blunt speech, it took Mari a couple of seconds to respond. Sarcasm leapt out before she could stop the words. "Well there goes my hot oil and chocolate fantasy, then," she snapped. "What the hell? I'm not interested in you, Mr. Hestworth, and despite that aberration in the Walk office, I'm not sure how you got the impression that I was. The clarification is appreciated, however."

She left him standing on the sidewalk in the sun. By the time she got to Lydia's Besom Shop, with its gigantic broom hanging outside, she was muttering in fury.

She walked in, and Lydia took one look at her and gasped. "Whoa! You're all but smoking. What the hell happened?"

"Pere Hestworth."

"Oh, dear," a lighter voice said, coming from the back area where the tarot-reading booths were situated. "I'm afraid I know what's going on."

Estelle Hestworth stepped out into the shop, and the concern on her face, and the resigned slump of her shoulders told Mari there was more trouble here than Mari's harsh words with Pere.

"It's all my fault, you see," Pere's mother said.

Lydia looked from one to the other, then stepped to the door and locked it. She put up the "Back in Ten

Minutes" sign.

"Let's have some coffee and figure this out."

## CHAPTER SEVEN

The week started with rain, rain, and more rain. Neither she nor Pepper had enjoyed their morning walk as they strode around the neighborhood. She'd thought about bringing him in with her, and Carol was eager for her to do so, but Pepper had given her a look of serious distaste when she suggested he go out in the rain again.

Mari smiled at the thought as she looked out the windows of the Walk office, thinking about the prediction of rain for the Gala. She watched the puddles form in the street, and the people hurrying along with umbrellas as they went from car to shop, or car to office. She was waiting for Gus to arrive, as usual, and for Marcus's helper to finish screwing on switch plates. The builder's young assistant, Jeremy, was going with Gus out to the storage space and bringing back the boxes with the final three years' worth of records for the auditor. Gus had put it off yesterday because of the holiday, and now, Tuesday, had said they would go.

"I'll bet he says no way, because it's raining," she muttered to herself, watching Gus jump a puddle on his way across the street. He was a big guy, with a belly, limping a bit after the jump. She knew he'd been a running back in high school, studied sports medicine, opened the first of his storage businesses right out of college, then inherited half of the urgent care businesses with his brother who lived abroad.

He'd made them each a success. So what was up with the Walk?

The minute Gus was in the door, he said, "No way we should go get those records today." He shook like a wet dog, and she stepped back to get out of the spray. "Sorry," he said absently. "But those boxes are all cardboard. With the way it's raining, they'll get ruined." Now he gave her a smile with a superior and nasty edge. "Don't want anyone saying I let the rain destroy important documents, now, right?"

"Of course," she said, turning on a smile. He looked puzzled when she didn't rise to his bait. "The auditor won't be back till Thursday, so no harm in waiting until tomorrow."

She'd just bring Pepper down here to the office tonight and spend all evening reading years four, five and six for the Walk. Geneva had finished those. Mari'd done this long enough that she knew what kind of things to look for. There were only so many ways to hide the money in a regular set of books on an event. Even if they were sloppily kept, she'd probably be able to figure it out. People who stole were never as clever as they thought themselves to be. She wanted to see the books. The auditor would make it official, but she was fairly confident she could spot fraud, if that was what was going on.

"Glad you agree, 'cause Hestworth's going to be breathing down my neck about it." He returned the smile, this time with real warmth. "Why don't you give him a call and tell him why we're not getting the stuff in today? I gotta deal with this break-in shit that happened at my other business."

*Condescending asshole.*

"I was sorry to hear about that." He wanted her to do the dirty work. She was fine with that. Pere would recognize the tactic. "And I'll be happy to call Pere," she said, surprising him. "I'll also let Jeremy know he doesn't have to stick around."

"Good." Gus headed for his office, shouting at Carol to bring him coffee, and to get Chief Strongbow for him.

"Asshole," Mari muttered the expletive aloud as she turned to the new door and her new office. The lanky, just-past-teenage, young man who opened it from the other side nearly fell over himself apologizing.

"Sorry, ma'am! Really, sorry," he fumbled.

"Its fine, we just happened to have the same direction."

"Yeah, happens to me all the time," Jeremy said with good-natured charm. "I'm all done in there if you're ready to go get the boxes."

"That's been postponed," she began.

Jeremy snickered. There was no other word for it. He had the grace to blush and duck his head, embarrassed. "Sorry, but I kinda figured Mr. Gus wouldn't want to try haulin' the boxes in the rain."

"Yes, so we'll go tomorrow morning, bright and early, if you can help then?"

"Yes, ma'am," he said, and actually tipped his dusty, paint-spattered ballcap. "See you in the morning."

She watched him go out into the rain, but unlike everyone else, who'd ducked their heads and run to escape the rain, Jeremy tilted his face up and smiled, letting the downpour wash over him like a balm as he strolled down the street toward the construction truck in which he'd arrived.

She went into her new office and finally, there was

something for her to actually smile about. The warm toffee-colored walls glowed, the tin ceiling was a uniform bronze color, the desk and hutch behind it streamlined but large and efficient. She already had a phone, some of her own books and awards, several plants and a huge bouquet of flowers on a small round conference table nearby, to warm the space. The flowers were from Aunt Vinnia and the Hachette cousins. She'd nearly cried when the bouquet had shown up Monday morning.

The cheerful faces of the blooms, and light, sweet scent had her stepping over to bury her nose in the blossoms, just to calm her irritation. She didn't want to call Pere. She didn't want to speak to him or hear his voice. Especially now that she knew what he was thinking about their encounter.

Tension roiled in her gut. It was stupid, but she felt like the new kid in town all over again, just as she had all through her childhood. It was as if she'd regressed to the awkward, nerdy teen reporter from the high school yearbook, calling the football star for a pretend report just so she could talk to him.

"Get over yourself, Mari," she grumbled. "Find your big girl panties and deal, for heaven's sake."

She took a deep breath and was about to dial when Carol poked her head in after a brief knock.

"Hi, sorry, the intercom thing isn't working on your phone yet. Um, did you want coffee? Or tea?" she said, then shook her head. "Um, not what I came to say. Um, Chief Strongbow is here to see you."

"Me? Why?" She set down the phone, and stood, then smiled at Carol's anxious hand wringing. "Never mind, Carol, show him back. He probably just wants to say hello and get acquainted."

Carol's face lifted at her words, and she smiled. "Oh, yes, you're probably right. He hasn't met you yet."

Lydia and the cousins had told her about Chief Strongbow, about his family's roots in the community going back to the founding of the town. Evidently the Native Americans in the area had accepted the renegade witches easily, whereas other settlers throughout Massachusetts had been targets until long after the Revolution. According to Aunt Vinnia and Cousin Caroline, Mari wasn't related to the chief—Mari fought down her amusement at the thought of him being Native American and a chief, even if it was of police and not a tribe—though Aunt Vinnia had said that the Strongbows, the Hestworths, and the Parrises were about the only families she didn't have some direct kinship with.

Indirectly, she was related to Pere through the Aldens and the Prescotts.

All this family stuff was beginning to weird her out. She was related to Gus in two different ways, and Carol in three different ways.

A tall, black-haired man stepped into her office, wiping his hand on his pants before offering it to her to shake. "Sorry, still raining outside," he said as they shook hands.

His voice was deep and resonant, his eyes a golden brown, but any other preconception about his genetics stopped there. There were none of the distinctive features of the Southwestern tribes she'd encountered, just a sense of grounded strength, which didn't have anything to do with race or genetics.

He introduced himself, as did she. "Please, have a seat. Can Carol get you some coffee, something cold?" she asked, seeing Carol hovering in the doorway.

"Thanks, no. I won't take much of your time," he said, sitting in her new guest chair. Carol discreetly closed the door, and Mari smiled. "My wife said she met you yesterday," he said, surprising her. "She's a jeweler at All That Glitters."

"Oh, yes. Susan. She mentioned she was married to the police." The brisk, petite woman had been all bright chatter and movement, with a dash of bitterness thrown in as she changed the battery in Mari's watch. The woman had gone on and on about how pretty and expensive the watch was.

It seemed an odd pairing given that the chief felt like a still pool, with none of his wife's frenetic energy.

"She kept her own name, so it isn't obvious," he said, then switched topics. "You're wondering why I'm here."

"Yes, but I'm happy to meet you finally. Working smoothly with law enforcement is key in the Walk's success."

"True. I understand you've met Saul Turner, from the traffic committee."

"Yes, we met and I was really impressed with that group's work. Was there something about that committee's work that you needed to see me about?"

"No, it's about your car."

Mari frowned. What was it with the cars? "My car? It's a rental. I didn't move my old car across country. It was in the shop more than it was running, so I made a clean break."

"Huh. Yeah, wondered about that. So it's a red sports car. Unusual for a rental," he said, and made a note in the notebook he'd pulled out. "Do you by any chance know the license plate?"

"No, I know it's a red Ford Mustang." She stopped, thinking. "Oh, wait, I have the rental agreement in my briefcase. That should have the license plate number."

He nodded and made another note, just one word, but she couldn't read what it was. She dug out the agreement, handed it to him.

"Why the interest in my rental car?"

"Did you pick it up at Logan?" he asked, naming Boston's international airport.

"Yes, I did. I flew in with my dog, and general luggage, and the moving truck came a few days later."

"Got it. So did you know Lissa Halliday?"

"Who?"

"Lissa Halliday. She owned a gaming business Pere

Hestworth bought out. I understand they had dinner together at the Judge's Chambers. You ran into them there."

"Oh, the blonde with the killer shoes. I was so sorry to hear about her accident." Mari paused waiting to see if the chief would say anything, but he didn't, so she continued. "I didn't meet her, exactly. Just ran into them as Lydia Webb and I were going for a drink. Why?"

"Nothing much, really. Just checking on some things. Her rental car and yours are identical." He handed back the folded pink rental car receipt. "According to this, they're the same down to the year, model and paint color. That's not so unusual," he admitted, then added, "However, the Walk has had some controversy, a few mild threats. Just covering the bases."

She thought about telling him about the calls she'd gotten when the Hachette ladies came by. The ones that were supposedly from Carol, but actually hadn't been. Mari decided it was just coincidence. Like the red-car thing.

"Ms. Beecham," he began.

"Mari, please. We'll be working together a lot."

He smiled, a slow, even curve of the lips. "All right, call me Jake. Mari, my job here is to keep people safe. If there's anything going on, I'd rather catch it early."

"But it was an accident, right?"

The chief tilted his head fractionally, from side to side, as if to say maybe-maybe-not. "Could be, but there are some signs that argue for it being something else. Pere Hestworth mentioned that your car was similar."

"Of course. Did she have enemies?" She shook her head. "What am I saying? Obviously she did, or you wouldn't be here telling me there might have been foul play."

He smiled briefly. "Yes. I don't like to think this was something directed at you and she just happened to be driving a car like yours."

"To me?" Mari managed to keep her voice from squeaking in shock. "But…"

"Strong feelings about the Walk," Jake repeated. "And some picketing, according to my officers. Some threatening talk from the pulpit," he added, looking disgusted. "Which is just wrong." He shook his head. "Forget I said that. What I'm getting at here, Mari, is that this wasn't just a traffic accident. So if there's anything that happens, even if it's just the picketers coming back, I want you to call us." He laid a card down on her desk. It had the main, non-emergency line in bold, along with an embossed 9-1-1 and the Chief's name and cell number. "Have you had anything happen, Mari, that might have been tampering?"

"I don't know," she said, taking the card. "There've been several things."

"But?"

"My car broke down. Some wires had been pulled. That was easy enough to fix. I had a flat. Again, that could be coincidence. A car swerved toward me on the road when I was out for a run, I had to jump onto the bank not to get hit. Again, could just have been somebody texting and driving."

Jake nodded, made notes. Said nothing.

"But I had a prank call Friday night. Several actually. It was someone pretending to be Carol. Saying it was urgent that I come to the Walk office. It was late when I realized I had voice mail."

Jake made notes. "What's your cell number?" He wrote it down as she dictated it. "What did you do?"

"I called Carol." She felt the blush heat her cheeks. "I woke her up and scared her half to death, because it wasn't her. She'd been asleep since ten-thirty."

"What was the number of the caller, if it wasn't Carol."

She pulled out her cell phone, scrolled to the Recent Calls screen and handed him the phone.

"Unknown caller," he read. "Great. What made you

think the calls were from Carol?"

"I know," she said, ruefully, closing the phone. "And although the messages were really crackly, the caller was a woman and sounded like Carol and she said she was Carol, calling to ask me to come to the Walk office."

"So you called Carol." He nodded. "And it wasn't her after all."

"No, it wasn't."

"Cell company could pull something, probably, but there's no cause for a warrant yet for that sort of thing. But I'd advise you to do just what you did. If someone calls and wants you to come somewhere, especially at night? Double check, then call me."

She started to nod, but he wasn't finished.

"You're gonna feel foolish, like it isn't a big thing," he continued. "It is a big thing."

"Words of wisdom?"

He smiled, "If you like. In this town, we're not afraid to say we've got a bad feeling or a hunch and have it be believed." He stood and held out a hand to shake. "I've got a bad feeling, so we're going to double down on caution, all right?"

She shook his hand and returned the smile. "All right."

The chief's next stop was MicroMechanics.

"I thought all you crazy-rich Internet mogul gamer guys decorated with gold leaf and diamonds," he teased as he looked around. "This office is for shit, Pere." He plopped into the chair and regretted it immediately. "By the Green Man, Pere, can't you at least get comfortable chairs? What's up with the hard-cushion thing? You want guests to leave quickly?"

"Dude, we started out as poor, stupid gamers with an idea that we managed to grow while eating ramen noodles and Beanie Weenies." Pere said, laughing as he leaned back in his own chair, swiveling it slightly. It creaked.

"Got that, but you've moved beyond, dude." Jake

looked around again. "You need a decorator. Your office is a dump."

Pere laughed and looked around trying to see it from Jake's viewpoint. He and Jake had been friends since high school. Jake had played football too and he'd remembered Gus, just the same way Pere did. Jake had gone on to play for West Point.

He'd survived high school, thanks to Jake, their friend Dan, who'd come back last year to run the library, and Sam Samuels. Sam was back as well, a doctor at the small, regional hospital, which had to be quite a come-down from the impressive position he'd held in Chicago.

He was sure Jake had seen plenty of worse—real—dives, far fouler than his office, as a Marine. So, since he trusted Jake like few others, he tried to take a new perspective, and took a good hard look around the space.

"You're right." He realized it as he said it. "It needs an overhaul."

"You need more security too. Lots more strangers in town, and you've hired some unknowns from a company with some problems."

Pere sighed. "I know. Lissa Halliday's company does come with its share of disgruntled employees. I'm weeding out the hackers and baddies before I bring them here and give them access to anything." It frustrated him, so he got up, paced, sat back down, this time next to his old friend. Jake was right, the chairs sucked. "I can keep the systems safe, the hardware and software. The building? Not so much." He grinned. "Although it's smothered in safety spells, thanks to Lydia and Dolores Webb, Madame Sabina, and my mother's coven, so we'll eliminate some trouble right off the bat."

"Yeah. That works. But belt and suspenders, dude. You need magick and tech on security. I've got a friend."

"I'll bet," Pere drawled, laughing. Jake had an uncanny knack for knowing someone you'd need almost before you did. "With the security or the design?"

"Both." Jake said, and took out his notebook, scribbled a note, then looked back up. "Tell me more about Lissa Halliday."

At Pere's growling noise, Jake smiled. "Yeah, I get it, she wanted you to be her boyfriend. Never shouldn't'a slept with her, bro."

"Too right. I wanted her gone, but not *gone*."

"I know. Besides, you were playing poker with Dan and Sam when she was run off the road."

"Yeah, I should have been home in bed, for all the good it did me."

"Better that you weren't," Jake said, lifting his little book. "You have an alibi."

Pere felt suddenly cold. "It wasn't an accident?"

"No. But I'm not looking at you. Your deal with her was done. You'd gain nothing by her injury or death, other than a little peace and quiet."

"Not to deny the value of peace and quiet, but that would be too high a cost for it."

"I know. And I know you wouldn't raise a hand to a woman, even provoked. So," Jake murmured as he straightened. "Who gains?"

Pere wasn't sure Jake was actually looking for an answer, but he gave one. "No one, as far as I know. I wasn't privy to her private life, much as she wanted to believe I was in love with her."

"Would she have run herself off the road, for sympathy?"

"Her accident wasn't really an accident then." Pere realized Jake hadn't confirmed that. Obviously he wasn't going to, but Pere knew now. He felt the troubling rise of a vision, of cuts and bruises and the blood flowing from Lissa's body to stain the ground. He blocked it, but it lurked at the edges of his mind.

*Dammit.*

He'd been having more trouble blocking the visions since Mari Beecham came to town.

"No, she was too much of a narcissist to hurt herself," Pere said, his voice heavy with dislike. Jake just looked at him, waiting. "Look, I really don't know her. I dated her briefly, slept with her twice. Months later, I found out she owned a company I wanted to buy. She was more open to the buyout because I was the guy who made her feel good—her words—and yes, I used that, but I wasn't her confidant, I was her rival. I bought the company. She decided it was a merger. It wasn't. I told her, repeatedly, that she had no place in the new structure and that we wouldn't be seeing one another again. I didn't shut her down hard enough, not until the other night."

"Not even in the Hamptons?"

Pere rolled his eyes. "I hate the Hamptons."

"Mari Beecham drives the exact same rental car. Same make. Same model."

"I know."

"I think she was the target, but whoever set this up got Lissa instead. Female driver, red sports car."

Pere closed his eyes, and immediately an image of smoke, fire and blood bloomed in technicolor behind his closed lids. Mari, bleeding.

He opened his eyes, to meet Jake's. "You going to have someone watch out for her?"

"Of course. My guys will patrol near her house. I gave her my cell number. I talked to the sheriff, his team'll be on the alert in the other parts of the county, if she goes driving. I'm going to have Lydia do some protection charms for her."

"Good call. Think she'll take them?"

"They get on well," Jake said, shrugging. "Susan didn't like her, so she's probably a good person."

Pere stopped himself before he said something rude. Jake had married Susan Crane on shore leave after his first, terrible tour as a Marine MP. She'd been bright, happy and everything America and home could offer a sorrowful soldier. She'd even liked being a Military spouse. When

Jake was deployed, she did what she wanted, and the homecomings between deployments were celebrations and wild fun.

However, the day-to-day of living with her man, now a small-town police chief, brought out the mean in her. She'd told Jake to his face that she didn't regret her affairs during his deployments. But Jake never asked for a divorce.

"You say that with such ease," Pere finally commented. "Don't you think it's—"

Jake interrupted him, his face closed and eyes grim. "I keep my promises."

"I know," Pere said, and let the matter drop. "So what's up with Lissa's not-an-accident that you're keeping it so hush-hush?"

"Beyond thinking that they got the wrong target?" Jake stuffed his notebook back in his shirt pocket. He seemed relieved Pere let the matter of his failing marriage go so easily. "It wasn't obvious, but there were signs that whoever ran her off the road checked on her, opened the car door. Nothing too overt, but most of the time, windshield glass doesn't make the kind of cuts she had gotten from the windshield. There was a lot of blood. Somebody besides Lissa and the EMTs was in that ditch that night."

"How do you deal with that, the blood?" Pere repressed a shudder at the continued feeling of the vision, lurking. He wasn't great with real blood. Despite the games he designed being full of ax-wielding Vikings, and barbarian swordsmen and women, he didn't want to deal with bloodshed one-on-one. "It's gotta be hard."

"Yeah, it is," Jake said, noting Pere's distaste. "Still a problem? With blood?"

"Yeah."

Jake's phone pinged, and he straightened, pulled it out and looked at it. "Gotta go. I'll forward you names on the designer and the security guy."

"Thanks. Jake," Pere said, before his longtime friend could get to the door. "You don't think this is a one-off." It wasn't a question. Not really.

Jake looked back at him, dark eyes filled with trouble. "No."

####

It had felt so good! The woman hadn't been the new executive director of the Walk, but oh! When she'd come speeding around the curve, and then off into the bushes and into the tree because of the other driver, the triumph surging through him had been...

He blushed a painful scarlet, and dropped to his knees to pray.

"Lord, forgive me for impure thoughts. I know that I should have called the police," he said, and tears tracked down his face for a moment as remorse filled his heart, he almost—almost—captured the true feeling of sorrow and pain. But the Bible he clutched to his chest warmed in his hands and distracted him, and the hatred returned.

"They're witches," he said after a moment, and a glittering anger filled his heart and tinged his vision with red. "They are the limbs of Satan himself." Gus Wilkerson and Jake Strongbow had been the worst of the lot, allowing these people to run rampant, to be part and parcel of the very fabric of the community. The mayor, the council with its coven members, the churches. The sheriff even.

They were all in collusion to create a hotbed of evil, of satanic activity.

But he'd gone along with it. He'd felt that the godly thing was to work in concert with these people, save souls where he could, and be an example of living a Christ-like life. He'd found a way to deal with Gus. But Jake resisted his efforts.

Then, the woman's blood had flowed under his hands, the knife he'd pulled out to cut her free of the seatbelt had ended up making her cuts from the window glass and the flying debris in the car bigger, bloodier. The glass had shattered when she hit the tree, the bruises on her face from hitting the airbag. The feel of that blood on his hands had been like the heavens had opened and the glory of God had rushed through him.

The power of it had been like the first time he read the letters he'd found in the oldest church records. The ones he'd found locked in the first pastor's office, beneath a floorboard that broke under his foot. That rush of pain and power had been so like his long-ago conversion, his baptism, that it couldn't be wrong.

A moment of clarity screamed at him that he was snared himself, caught in the clutches of evil.

"No!" he exclaimed out loud, clutching the book to his chest. He'd put the letters there, where he could read them. No evil could come from the Bible.

An idea formed in his mind, so clear, so perfect that he had to smile.

"Yes. Oh, yes. That's perfect."

As he bowed his head to pray, he didn't even notice the faint reddish glow that engulfed the Bible he clutched.

## CHAPTER EIGHT

Mari believed in being careful, and being prepared. She'd taken precautions, hadn't she? She locked her doors, checked her windows, made sure the perimeter was clear. She laughed at that, thinking of her father's military lingo.

She'd been smart, hadn't she? She'd talked herself out of taking Pepper down to the Walk office at night. With everything going on, she wasn't sure it was safe to be there alone.

But putting out charms? That was just a little freaky.

"They're for safety," Lydia said, catching her in the driveway as she was about to leave for work. "Hey, if our top cop thinks you need them, I'm going to be sure you get them, okay? Besides, he's paying for them—a welcome and be safe present."

"What's so magickal about it?" she asked, taking the intricate copper-wire star, with its beautiful crystal point hanging in the center. Once it was in her hand, she felt a sense of peace and delight in just touching it.

Lydia looked smug and nodded. "See, you feel it. It's smoky quartz, and the copper is a fabulous conductor for magic. It's imbued with magickal protections to ward off evil, to ward off intruders, and to make anyone think twice about messing with you.

"And besides that," she added, still looking pleased with herself, "It's pretty."

"It is pretty," Mari agreed, and walked back up the front steps to hang it on the nail that was already embedded in the brightly painted front door. "There, it looks great."

"It does. Let's hang the one on the back door, and then both of us can get to work."

"Deal."

Mari considered the stars and the kind gesture as she drove into the Walk office. It warmed her to think that people were accepting her, just as it chilled her to think that someone wanted to hurt her. Lydia had promised a charm for her car as well, and for Pepper's collar.

Lydia had refused to let her pay for the charms for the doors, or for the salt she'd sprinkled over the thresholds, but, with a grin, had said she'd definitely take payment for the collar and car charms.

Mari spent the rest of the day with that in the back of her mind. More frustrations with Gus were leavened by really excellent interactions with the grounds and Walk volunteer coordinators, and a talk with two of the vendors who'd been at the walk in prior years. After discussing their concerns and assuring them that they would be accommodated, both committed to return to the Walk, even at this late date.

Mari was still trying to figure out the bands and trucking companies who weren't visible but had been paid. She didn't have the checkbook, but she knew how to do it once she had access.

Mari loved the growing excitement around town. That energy was what made events so wonderful, in her opinion.

"Here's the paperwork for the latest vendors," she said, handing the newly completed forms to Carol.

"I'm so excited." Carol beamed. "I've got just the place for them and it totally solves the issue Mrs. Jamison has of being too near another tarot card reader." Carol positioned a pin with Jamison's name on it in a strategic place on the Faire grounds. "This way, she's not too close to anyone in town who's doing readings, like Madame Sabina, and she's several rows away from the gals who work out of Lydia's shop, who are here," Carol pointed out a different row and a different booth, right next to the one marked for The Besom Shop.

"So Lydia keeps the shop open and has a booth for the Faire?"

"Yeah, she's really popular." Carol said, opening an enormous three-ring binder and slipping in a page with Mrs. Jamison's information on it. "She has brooms and herb and lotion samplings in the booth, and then people can go to the shop for more selection or other things. She also hires a bunch of the track kids from the high school as runners. She gets them these really cool broom shirts and hats," Carol grinned and opened another binder, full of pictures. "See?"

The picture was a group of teens laughing at the camera, all of them with brooms emblazoned on their shirts in gold. They had on hats with brooms sticking out of the front of the brim and the back of the hat, as if it had been pierced by the broom, and they glittered in brown and gold, including their sneakers.

"These are great. What do the kids do?" Mari had a good guess, which Carol confirmed.

"Oh, they 'fly' back to the main store from the booth, to get a customer whatever they want, just in case they want something but don't want to walk to the store."

"Great marketing."

"That's Ms. Lydia for you."

Mari made a mental note to have a long chat with Lydia after this year's Walk was over. She obviously had unique and clever ideas about marketing.

Gus flung open the door, at that moment, and strode in pushing a hand truck loaded with file boxes. "Carol," he grunted, pushing the cart over the thick carpet. "Get the office door."

Carol rushed to do so, and the faint musty scent of paper and dust reached Mari as Gus breezed past. She followed him to the door of the office where Geneva had been working. He unloaded the boxes onto the only spot on the desk where there was any space. With more and more Walk paraphernalia coming in, space was at a premium. Teams of volunteers had begun making up Walk gift bags and Walker packets, which now filled bin after bin in the conference room and spilled over onto table after table in the new space. They'd be taken to Salem the first of next week, ready for the walkers.

"Are those the last of the records?" Carol asked, whisking Geneva's files off the desk as Gus hefted, then plunked down, the latest boxes with a dusty thud.

"Last that're in storage," Gus said, wiping his hands on a rag he took from his back pocket. "I got the latest two years at home 'cause I was going over them before the Walk prep this year," he said, turning his head to wipe his brow on the edge of his shirt. "I'll have to get those put in a box and get them back in here."

"I thought Jeremy was going to help you?" Mari spoke for the first time, her heart sinking at the thought of Gus having all the most recent records held captive at his house.

"Yeah, well, he's busy," Gus snapped at Mari's question. "Walk stuff. So I brought this last bit over myself. Auditor's gonna be back tonight so she can get to work tomorrow morning bright and early. I want her to be able to get started on this."

Mari looked forward to Geneva's return, but she was going to dig into these boxes as soon as Gus left for the day. Pere said Gus was up to something and it was up to her to figure out what before it sank the Walk. She had a really bad feeling about it, and she never went against that.

Her lips twitched, thinking about what the police chief had said about hunches. Haven Harbor was obviously a place where her mild brand of intuition would be taken as absolutely normal.

When Mari finally left, heading for home and dinner, it was only because Gus had waited her out. She decided it was the better part of wisdom to leave, and then go back. This time, she'd let the Chief know, so she'd have back up. She was going to get to the bottom of this business with Gus and the Walk finances.

Nothing prepared her for what waited on her when she got home.

Police tape and two police cars, along with an unmarked panel van, were parked in front of her house. She pulled up behind the van and got out, walking over to Chief Strongbow.

"Hello, Chief. What's going on?"

"Ms. Beecham, I was just about to call you," he said. "I got Gus at the Walk office, so I was going to go for your cell. Seems someone wanted to do more than picket." He motioned to the porch where two clear quart jugs sat on the porch filled with a dark, red liquid. Three more empty quart jugs were lined up with them.

"They painted an enormous cross on your porch," he said. "It's drawn in blood with some other blood splashed around as well. We don't know if it's human or not, but no matter what, it's just wrong, so we'll be clearing it up for you."

"Thank you," she said, suddenly feeling shaky. What an ugly, ugly thing to have done. "Why would someone do this? Has Gus ever had this kind of thing happen?"

Strongbow shrugged. "Most people know Gus, and need his businesses, so no, he hasn't had this kind of thing. You're new, and whoever's up to this nastiness is trying to scare you off. They also have you in their sights because you're coming on to grow the Walk, make it bigger, broader with a greater appeal."

"It won't work," Mari said, hoping her voice sounded strong. "I don't scare easily."

"That's a good thing," the chief said, moving away from the steps and back toward her car. "Let's move over here where we won't be overheard. Someone tried the doors. There's boot prints in the mud next to the back steps, unless you have bigger feet than I think." He made a point of looking down. "That would be a no, on that one," he said, smiling. "Then someone was on your back porch. They didn't get in."

"I'm so glad."

He nodded. "I guess Lydia dropped by before work."

"Yes, how did you know?"

"Because your intruder didn't get in and splash the mess in the last two jugs all over your house."

Mari felt her mouth drop open in shock. She'd always read that phrase, but thought, *really, does that happen?* She was now proof that it did.

"Between the charms and the salt across the threshold, they couldn't or wouldn't pass."

"Well, I'll be damned," she said.

Jake grinned. "I hope not."

"What?" His response took her totally aback.

"I doubt you'll be damned."

"Ha! Yeah, turn of phrase gets you in trouble around here," she muttered, still looking from the techs to the front door. The crystal in the lovely charm Lydia had helped her hang was crazed and cracked as if it had been heated. The copper wire was dark and looked bent in places.

At her side, she felt as much as saw the chief shift

when his phone rang. "'Lo" he answered, but although she couldn't hear what was being said, she could see the change in body language to a more tense stance. He nodded at her, and moved toward his cruiser. One of the other officers converged on the car as well, and when the chief spoke to him, he blanched, and nodded, heading to his police car.

"We've got a call," Jake said, walking back to her. "But you're in good hands. I presume you'll press charges if we get whoever did this?"

"You bet I will."

####

"What the hell are you doing?" Gus hissed into the phone. "This is unconscionable! Not only that, you know the witches in this town will figure it out!"

"No, they won't. Not if you don't tell them."

"I won't have to. You don't get it. They'll use magick. They'll figure it out."

"No one finds out who I am and what I do without evidence, and no one left any."

He knew it was useless to try and explain the powers of the witches in Haven Harbor to an outsider, to a non-believer. She just wouldn't listen. He was going to have to bring his idiot brother into it after all. Carl didn't have much innate magick, which is why he'd turned to the darker stuff, and to drugs, though he'd deny that.

"This week's shipment will be double the size, so be waiting."

"No, I can't handle double," Gus said, panicking. "I promised I'd handle this end till the end of the Walk this year, but with all the uproar, you've made that impossible." She just didn't get it. The witches would know. "I gotta lie low."

"No. We have a deal. You have been paid."

"Not this time. I'll send the money back the same way. I can't take double. Just the usual. The chief is suspicious, and I need to back off or we both risk getting caught.

Once I'm not doing the Walk anymore, I'm gonna have to bow out all the way." He hated it, would miss the extra money, but he had to get this straight. He hadn't thought much of it until that woman was nearly killed. That had sent him a hard, cold message about who these people really were.

He knew his contact wasn't the top dog, she just moved the drugs he'd gotten hooked on two years ago when he'd busted his leg. When he realized it was too dangerous to get them through his business, he'd gotten it from his brother, Carl, and from her. Sure, she was sexy. A temptress.

For her, he'd kicked the drugs, and for her, he kept selling them. He'd fooled himself that he did it for Carl, because his idiot brother couldn't keep clean.

But really, he liked the cash.

But it was too dangerous now. He was sure they had someone in Haven Harbor, watching him. Reporting on what he was doing. They knew too much for there to be any other answer.

"Just let me handle it, okay?"

"No." Her voice was cold now. "I gave you time, and you wasted it. It's been handled. Deal with the rest of it. Including the double shipment. Or else."

He started to protest, but she was gone. He winced as he dropped the phone in his pocket. Where was Carl?

"Idiot," Gus sneered to himself scanning the street for his brother. He knew what Carl courted in going the darker path, and he also knew that Carl was up to something, trying to get to Mari Beecham. If the woman was seriously injured or killed, there would be an investigation, Gus would be stuck in the middle and Carl wouldn't care. "He's going to have to care now," Gus muttered, checking to see if anyone was on the street behind the Walk offices. Carl had gotten him into this; he could sure as hell help get him out.

They were going to have to risk the witches of Haven

Harbor. Those records had to be destroyed.

When his brother walked into the office, Gus started to smile. Then to chuckle.

Let them watch. Tonight, there would be plenty to see.

####

"Mari, its Jake. You need to come to the Walk office. There's been some trouble."

That call came in just as Mari brought Pepper back inside, so she grabbed her keys and headed into town.

Mari had been on a second, equally bland date with Kevin, the lawyer. He'd been interesting, and a gentleman, but his goodnight kiss left her cold, and on the drive home from the restaurant in Pennyfield, she'd resolved not to see him again. Now, dating was the farthest thing from her mind. Mari looked at the mess in her office.

"What a mess," she said into the relative quiet of the new office space. In the outer area, Jake and Pere were checking the damage to the window glass in the door, other officers were taking pictures. They hadn't been able to get Gus on the phone, so they'd called her.

The office portion of the new space was trashed. The vase her flowers had come in was smashed, her awards and desktop knickknacks tossed to the floor, her papers and books scattered. Gus's office had received the same treatment. His chairs were smashed to kindling, his desk bore heavy gouges, and papers, files and books were tossed everywhere. Geneva's office had been locked, but that hadn't helped. The door had been kicked in, and boxes were strewn all over the room. There were boxes missing, and it looked like all the records boxes had been taken.

Oddly enough, to her eye, it looked like nothing else had been touched.

"It's weird," she muttered, thinking hard.

"What?"

"Good Lord!" she cried, nearly jumping out of her skin. "Warn me or something," she snapped, as both Jake and Pere came into the room. They looked abashed at having scared her.

"Sorry," they each said.

It was Jake who broke the immediate, embarrassed silence. "What's weird?"

"If this is about stopping the Walk, why were the offices trashed, the records taken, but all the Walk materials are untouched?"

Both men looked around. Tables had been set up in the long, narrow "neck" of her new office space. They were loaded with boxes of Walk volunteer shirts, Walk participant shirts and packets, hats, florescent vests for traffic management volunteers, directional markers, signs and all the paraphernalia that accompanied a huge event. Beyond the open door, the board room table was equally laden, and the map on the wall in the main room was an explosion of colored pins—untouched, undisturbed pins.

"It's just our desks, and the Walk paperwork."

"That is odd."

"I think I need to find Gus and have a very serious talk with him," Jake stated, hands on his hips. "I'm driving to his house. Chase is here, taking pictures. I'll be back," he said, leaving her alone with Pere.

"I'll help you clean up." Pere bent to pick up books and stacked them back on the shelves of her credenza. They reached for a broken award at the same time and, picking up the separate halves, each cut themselves.

"Oh for heaven's sake," Mari griped, irritated at her own stupidity. "That was stupid. And we both did it."

"Yes," Pere agreed, dumping the heavy, offending glass award into the newly righted trash can with a resounding clang. "Here." He held out a wad of tissues from the box on the floor. It had split open, but the tissues were still pristine. She pressed them to the cut, and he did the same with his own.

"That's twice in one week," she said on a sigh, mentally cursing a blue streak.

They stood, awkwardly staring at one another. He said nothing, and she sure as hell wasn't going to bring up that his mother had told her what was going on with his reluctance to connect with her. Anger surged within her, but she tamped it down.

"I'm supposed to head for Moulden in an hour," she said. "A late meeting with the committee for the overnight spot there."

"I have meetings as well," he said, looking around the room. He frowned. "You're right. It's weird."

The anger faded, and she shivered at the thought of someone wreaking such havoc, yet leaving all the Walk materials serenely untouched. What did it mean?

When they heard the scream of sirens outside, Mari and Pere raced into the main Walk reception area in time to see the fire truck and ambulance that had been sitting outside make a racing turn down Rowan, headed toward the river.

"What on earth?"

Pere turned to Chase Pickett, the young officer who was taking pictures. "Chase?"

"Jake just called in from Gus Wilkerson's house. It's been smashed up and Gus is hurt."

Mari's hand flew to her mouth. What was happening? If it hadn't been Gus damaging the offices—a conclusion she knew that she, Jake and Pere had immediately leapt to— —then who? If Gus was hurt, at his house, he couldn't have trashed the Walk offices, could he?

She said as much to Pere when they went back to her office.

"I don't know, Mari," he said, looking frustrated, concerned, and a whole lot pissed off. "It would seem that Gus would have the most to gain by having those records disappear, but if he was hurt, there may be more to it." He looked around at the barely restored office. "And there could be worse to come."

#### ####

Pere knew he shouldn't have said anything about the

situation getting worse when Jake woke him at three in the morning.

"I think you're going to want to come down to the courthouse," he said, and Pere could hear the crackle of radios and the hiss of water hitting the dry earth, even through the phone.

"What's going on?" Pere said, pulling on his pants and snagging a shirt as he headed out of the bedroom.

"Fire. In the big cauldron out front of the courthouse. I think it may be all the Walk records that went missing."

"Shit."

"In a word," Jake said, sounding both pissed and worried, a combination of emotions Pere understood.

"On my way," was all he said, ending the call and snatching up his keys to head out.

Haven Harbor was as empty as a ghost town in the early hours. Pere was only to Yew St. when he started to see the reflected glare of the lights from all the fire and law enforcement vehicles. Neither the police nor fire department was large, but they had good equipment, and most of it was out front of the courthouse.

At this point, only steam rose from the enormous ceremonial—and now, only decorative—cauldron that sat in isolated splendor at the bottom of the courthouse steps. Every year, the Haven covens kindled a fire there for Samhain, for Yule and Beltane, and the high school seniors usually staged something with bubbles or balloons at the end of their school year, but otherwise, it sat empty.

Now it was the focus of several fire hoses.

"Isn't that overkill?" Pere said, walking up to where Jake stood by his Blazer.

"Not really. They're worried about the courthouse. As old as it is, it wouldn't take too many stray sparks to set it on fire. They're preventing that, as much or more than they're putting out the fire." Jake turned to look at him. "It's the Walk records. I'm sure of it. There are some unburned pages lying at the base of the plinth the cauldron sits on, like a box busted or something. There are a few pages under the feet too." Jake looked back as the fire chief called a halt and told his people to rake the ashes for hot spots, and roll the rest of the unneeded hoses.

"Worry about the courthouse explains the sheer number of units here. Is anyone out patrolling the streets?" Pere was trying to lighten the mood, but it didn't help him, or Jake.

"I've got the sheriff on it, he's shifted his patrols to cover us. Chase got the Walk windows boarded up. Gus is at the hospital. Sam was on duty tonight and said he took some hard blows." Jake's jaw tightened and he looked remote and dangerous in the flickering, colored lights. When he turned to Pere, his dark eyes were hard as well. "I'm not buying it. His house was totally trashed, more thoroughly than the Walk office, but there's something wrong about all of this."

"Other than the obvious, you mean?"

"Yeah."

About that time, an older man walked up to them. "Chief Strongbow, Mr. Hestworth."

"Pastor Walthers." Jake acknowledged the man, and with that naming, Pere recognized the older man.

"Sir," Pere said, according him respect due his age and position. He didn't have to like the man's beliefs to give him respect.

"I see there's been some trouble. What on earth happened?"

"We're not sure, Pastor," Jake said, and Pere realized how closely Jake was watching the man. "What brings you out this late, sir?"

The pastor sighed. "It's harder for me to sleep since my Melinda died," he said, looking toward the courthouse. The colored lights made his face a study in pain, and gave him an eerie doubling of his features. Pere was sure he saw a tear track down the man's face. "I was at the church, praying when I heard the sirens."

"You didn't by any chance see anyone or anything when you came to the church tonight, did you?" Jake asked, taking out his little book. Pere wondered, as he always did, why Jake didn't get something bigger on which to write, or use his phone to take notes. "What time did you arrive?"

The pastor grimaced. "I left home around eleven and have been in my office or the sanctuary. But neither of those faces the courthouse."

Jake nodded, putting his book away. "You should get home, sir, get some sleep."

The pastor nodded, and reached out, as if to clap Jake on the shoulder. Mid-reach, he stopped, as if realizing he didn't know Jake well. "You're right, young man. I will. And I'll pray that you catch whoever did this." He looked back toward the cauldron, a faint smile creasing his cheeks. "I did enjoy this year's senior prank, though."

They all smiled at that. The Haven Harbor seniors had filled the cauldron to overflowing with water balloons. It had prompted a water balloon fight on the courthouse grounds amongst both students and townspeople that was still being smiled over nearly three months later.

When the pastor had walked away, heading for his church, Jake frowned.

"What?" Pere said, walking up.

"He's grieving still."

"I didn't know you knew him," Pere said, surprised. From all he knew of the pastor, the man wasn't well liked among the majority of Haven Harbor's mostly pagan populace. His church was not one of the tolerant ones.

"I don't, but it's sad to think that three years on, maybe four, he's still so deep in his grief."

Pere nodded, knowing in part that the end of Jake's own marriage would never engender that kind of grief. It made him wonder about what he would feel when Mari left town at the end of her contract.

####

145

The fire that night, in front of the town council offices, and the break-in at the Walk office and Gus's house were the talk of the town the next day. Mari'd been in the office with Carol all day, cleaning up. Just before they left, the repair team with the replacement window glass had arrived. With little else accomplished, and Gus in the hospital overnight for observation, there was little else to do until tomorrow.

"So thank you, again, for the charms," Mari said, back at home. She was talking to Lydia as she dumped the debris from the front porch. This was the first moment she'd had to sweep. She shifted the phone from one ear to the other, pressing it with her shoulder so she could use both hands to put the broom and dustpan away. The crime scene people had taken most of the mess with them. Now that she was home for the day, Mari wanted the rest of it gone. "They obviously worked."

"Of course they did." Lydia's smug reply turned solicitous. "You sure you're okay though? Want to come hang at my house for a few nights?"

Mari felt a pang of something—homesickness? loneliness?—in her gut. She didn't know many people who would offer a virtual stranger refuge, especially from what many would consider just minor inconveniences.

"Thanks, but I'm good. It means a lot that you'd offer, though. I appreciate it."

"We gotta stick together," Lydia said cheerfully. "Only way to stay safe."

Safety. That was something she'd seldom had to consider, not really. It was a strange thing to have to consider it now.

"It's comforting to have a friend in town," she began, but the doorbell interrupted her. Frowning, she headed for the front of the house. "Hey, I've got company, I think. I'd better go."

"Call me later, or if you get wigged out or anything, okay?"

"Will do." She ended the call just as she reached the foyer, and a madly barking Pepper dancing on his hind legs, scratching at the door. Picking him up, she started to open it, then hesitated, and peeped through the security peep.

Pere Hestworth.

What did it say about her that her heart leapt into a pulsing rhythm of anticipation and her mouth dried out just seeing him?

"Nothing, absolutely nothing," she scolded herself. "He's off limits."

She opened the door just as he was reaching to push the bell again.

"Hi," she said, then felt totally lame. God! Why was it so difficult to talk to the man?

"Hi," he said, stuffing his hands into his pants pockets and rocking back on his heels. "I wanted to come by and see if you were okay."

"I'm fine, thanks," she said, struggling to restrain Pepper, who'd decided that this new person needed to be properly greeted. He wiggled so much she nearly dropped him.

"Hey, pup," Pere said, reaching out a hand for Pepper to sniff. Pepper promptly licked his hand and wriggled even more enthusiastically. Pere grinned and Mari nearly melted on the spot. The open, happy expression turned the severe lines of his broodingly handsome face into that GQ gorgeousness she'd thought of before. But better. More...real.

She let the dog jump down just to give herself something to do besides stare. She immediately regretted it, because now she had nowhere to put her hands. Thankfully, Pere crouched down to pet the dog and didn't see her fidgeting.

He looked up, and his smile nearly stopped her heart. His eyes changed first. The smile faded and his look grew more intense. "Marisol," he began.

"Peregrine," she said, her voice clashing with his.

It broke the moment and the smile returned, though it showed strain around the edges. "What's your dog's name?"

"Pepper. When he was a baby, his fur had black tips, as if he'd been dusted with pepper. He grew out of it, but by then the name had stuck."

*She was babbling, wasn't she? Why was she babbling?*

Because he intimidated her on a primal level. She wanted to touch him, see if his skin was as hot as it looked, as rough and tactile as she wanted it to be.

"May I come in?"

It took her a full two seconds to process the request. Red flushed her cheeks as she stepped back, opening the door. "Sure, please. Come on back to the kitchen. I was just making dinner."

"I'm sorry to interrupt," he said, his resonant voice making her nerves ping. "I can come back another time."

She wasn't sure she'd survive that.

"No, of course not. It's fine. Here, have a seat," she said, pulling out a chair at the little bistro table. "It won't take me a minute to stir this. Can I get you a glass of wine? Or a beer?"

She had beer, thanks to the Hachette cousins. And wine too. She had a bottle open.

"The red wine is fine. Thanks."

She bobbled the wine glass she got out of the cabinet. She nearly dropped the wine bottle.

"Dammit." She put down both bottle and glass and stomped over to him. "You make me nervous," she declared, crossing her arms and glaring at him. "And I hate being nervous."

To her surprise a slow, sensual smile curved his lips. He stood up slowly, moving into her space. She refused to back away, back down. Peregrine Hestworth would *not* intimidate her.

"I–"

"Here," he said, softly, his hand coming up to cup her cheek. "It's this," he said, his head dropping slowly toward her. He was going to kiss her. OhmyGod. "It's this energy between us," he said. "It's electric."

She slapped her hands to his chest, stopping him, this seemed like such a change. "I don't like to play with fire."

Such a lie.

"Liar," he echoed the thought, but didn't move in, didn't continue. If he had, she could have slapped him down, called him a chauvinist, gotten past it. Instead, he just watched her, letting that raw hunger show in his gaze, letting her feel the accelerated beat of his heart. His skin was hot through the shirt, a burning wall of muscle beneath her hands. She wanted to shape that muscle, pet him, slick her hands down the hard planes of his body.

"If you keep thinking that sort of thing, I'm going to spontaneously combust," he growled.

"Thinking what?" she squeaked, wondering how he knew.

"You're touching me, and for once, I'm not having visions of smoke and fire but of sex and heat. If that's not you projecting it, then I'm in trouble."

Her gaze flew to his. "You've been having visions of smoke and fire around me? I've been having those every time I touch you."

He nodded, his eyes narrowing. "Yes, I thought you might. It's why I was against hiring you. Something about you being here will bring fire and smoke and death."

"What?" Shocked, she tried to back away, but he'd put his hand on her hip when she wasn't looking, held her fast. "I'm not going to start any fires."

"Not you," Pere said. "Never you. But you've changed the dynamic. Shifted something. I told you, Gus is hiding something. Then all this mess today. It has something to do with him."

"And…and…and this other thing?" she said, unable to ignore the pounding of her heart, the heat that rolled off him in waves. "Between us?"

"I don't know," he said, gaze locked with hers. "I think my mother is tampering. I need to tell you about that."

"She already told me," Mari said, and Pere looked like he'd been slapped. "She says she hasn't put any charms on me or you. Lydia confirmed it."

Pere stood frozen for the space of several heartbeats, his gaze abstracted, as if looking inward. "I have to see," he said. His gaze flashed to hers, hot and urgent, but then his lashes dropped down and the look was gone. "Do you have a candle and some matches?"

"Yes." He took the items when she found them, and with a toothpick drew some lines and words into the candle wax. Lydia had done something similar, but added herbs and some chanting. It hadn't freaked her out in the light of day in the pretty, fun space of The Besom Shop.

Now, in her kitchen, with night falling, it was making her shiver.

"This would work better with a dark candle, but we'll make do." He muttered some things under his breath as he struck the match, and said more words, something about showing spells, as he lit the candle. "Stand here, in the middle of the room," he said, tugging her into place.

He walked around her clockwise, three times, and the candle flame pulled along with him, seeming to stretch out in an unnatural way as he walked. She felt surrounded, like she was in a pressurized tube.

"Let the smoke show the spell where the flame has passed," he said, his voice deep and resonant. Then he blew out the candle. It put out a huge amount of smoke, all of which curled around inside her invisible tube, twisting and twining but showing only curlicues and flowery, star-shaped shapes.

She'd almost expected it to glow in fiery letters like the ring in The Lord of the Rings.

He frowned, made a gesture and said, "I dismiss you,

and thank you, all Powers that Be."

"Who? What?" she said, wondering who he was dismissing.

"The power," he said absently, staring at the now-cold candle wick. "You don't have any spells on your person."

"I know. Lydia checked."

For the first time since he lit the candle, he actually looked at her. And smiled.

She felt her insides quiver at the sensual promise in his eyes. "If you're not under a spell, and neither am I," he said, his voice still in that intense, rich bass tone that made her want, "then I think we should find out what would have happened in your office, if we had continued."

She licked her lips and he focused on her mouth like it was gold. "But, what about the 'nothing personal'?" she said, her voice going husky at being the focus of that intense energy. "You said—"

"I don't want to be attracted to you," he said, his voice still holding that deep, growly note. "But it isn't going away. And it isn't a spell."

"No, it isn't." Somehow her hands had flattened onto his body again, slipped under the edges of his jacket to lie on the hard wall of his chest.

"What are we going to do about it?" he rumbled.

She was insane. She was certifiably crazy. Seriously. Nothing freaked her out more than aggressive, gorgeous men. She avoided them like the plague. Kevin was attractive, probably considered powerful, but to her, Kevin was bland and uninteresting. She'd dated other men who were CEOs or in the tops of their fields. None of them had made her feel like this.

"This, I guess," she managed before rising on her toes to press her mouth to his.

The rush of heat was almost unbearable. A torrent of sexual, sensual force rushed through her and had her gripping the fabric of his shirt like a lifeline. His hands slid to her back and pulled her closer, and he angled his head to deepen the kiss.

*OhmyGod can he kiss.*

The words repeated over and over in her mind, when she could form any coherent thought at all.

She slid down one hand to the curve of his butt, pulling him even closer, feeling his arousal, and making herself moan at the thought of him being with her, being inside her, driving her to peak after peak of pleasure.

"Mari," he rumbled the words against her mouth. "If you keep that up, I'm going to embarrass myself, like some randy teenager."

"Keep," she said between kisses, "what?"

"Thinking about us, together."

She broke the kiss, panting. She felt like some ravished heroine from a movie. Her equilibrium was off, and she knew if she drew away from his arms, she'd stagger.

"I wasn't thinking anything," she lied.

To her surprise, he laughed and rolled his eyes. "Aren't we past that? You were thinking about us making love, and me giving you orgasm after orgasm." He closed his eyes and took a sharp breath in.

"Code. I'm going to think about HTML and Calibre Security and a decorator. And security," he repeated.

Totally nonplussed, she drew back. "What?"

He opened his eyes, and they were just as hot, just as intense. "I nearly came just thinking about making love to you," he admitted. "I'm trying to get a grip, but you're not helping me by thinking about my cock."

Shocked, she blushed, then, she couldn't help it. She giggled.

He grinned.

She laughed and Pepper, who'd retired in disgust to his dog bed, bounced over to bark at them, pawing at their legs. Before she knew it, the two of them were whooping with laughter. The more they tried not to laugh, the more they did.

"Stop," she said, gasping and leaning on the kitchen

granite. "I'm going to wet my pants."

"Don't say wet and pants in the same sentence," he said, snickering. Then he looked at her and she snorted out another laugh. "Seriously."

"I'm going to the bathroom. Stop laughing," she said, all but running for the nearby powder room. She shut the door and leaned on it. What the hell had she just done?

She looked in the mirror at her tousled hair and flushed cheeks. "You kissed freakin' ice man Pere Hestworth, that's what you've done," she whispered, and grinned for all she was worth.

It took her two tries to get her pants undone and actually pee, and she was still half-giggling as she managed it.

She stopped outside the kitchen, trying to get herself together.

"You might as well come on back in, I know you're there. I heard the door."

The laughter was still in his voice, so she came around the corner. Part of her had dreaded that the cold mask he habitually wore would be back in place. Thankfully not.

"So," she said, going to the counter to grab her wineglass and take a gulp. Watching him pet the dog into a puddle of delight made her want to switch places with the dog. Instead, she opted for confrontation. "What the hell was that?"

"You planted a wet one on me," he said, smiling, lighter in his whole being than she'd seen him. She hadn't known he could smile like that. "Being a gentleman, I was compelled to accept."

"Riiiiight," she drawled. "So are we going to do it again or forget it happened and move on?"

"Good question." He frowned. She poured a glass of the red and brought it over, being careful not to touch him at all. He figured that out, because his lips tipped up in another brief smile. "I really did just come to check on you."

She cocked her head sideways. "Why? Do you check up on all the new gals in town, or just me?"

He laughed. "Just you, apparently. I felt compelled to." Now his frown was back, darker and deeper than it had been before. He turned to her. "I was sure...when did you meet my mother?"

"Uh, well, not the usual question, but I met her in The Besom Shop in my second week. Then again, yesterday, with Lydia. That's when they checked me for spells." She frowned. "What they did was different."

"Every witch has a different Gift and a different style. That's what makes witchcraft and magick more than a religion or a lifestyle. It's more personal."

She thought about that for a moment, still trying to reconcile Lydia's way with Pere's actions. She shrugged. "But you asked about your mother. She was there, at Lydia's." She took another gulp of wine. Was she really in her own kitchen talking with Pere about his mother? Had she really just been checked for spells, for the second-freakin-time?

*I'm living in Oz. Cynthia and Babs are going to have a fit when I tell them...*

The thought stopped her cold. She wouldn't be telling Babs or Cyn anything, she realized. Now Lydia's comments about "normals" made more sense.

"We're having coffee in a few days, your mother and I, if you'd like to join us."

"You're having coffee?"

"To talk about the Gala."

"Gods, it's upon us, isn't it?" he said, still frowning.

As much as she was relieved they were talking normally, her body ached from touching him, from being touched. It wanted more. She struggled to focus on the normal, on the job.

"Just about. Tents and set-ups arrive next week. Carol said the final shirts came in today at lunch, so I brought one home." Distracted from her arousal, she bounced to the counter and held up the bright purple shirt with a black cauldron and two footprints and the words Witches Walk 2016 on it. "These are the volunteer shirts. The Walkers have shirts in a gorgeous royal blue with the Walk logo on it—you probably saw those—but these, I was worried about these. They should have been in before the others."

"Nice," he nodded. "The logo turned out well this year. Some years it's silly. This year's is good."

"I'd like to get the shirts from each year framed and put up on the walls in the new space."

"That's a good idea."

"I have a few."

There was an awkward pause before he spoke again. "Mari, you're in danger."

"I know," she said automatically, and realized as she said it that she *did* know that, but hadn't really felt like it was a big deal. Women who lived alone always had a low grade danger level anyway, even if they had a dog. That sense of danger looming, however, was so subtle, she'd managed to ignore it. Then again, she'd also had those flashes of fire and pain when she was around Pere.

Pepper had abandoned Pere when Mari went to the counter, and now jumped up on her legs for a pet. She obliged him, scratching behind his ears and making his tags jingle.

"You'll be careful?"

"Of course I will."

He rose and moved to her. "I'm not sure what this is between us."

"But you don't like it," she stated, knowing from his reaction that it was the truth.

He shook his head. "I don't trust it—didn't trust it— that's completely different."

"Don't trust it?"

"I thought my mother was meddling."

"Yeah, about that. I thought her specialty was weather." Lydia had mentioned something about Mrs.

Hestworth and the weather, but Mari'd discounted it. "She said you were worried that she'd charmed you or hexed you."

"Hexed?" he laughed. "No, that's a darker magic, Mari. But she's no slouch at charms, even if she is a weather worker. She wants grandchildren. She and my dad were older when they had me, and she feels the pressure of time. She wants me to get married and produce little Hestworths to carry on the family name."

"And you don't buy into that?"

He reached out a hand, brushing the backs of his fingers over her cheek. The touch burned a path along her nerves, setting her skin tingling and sending her body right back into that hot zone of awareness they'd created. "So lovely," he murmured, sliding a hand along her wildly curling hair. "Such intensity."

She had to get control over this situation, somehow. "Me? Intense?" She shook her head, which had the effect of burying his hand in her hair. "No, you're the intense, brooding one."

"Am I?" He was getting that look again, the devouring, you're-my-everything look. "I don't know why you draw me so."

"I do?" She wasn't insecure about her attractiveness, but this wasn't just some random guy. This was Pere Hestworth. Town council chair, CEO/gamer, man about town.

He was, in some ways, her boss.

That stopped her cold, just as his lips touched hers.

"We can't," she said, gripping his wrist and pulling back at the thought. *Shit.* "I work for you."

"No you don't." He closed the distance, bending to brush his lips over his. "You work for the Walk."

"I serve at the pleasure of the town council," she insisted, aching to kiss him back, but slipping away to stand in the middle of the kitchen. "That's you."

He looked even more frustrated than she felt. "You're

right."

"I am?" she said, startled. Then realized how that sounded. "Yes, I am right. This is nuts." She fisted her hands, sternly telling her hormones to calm down. "Obviously, we're attracted to one another."

"Obviously," he drawled, still half turned away from her, and leaning on the counter. "You're lovely, smart. You're a keen businesswoman, and advocate for my town. What's not to like?"

Peregrine Hestworth had just told her she was lovely. It was going to start snowing in Hell at any minute. Wow.

"Thank you. You're…" She stopped. He wasn't lovely, but oh, my God he was—How had Lydia put it?— hotter than a matchhead.

"I'm what?"

What the hell did she have to lose? "Smokin' hot."

He hesitated a moment, as if processing that, then threw back his head and laughed. The sound was as full-bodied and rich as the wine they'd been drinking and she loved it.

"Thank you, I think."

"You're welcome." Oh, my God, she wanted him so bad. Even more so when he laughed, when she could see the man inside the armor. *Double fucking shit. She had to be the sensible one. It sucked wide.* "And now, I think you should go."

He nodded. "Yes." Just the one word, but it seemed to echo in the room. He set his wineglass in the sink, a little consideration that tugged unexpectedly at her heart. At the kitchen door, he stopped. "I'm not sorry I came."

"No," she agreed, walking him to the foyer. He stopped, and so did she. Once again, he caressed her cheek. That was a hell of a move. She didn't know why, but it set her every nerve on fire and melted things inside her. "It sucks to be sensible."

*Sensible, sensible, sensible.* She chanted it like a litany because she wanted to jump him right then and there.

*Must. Be. Sensible.*

"It does. I should go," he said, but made no move to reach for the door. "I really want to kiss you again."

"I want that, too." Oh, my God, did she want it. "But if we do, I'll end up tangled up in something hot and dangerous with my boss, and I don't do that," she said, holding on to sanity and common sense with both mental hands.

She would not sleep with her boss. She would not sleep with her boss. *She would not.*

"Just once," he said, stepping closer. "Just to see."

She didn't consciously move into him, but the whispered words were a siren call and she couldn't refuse. She was the one who closed the distance and looped her fingers into his belt loops to anchor herself as their mouths met, fused, and they scorched one another with one of the hottest, most amazing kisses Mari had ever experienced.

He wrapped his arms around her, one hand on her ass, the other pulling her tight to his chest. Breathing didn't matter, moving didn't matter. Nothing mattered except the power of his mouth, his tongue, and the heat between them.

When he lifted her, she wrapped her legs around his waist and let him back her against the door. He held her easily, which thrilled some primitive part of her brain that loved the caveman power of his strength. He also never lost the rhythm of the kiss, the furious dance of mouth on mouth.

They might have stayed there for hours, or she might have given in, and taken him right there in the foyer, but Pepper barked furiously, and within seconds, the doorbell rang.

# CHAPTER NINE

God had led him to the right place.

He'd been there when the hulking SUV had run another red car off the road. He wondered who they were after. Perhaps the new director of the Witches Walk. He'd watched it stop, seen the flashlight shine down into the ditch, glinting on the water, on the broken glass.

When the truck had sped away, he'd gone to check on the passenger, as he'd done before.

He saw another stranger, her face cut and bloodied by the windshield glass and the items which had been thrown around in the car as it skidded out of control. When he touched her, she'd shuddered and he'd nearly fallen into the muck in surprise. He'd expected her to be dead.

Clutching his Bible, he'd moved closer again with the idea of rendering aid.

"Ma'am? Ma'am, can you hear me?" he said. "I'm going to call for help. Don't you worry."

But something had stopped him. The heat from the Bible, the warmth of it, tucked against his chest. The notes in the margins of the old letters he'd put inside sang to him. Something told him to touch it to her, to let it feed on her while he went up to the road to make the call.

*Feed on her?* Where had that thought come from?

She groaned and that decided him. He would leave the Bible with her for succor, for comfort. He set it on her chest and she shuddered once more. He started to climb, but his hands itched to bring out his knife. A red haze clouded his vision and he felt for the knife in his pocket. It was old, worn. He'd had it for years.

His hand closed upon it and he smiled.

He came to himself in the ditch, the rain beating down on his head. Another car. Another woman at his mercy. He hadn't been out for more than a few seconds, nor had he climbed very far up the hill.

*Another chance to feed.*

The whispered thought in his mind didn't slow or deter him this time. He didn't hesitate. He pulled out his handkerchief and used it to open the car door. The big SUV had screeched away toward the bridge, and I-95. They wouldn't be back.

Moving the Bible from the woman's chest, he was surprised at how heavy it was.

With a bit of an effort, he set it aside, out of the rain. Then he pulled out the knife.

####

"Chief Strongbow!" Calvin yelled at Jake the second he pulled up in the Blazer, and Calvin's face was a study in relief. He waved muddied arms at the ambulance and the fire truck that followed right behind it. The two of them moved to the side to give the rescuers room.

"Calvin?" Jake gripped his arm, kept him from slipping in the mud as they stepped back. "What's up? You said a car off the road?"

"There!" He pointed downward, and Jake pivoted the

spotlight on the Blazer down into the ditch. In the darkness, it glinted on crushed metal and twisted rubber.

Two people from the fire department, sexless and unidentifiable in their fire gear, were already climbing down into the deep ditch, Hurst tool in tow to cut away the car's top. Two more were right behind them with the backboard.

"We should help," Calvin said, starting back toward the edge.

"No." Jake grabbed his arm, pulling him back. "They know what they're doing, and space is tight down there. The ditch is already picking up more water from the rain. We don't want to make the slope worse than it is, and we may have to pull them up. If we go down, we're all down."

"I wish I'd come sooner," Calvin said, wringing his hands. "I might have seen her go off the road, helped somehow."

"Why don't you tell me why you were out this way and what you did see?"

"I'd been over to the hospital to see Mrs. Brantley," he said. "I was on my way home, but I was afraid I wouldn't sleep." He grimaced, and explained. "I've had a bit of trouble with that lately. Anyway, I thought I'd go into the church and do some work. There's a lot to catch up on, with Brother Walther's troubles and all." Calvin spoke quickly, as if by imparting the story faster, he could help the woman out of the ditch.

"That wouldn't bring you down here." Jake knew where Calvin lived, and this wasn't the route.

"Not normally, no, but I'd made the turn for home, headed that way, then decided about halfway there to just go into the office. Turned around and came this way."

That wasn't implausible, but it wasn't really a straight tale either. Jake didn't have the Gift of sensing truth, like some of the Haven Harbor witches did, but he had a cop's instincts and they were twitching.

"Lucky for our mystery lady," Jade murmured.

"Yes. I pray she's all right. I hated to leave her but I knew you wouldn't see where we were unless I came to the top."

"Too true," Jake said, watching the pastor closely. He wasn't sure what was setting his spidey sense off, but something was. Calvin had always been a little fanatical—in school it had been about a particular girl—now it seemed to be Christianity and CAWW. He hadn't gone quite so far as to be a stalker back then, but he hadn't been far off that mark, either. Jake hadn't been happy when he found out it was Calvin was driving CAWW to new heights of anti-Witches Walk sentiment. Now that Calvin had found religion, in the most evangelical of ways, Jake didn't trust him.

In this case, however, he seemed to have truly been in the right place to help.

"CHIEF!" The call came from the bottom of the ditch. It sounded like Mercy Clark, yelling for him. Jake hustled to the edge of the tarmac, looked down.

"Here!" he called back, puzzled as he saw all four figures coming back up the steep grade.

"There's no one in the car!"

Since there was blood staining Calvin's shirt and more darkened the mud lit by the glare of the spot, he knew there had been someone there. To have her be missing, now, wasn't right.

"What the hell?" he said, surprised. What the hell was hunting in Haven Harbor?

"That's impossible!" Calvin said from right next to him, startling him. "She was there, I swear it."

Jake started to say something, but Calvin pressed on. "Chief, you know me, I would never make a false report. We have to look for her."

"Yeah, we do."

They called in other officers and off-duty sheriff deputies and formed grids as the rain poured down in earnest, but they found no sign of the woman from the car, someone Calvin was sure was critically injured, maybe dying. There had been considerable blood, but the rain had washed it, and any trail the woman might have made, away.

The rain stopped as dawn stole over the bluffs, but they'd found nothing and the rain had washed away any traces that might have allowed any further searching.

"Thanks, Calvin. I'll be back in touch if we find anything." Jake clapped a hand on the man's shoulder but got no sense of him, nothing that further troubled his mind or intuition. Sometimes he could get that sense, if he touched someone or they touched him. "You head on home now, get some sleep."

"I don't think I can sleep," the pastor said, shaking his head. "I'm wide awake and troubled." He frowned. "Once I turned toward the church I started to feel sleepy, almost turned around, which would have been silly since I'd decided to go work because I couldn't sleep." He shook his head again. "Crazy, right? That SUV might have run me off the road if I hadn't just rolled down the window for some fresh air. That woke me up, so I turned around and headed for the church."

"Wait, what? Why didn't you mention this sooner?"

"Yeah, I heard it," Calvin said. "The SUV. But it roared past me, headed for the highway so fast it blew my little car around in the road. That was before I even saw the car in the ditch." Since Calvin drove an old Corolla, Jake figured from that description that the SUV had been going a lot faster than the posted limit, but it wouldn't take much to buffet the smaller vehicle.

"Can you describe it?"

Calvin looked worn. He was always pale, but his skin looked pasty harsh in the breaking light. His eyes were hollow. "Good Lord, do you think that's what happened? That the SUV ran her off the road?"

"Could be, or they might have seen who did, so what

do you remember?"

"But they couldn't have come back here, not in the time it took me to climb back up to the road!" he protested. "I would have seen them. The SUV was heading for the bridge," he insisted. "I know they didn't come back."

Calvin dredged up a few details, but reiterated that it was the sound of the crashed car's radio that had led him to stop, get out and peer down into the ditch. "It's all a blur, from there," he said, much to Jake's irritation.

"Did you see anyone else? On the road, in the trees? Any other cars come by?"

Calvin frowned, rubbing at his chest, then clutching at the gold cross that hung around his neck. "I'm not sure."

"Calvin, are you all right?" Pastor Walthers hurried up, clutching his Bible and giving Jake a tense smile. "I heard there'd been an accident, and I heard your name as Mrs. Winona Aylesworth left the diner this morning."

"Oh, Brother Walthers," Calvin said, leaning on the older man's arm for a moment. "It's terrible."

Jake let Calvin explain the situation, listening carefully for the nuances of the narrative as Calvin told it. Again, something was twitching his intuition, but he couldn't put a finger on what.

And wasn't it odd that both the pastors of the Christian Reformers church had insomnia?

#### 

Jake Strongbow looked down the gully at the car that lay upside down and mangled. Full daylight had come, begrudgingly, it seemed, and along with it, more occasional rain. The garage crew was in the process of winching the vehicle out of the ditch. Oil and gasoline sheened the mud, and he could smell the fumes from the ruptured gas lines.

To have one accident that might or might not be accidental, in his town, was one thing. For those accidents to both involve red rental cars? Not a coincidence. For there to be two accidents, and one of them a likely to be a fatality, and with the woman missing? That really pissed him off. Lissa Halliday was on the mend, but he'd seen enough injuries in the military, enough blood trails, to know that Geneva Banks, whose rental car this was, might not make it.

And here again, it was a red car. A rental. He hated coincidence. In fact, he didn't believe in it.

Geneva Bank's car wasn't the same kind Marisol Beecham drove, but the same rental company, the same color. Lissa Halliday's car had been exactly the same. A red Mustang. He'd be damned if someone was going to get away with randomly hunting and snatching injured people in his town. He and Mari Beecham had joked about the oddity of all the red rental cars. Now, with this, he was cursing. He, for sure, wasn't about to let Marisol Beecham get killed either. He pulled out his phone.

"Pere? It's Jake. You got some time later?" He got an affirmative reply. "Call Sam and Dan. The usual place."

Between them, just as they had in high school, the four of them would find some answers. For now, he'd do the job.

Later, he'd set up some safeguards. And some traps. Then he'd catch the son of a bitch who thought he could get away with murder in Jake Strongbow's town.

####

"What do you mean you can't get someone out here until Friday? I can't be without a car until Friday." Mari was pacing the foyer, arguing with the rental car company. When she'd gone to start the car and go into the office, the engine wouldn't crank. She'd looked under the hood, but it wasn't just loose wires this time. She didn't know what it was, but all the wires she'd seen dangling the last time were still firmly in place.

She'd immediately called the rental car company, but this was their answer. Two days before they could get her a new car. They'd put her on hold to see what they could do. She wondered if Uber or Lyft was available in Haven Harbor. Probably not. It was such a small town.

"Thank you for holding, Ms. Beecham. With you being a platinum member with us, we are, of course, doing our best to help. Is there any way you can get into Boston? We can get you another car for the time being if you can get to us. I know there's a train that runs from Newburyport." The young woman trailed off. "I hate to inconvenience you that way, but we're desperately understaffed." Mari could hear the worry in the other woman's voice. "I know that's not your issue, but ours, but I did want you to know why we weren't on our way to you immediately."

"Thank you. I'll see what I can do."

The woman gave her a direct number and contact information so that she could call back and reach the same person. Her next call was to Jake Strongbow. Having her car just stop might be nothing, or it might be sabotage. No way to tell this time, since she couldn't see any damage.

"Hi, chief," she said, hearing the roar of traffic behind him. He must be standing outside.

"Mari, how can I help you?" Jake's voice was terse, tense. It wasn't like him.

"My car may have been tampered with. It won't start."

She heard a growling sound and realized it must be him, making a sound of frustration. "Dammit. Have you touched the hood?"

"Yes. Sorry. I looked to see if it was the wires again. It won't even turn over. I opened the hood, but when nothing was obvious, I called the rental company."

"Let me get over there with the tech first, before they take it."

"No problem as they can't get to it till Friday. I have to figure out how to get to Boston and get a replacement car."

"We'll help you with that, somehow. Let me make some calls."

"Thanks."

She called Carol and let her know why she wasn't into the office yet. "Oh, Ms. Mari, I'm sorry that's happened. And yes, I'll let Mr. Gus know, he's back. Mr. H is here too, so I'll tell him. I think he was wanting to meet with you."

"Thanks, Carol."

She wasn't sure she wanted to see Pere for any reason. Their abbreviated make out session had been stopped by Jake's arrival the previous evening, and she'd been alternately burning up with remembering it, and mortified that she'd practically jumped him. Jake had looked from one to the other of them, the faintest of smiles curving his lips. It was totally embarrassing.

Jake hadn't wanted to discuss her case in front of Pere, so after several awkward moments, Pere had said goodnight and left. Jake had come to tell her that the blood from her porch wasn't human, and to ask more about the calls she'd gotten.

It was surprising to her, however, that Gus was already back in the office. She'd heard Jake say that the doctors had kept him overnight for observation.

"Just because you expected him to slack off, take more time, doesn't mean he will." She let the words echo in the empty house. Gus was, she reminded herself, dedicated to the Walk.

It was really strange. He was dedicated, and yet…More than ever, Mari understood what Pere meant when he said he thought Gus was hiding something or up to something. The fact that he was already back at work and the records had burned, he should have seemed relieved. Instead, he was more on edge and snappier with everyone. Everything that had happened would have been more plausible if Gus hadn't looked so guilty and furtive when he said anything about the break-in at his house, or at his business.

Now, he was also pressing more of the details of the Walk onto her shoulders. It was a total shift from his attempts to keep everything in his hands. It just made him look more guilty.

She finished setting up to work at the kitchen table just as her doorbell rang. Somehow she knew it was Pere.

"Hey," she said, opening the door, but not inviting him in. He smiled.

"I hear you need a ride into Boston. Can you leave in an hour?"

Surprised, she nodded. "Sure. I have to go to Logan and get another car. That one," she said, as she gestured to the inoperable car sitting in the drive, "won't start and Chief Strongbow wants to check it for tampering."

"Yes," Pere said, scowling fiercely. "There's been another accident. Geneva Banks was run off the road on her way back into town either late last night or early this morning, maybe just before the fire. She was headed for the hotel, evidently. She'd told them she'd be in very late."

"Oh, no!" Mari cried, her hand flying to her chest as her heart pounded. "Is she all right?"

"That's just it, they don't know. When Jake got to the scene and they went down to get her out, she wasn't there."

"Good Lord." Mari shook her head. "This is nuts. Where would she have gone? Could she have crawled away from the car, thinking it might explode?" Visions of shooting flames and a red car leapt into her mind out of nowhere and she nearly staggered at the sense of heat and danger.

*Whoa. Freaky.*

She had to stop listening to stories about having an affinity for fire. It was messing with her imagination.

"Jake doesn't know. They rousted out all the officers, and got the sheriff's team too, but they couldn't find any sign of her. The heavy rain made it impossible to track where she might have gone, or track anyone who might have taken her. Jake let her office know, and he's put out and all-points thing, a BOLO, or whatever."

Despite the gravity of the situation, she smiled a little. Obviously Pere watched detective shows too.

*Another point in common,* a part of her brain whispered gleefully.

"Who would suddenly want to do this sort of thing? The Walk's been going for almost eleven years now. Nothing like this has happened before, right?"

Pere leaned on the doorjamb. She was studiously not inviting him in. They both knew why. They were a combustible mix.

"There were plenty of naysayers when it was started. When I moved back to town, I wasn't a huge fan, but I saw what the Walk did for the town and for the economy, and I got on board. Most people feel pretty good about it. It's a boon to Haven Harbor and we don't have to deal with the constant influx of wannabes year round the way Salem does, just that one week. That makes most people feel favorably towards it, even if it doesn't impact their businesses."

"But nothing like this."

"Some picketing. The formation of CAWW, and Calvin's rabblerousing there, but that's it." He shook his head, watching her. "So no, nothing like this."

Mari made a gesture and the glint of copper at her wrist caught his eye. One of Lydia's protection bracelets. That she would wear it made something in him relax.

What was it about her? She wasn't his usual type. She was compact, more like a gymnast, instead of the willowy, tall women he usually dated. She was dark-haired and dark-eyed. That shouldn't have added up for him.

But it did. He could feel the tug in his gut, and lower, just watching her, listening to her.

"We could speculate endlessly, but that doesn't get you to Boston." He drew his mind back to the moment. "I'll go do the things I need to do, then come back and get you. I think we can get you to the airport with enough time for you to still make it back to your lunch meeting with the

Salem Chamber people. I've got several things to do in Boston myself, so it's on my way."

"All right. I accept and thank you." She nodded briskly as if that settled some internal debate she'd been having.

"I'll see you in an hour then."

"Good."

They both stared at one another. "Mari—" he began, only to turn at the sound of a car pulling up. Jake got out of his Blazer, and a tech got out the other side, case in hand.

"Saved by the chief," Mari murmured, amusement ringing in her voice. "Again."

"Yes," Pere said, smiling. "We have to return to our discussion from last night, however."

"Yeah," she said softly. "I repeat, *Boss*, that might not be the best thing."

He gave her a sardonic salute, the sleek car pulling silently away from the curb. He waved at Jake as he pulled away from the curb. Jake and his tech, Missy, spent time with Mari's car, using the typical dust she'd seen on crime shows to find prints. With that done, Jake opened the hood. Mari took the time they were working to get herself ready for the meeting and gathered the paperwork on the car. When she came out, Jake greeted her.

"Hey, Mari. I can tell you, this won't start again. And your rental company's not gonna be happy."

"Why? What's wrong?"

"Wires from the starter to the battery are cut from underneath. Maybe the brake lines too."

"Cut?"

Jake nodded, closing the hood. "Definitely sabotage. Are you headed someplace today?"

"Salem. I'm meeting with the Chamber people there."

"Walk business." Jake seemed to be considering the impact of that. "And are you getting another car?"

"Yes, Pere Hestworth is going into Boston for

meetings, and has kindly offered to give me a ride to the airport to get a replacement for the rental car."

"Hmmm. Let me know the make and model when you get back into town. I'll be meeting with the Massachusetts State Police investigator about Geneva."

"That's serious," she said, suddenly chilled. Whenever the state police were involved, it was really serious.

"Somebody missing is serious at any point, but this kind of thing happening twice in one month, and a woman missing? Yeah. Deadly serious. My staff isn't big enough to handle something like this, if it's an abduction." She must have looked odd because he added, "I'm not too proud to ask for help, and this could be bigger than the Walk."

"Bigger?"

He nodded. "I have a bad feeling about it."

Jake helped Missy, the tech, pack her things, and Mari finally stopped watching them to get ready. She had just let Pepper back in from doing his business, but before she could close the door, Pere pulled to the curb. She put Pepper in his crate, picked up her briefcase and locked the door. She touched the lovely new door charm Lydia had made for her.

"Keep the house safe," she murmured. "And Pepper." His collar charm had jingled cheerfully among his other tags as she walked him. She hoped it would keep him safe as well.

She felt foolish about talking to the house, but no one had been there to hear her, so it didn't matter.

The drive took them by the accident site. There were still people there, working, as they passed. She decided they were crime scene people, or maybe the state police, because it looked like the car was already gone.

"It's so awful," she murmured, turning back to the road. "I hope they find Geneva quickly, and she makes it."

"I do too." He glanced her way as they crossed the

171

bridge toward Newburyport. "It puts Gus in a really bad position. The Walk records are destroyed, the office was trashed, and the auditor is missing. I don't have to be Jake Strongbow, or play a lawyer on TV, to figure that one out."

He was right. It did make Gus look horribly guilty.

"Something in the files implicates somebody, whether that's Gus or someone he's protecting. Whoever it is, they can't let Geneva talk about whatever she might have found in the records." Stating the obvious felt like idiocy, but there it was, out in the open.

"Pretty much."

"And Gus, despite being hit on the head and knocked out," she said, wincing at the thought of how difficult it would be to hit yourself on the head, "looks like the culprit."

"He had a break-in at one of his other businesses a couple of weeks ago."

"I know, Sarah at the Judge's Chambers told me. Now this. Does that make him less suspicious or more?" she mused. "It seems to me to point everything in his direction."

"I'd like it to be him," Pere said, a harsh note in his voice. "We've never gotten along."

She turned in the seat, the better to see his face. "Why?" Now that she had kissed him, wanted him, she was eager to learn anything about him. A surge of that bleak, new kid in town feeling hit her, but she shoved it away.

He glanced at her, frowning. "Why would I like it to be him, or why haven't we gotten along? And why do you feel sad?"

"Huh?" How had he figured that out?

"It's gone now." He said nothing for a few minutes as he negotiated the ramp onto I-95 and pointed them toward Boston. "What do you want to know?"

"Both, I guess. Do you want it to be him because you

don't get along?"

"Yes and no. I want it to be him because that would mean it was simple." The frown was deeper, darker, this time. "I'm not so sure it's going to be that straightforward."

"And you don't get along, because?"

Now the frown was sardonic, self-deprecating. "Because I've hated him since high school and part of me wants him to fail, to be embarrassed." He glanced at her again. "Not very adult of me."

She laughed. Somehow, she felt better. The bleak feeling of aloneness slipped away. "Been there. Remember, I moved a lot. I know that high-school-sucks despair from several sources. And yeah, just because we're grown-ups, doesn't mean we don't remember people pissing on us."

Now the smile was back, even though it was still grim around the edges. "Exactly. Gus and his brother were frat-boy pranksters in high school. They liked to haze the underclassmen, especially those of us who were junior varsity football players when they were varsity. Since their dad owned businesses in town, and was then head of the council, he got away with a whole lot more than he should have. His Uncle Roger was the Chief of Police."

"Great," she drawled. "Sounds like a recipe for major bullying."

"It was."

He packed a lot of emotion in the two clipped words. "Ouch. Okay, so you have personal experience with the hazing, and you don't like Gus, and he's obviously up to something, as you said. Playing devil's advocate," she said.

"Not the best thing to do in Haven Harbor," he said seriously. "We've had our share of troubles with the devils of this world."

"I was being serious."

He turned to her briefly, before looking back at the road. "So was I."

She suppressed a shiver of reaction, and shifted her legs, which bumped her purse and turned it over. "Drat." She righted everything, but in doing so, she managed to pull the bandage off the cut on her hand. It was healing well, but there was still a spot of blood on the bandage. The position of the cut, right in the webbing of her thumb, meant that she moved it a lot, and that made it bleed a little. "These bandages really suck; they won't stay on."

She pulled it off, and got another from her purse. The ones at the office had been old, so she'd picked some of her own up and stashed them in her purse, because the bandages kept falling off. She'd had to replace them a couple of times every day. She folded the old one and Pere opened the center console to reveal a small trash receptacle.

"Here, put it in here." He waited until she had then said, "I meant to tell you, you should be very careful where you dispose of anything with your blood on it."

She paused in the act of peeling the backing off the new bandage. "Why?"

"Blood can be used to do a lot of nefarious things, especially by witches."

"Surely not."

Once again, he glanced at her. "It may be the 21st century, but that just lends more credence to the things witches have known for centuries. Your blood is you. It's your DNA. Using the Laws of Correspondence, your blood can be used by magickal practitioners to lure you someplace, affect your health, and make all kinds of trouble. You'd be wise to destroy bandages, hair and nail clippings, and anything else on which you might get blood." He blushed faintly at the last statement and she realized he was trying not to say anything blunt about women and periods and that kind of blood.

"Okay, warning heard."

"And heeded?"

"Yes, I guess so. But I wish I'd known that a day or so

ago. I left all kinds of blood on paper towels in the Walk ladies' room. I think I even put some folded bandages in…my colleague's car after dinner the other night."

If he noted her hesitation over *colleague* it seemed he wasn't going to say anything about it. Then again, Kevin from the Salem chamber wasn't a witch and when she'd asked to drop the bandage she'd had to change in his little trash receptacle in his fancy car, he hadn't been pleased.

"As I said," Mari continued, setting thoughts of Kevin and blood aside, "I've seen a lot, and there are a lot of cultures that still believe that blood ties people to things or actions." She thought about his DNA comment. When you considered what DNA held, and how you could build a whole new person from it, through cloning, anything a witch with bad intentions might do didn't seem as far-fetched. "So should I get it back out of your trash and burn it?"

"I'll take care of it," he said, smiling.

They didn't speak much for the next few minutes as Pere negotiated the busy roads around the airport, pulling up at the car rental building within a few minutes. "Here you are, safe and sound," he quipped, and that boyish, real smile was back. Her heart skipped a few beats. "What?" he said, looking concerned now as he caught her hand. "What is it?"

She couldn't help it, she turned her hand, linked their fingers. "When you smile like that, open and easy, it really makes it hard to remember that you're my boss, and therefore off limits."

Now his smile took on a distinctly predatory, masculine tone. "Oh, really? I think I need to take advantage of that," he said and swooped in to kiss her thoroughly. It took someone beeping behind them to break them apart.

"You're my boss," she reiterated. "You're my boss, you're my boss. I have to remember that."

"I'm going to have to resign from the council, I see," he muttered, stroking a finger down her cheek.

"What?" Dazed, she tried to comprehend what he was saying, but the impatient rental car patron behind them beeped again. "I have to go."

"I'll call you later," he said. "I'd come around and open your door, like the gentleman my mother raised me to be, but I think it would be painfully obvious how much I'm attracted to you."

"Oh, my God, don't say stuff like that," she said, gathering her things. She couldn't help it though. She looked at him and smiled. Her gaze drop to his lap.

"Mari," he growled.

"I'm going. I'll talk to you later."

"Count on it."

It was the work of mere minutes, thanks to the helpful rental agent she'd talked to, to get in a new vehicle and head for her meeting in Salem. On one hand, she kind of dreaded it, because Kevin would probably be there. Then again, if she was nonchalant and played it cool, it wouldn't be awkward.

She worried over that all the way to the Salem chamber offices.

"Mari! Welcome back to Salem," Trista Reynolds was quick to take her hands and pull her forward for an airy kiss on the cheek. "I'm just so thrilled about the Walk this year. We've just gotten the last of our barriers into the lots for the start of the Walk. We're revved up and ready to go. Carol called and told me about all the trouble you had. I'm so sorry about that." She paused, taking a deep breath, but smiled again. "She also told me that you all would be fine, so I'm going to go with that positive spirit. She said all the Walk packets and shirts for the participants were okay and would come down this next weekend. Even though we had considerable tourist traffic for Labor Day weekend, we're totally focused on the Walk now. Our committees are ready to rock."

"That's excellent. Hello everyone," Mari said, taking a moment to shake hands and greet the representatives from

Mouldon and Pennyfield, as well as the folks from the pharmaceutical sponsor, and the HVAC company. "Where's Kevin today? In other meetings?" she said, keeping her voice light, so it didn't seem obvious to ask about him.

"Oh, Kevin had an accident and is home recovering. He broke his leg and got some scratches and such when his car ran off the road in Pennyfield the other night," one of the other women said. She looked at Mari curiously. "I thought you would have heard."

"No, I didn't. Is he all right, otherwise?"

"His car was pretty banged up," said one of the men. "But he's okay. Said he swerved to miss a deer or something, when it jumped out into the road."

Mari went cold all over. With everything that had been happening in Haven Harbor, she hadn't thought about warning Kevin.

*Then again, why would I?* Kevin would probably have thought she was nuts. His open amusement at the whole concept of the Witches Walk being based on real witches was something that had turned her off.

"Did you all send flowers to him?" she asked, "I guess we should too, from the Walk. He's a valuable member of the team, and I hate that he was hurt."

That seemed to stop the speculation in some of the committee's minds, because the talk quickly turned to jointly sending an arrangement of fruit—something the guys said he'd appreciate more than flowers—from the different stakeholders. From there, they got down to business quickly, ironing out some of the latest wrinkles in the plans for the Walk.

"I'll take all this info back to Gus and Carol, and we'll be sure to send you answers on those two other things." Mari shook hands all around again, and the group dispersed. After saying her goodbyes, she sat for a few moments in the car, debating whether or not to call Pere.

"He's not your boyfriend," she reminded herself, but

that just threatened to heat up her blood and libido all over again. She forced herself to stop thinking about his kisses and ruthlessly suppressed her feminine reaction to those thoughts. "But I should tell someone about this."

Jake. She needed to call Jake. She pulled his card from her purse and dialed his number.

"Mari, are you all right?" His instant leap to her being hurt was worrisome.

"Yes, I'm fine, I've gotten the new rental car. I'm in Salem." He asked for her to hold. She heard him tell someone he'd be a minute.

"What's the make and model?"

She told him. "A sedate sedan, and blue this time, so that's good. Anyway, I didn't actually call about that. I wanted to tell you that one of the committee members from Salem has been hurt. A car accident. But it was in Pennyfield."

"Pennyfield? That's out of my jurisdiction, obviously. What makes you think it might be related?"

Not that she wanted to share her personal life, but...

"I had a date with the guy who was hurt. Kevin Torsk. He had the accident that same night. He picked me up and we went to dinner at the Pennyfield Castledon Inn. He evidently had the accident on his way back to his house in Salem after dropping me at home."

There was a long pause, but Jake's voice was even and non-judgmental when he spoke. "He doesn't drive a red rental car, does he?"

"No," Mari said, on a half-laugh. "No, he drives a black BMW sedan. Why?" It took her about three seconds. "Oh. Our coincidence with the red cars really isn't feeling much like a coincidence, is it?"

"No, but this may be unrelated. So...did you kiss him, or otherwise have more, uh," Jake hesitated, "intimate contact?"

Anger and embarrassment rushed in in equal measures. Mari reminded herself that Jake was just doing his job, and she had, after all, called him.

"Oh, for God's sake, no. I kissed him goodnight, but it wasn't a big thing," she said, feeling the heat in her face as she said it. God, why had she called Jake? "Seriously, it was dinner. We both, um, realized it wasn't going anywhere. And why the heck would you even ask that?"

She really hoped Kevin had realized that they weren't going anywhere, relationship-wise.

Jake took a long moment to answer, and Mari's brain started on the crazy loop. This was stupid. Kevin had admitted that he always drove his BMW too fast on the curving roads in the smaller towns.

Frowning now, she also remembered that he'd said he hated to take the backroads because the small town cops were eager to ticket speeders. He always took I-95 when he could. Why had he gone home that way? He'd even complained about the road to Pennyfield when they were headed to the restaurant.

"It's a witchcraft thing, called—" Jake started to say, but Mari finished the sentence.

"The Law of Correspondence?" That was what Pere had called it today when he told her not to let her blood get into the wrong hands.

"Yes." Jake sounded surprised.

"Pere told me about it. Why would Kevin—" she began, then thought about sex and transference and blushed even harder. DNA was in all kinds of bodily fluids and if they had had sex…"Oh. Got it."

"Good. Then I won't embarrass either of us anymore," Jake said, and he did sound discomfited, which helped ease Mari's own mortification. "I'll check it out with my counterpart in Pennyfield. If he says anything about a dark SUV, we'll know it's related."

"Dark SUV?"

"Yes, Pastor Parris called in Geneva's accident, and he saw a dark SUV, like a Suburban or a Yukon leaving the area. It almost ran him off the road."

"Wow. That's scary. Have you heard anything about Geneva? Have they found her?"

There was a hesitation, but all Jake said was, "I don't have any news."

She didn't press him, but her heart sank. Jake probably knew something, but couldn't tell her, and that something wasn't good.

"Do me a favor," Jake said now.

"What's that?"

"Go the long way. Take the interstate back to town."

####

"You have Sam?" Jake said into the phone as he pulled away from the curb with Dan in the passenger seat. "Great, see you there."

"I thought we were headed to Pere's place to do some work on protecting the Walk."

"Plan's changed," Jake said, taking the road toward the bridge and then the branch that led down the Walk route through Moulden and on to Pennyfield. "Some dude from the Salem committee took a header into a tree down in Pennyfield."

"And that's relevant, how?" Dan said, his dry sarcasm ringing through loud and clear. Most people underestimated the quiet librarian, but neither Jake nor Pere ever had. He'd played baseball instead of football in high school, but he'd been the butt of some of Gus and Carl Wilkerson's hazing too. Dan, Pere, Sam, and Jake had formed their own group in those days, and taken back their school from Gus and Carl. And now, with all of them back in town, they still called on one another when they needed back-up.

"He was hitting on our new Walk director," Jake said with a grim smile. "Not that it did him any good. I think Pere's hit hot on that one."

"Oh, really?" Dan's drawl was amused. "I saw that one coming."

"Sure you did, in your crystal ball, right?"

180

"I seldom use the orb, as you know," Dan said, making his voice sound high and pompous. Jake laughed. "Although going old-school is sometimes the best. No, I just got the vibe when I met her. I could tell she had something intense, and someone here would match that fire. Besides," he said, leaning the seat back so he could rest his head. "*They* told me."

Jake didn't have to ask who "*they*" were. Dan was what Jake's people called a spirit talker. The rest of the witches in Haven Harbor called him a medium. He didn't practice it as a profession, preferring the quiet of the library and the gym to the chaotic world of the sprits. That didn't mean the spirits let him alone, however.

"And what did *they* have to say about her?"

"They keep talking about fire, smoke and blood when they're not talking about how her fiery energy meets and matches one of the town's highest." Dan made his voice prissy and old-maidish again as he said the last bit, and Jake realized it was a quote from some long-departed townsperson.

"Great. Fire and smoke and blood. Just what I need while trying to keep law and order."

"We never promised you a walk in Founders Park when you took the job, dude."

"Ha. And you'd have been right, since getting Roger's lazy lot out of the department was a pain in my ass from day one."

"We live to provide a challenge, my friend."

"Sure you do," Jake poked right back. "Not that you couldn't have done the job yourself."

Dan had spent the first four years out of college at Quantico, working in investigations for the FBI. He's been in what he jokingly called the "strange and unusual" department. His skills and his job had clashed too often, however, and knowing things he shouldn't know had not only blocked promotions but brought scrutiny he didn't want. So when he'd taken a bullet in the line of duty, he'd also taken a buyout and gone back to school. Armed with a master's degree in library science, he'd taken over the Haven County Library System and school libraries, when the previous, non-witch librarian moved on.

"So what are we looking for in Pennyfield, besides dinner?"

"Something that might have made Mr. BMW run off the road. It could have been our dark SUV," Jake said, but he didn't think so. "We'll see. The locals, including Chief Michaels, aren't suspicious. They think the guy swerved to avoid a deer, just like he said. I want to be sure, since there's some serious crap going down around the Walk and Mari Beecham this year."

"True, that." Dan cocked the seat back a bit farther, and closed his eyes. "Wake me when we get there."

"Got it."

Dan's even breathing deepened and Jake shook his head at how easily his old friend could drop into sleep. Given how much *they* kept him up sometimes, Dan had learned to take naps easily and often.

It wasn't more than fifteen minutes before Jake spotted Pere's snazzy Benz sitting on the side of a long curve on the two-lane country road heading into Pennyfield. Since Pennyfield was in another county, this one hadn't hit Jake's radar in terms of what was going on with the Walk. Jake eased his Blazer onto the shoulder as well and elbowed Dan awake.

"Let's check it out."

The four men met at the bumpers of the cars. "So what are we looking at?" Sam said. He was still wearing his medical center scrubs top, though he had on jeans and boots.

"Guy went off the road here," Pere said, pointing first at the tatter of police tape and then to the skid marks in the road. "It may have been a deer—"

"Or a dark SUV," Jake put in.

"Or that," Pere agreed. "But I'm thinking there was

something else going on. Let's walk the sides of the road up and back, just to check it out. I thought I caught a glimpse of something. Like a chalked rune."

The other three turned to him in surprise. "You Saw something? Something that wasn't related to business?" That was huge if Pere had broken his visionary skill out of whatever had locked it into "business only" mode.

Pere's brows drew down in a furious frown. "It's related to the Walk, which is related to MicroMechanics. And somehow, to Mari Beecham. Otherwise, it's the same as it always is." He grimaced and rubbed at his eyes. "Business is the only trigger."

Jake wasn't so sure, but he nodded. "Okay, Pere, you and Dan take the other side of the road, Sam and I'll take this one."

"Freaks on that side, Geeks on this one?" Sam joked, and Dan socked him in the shoulder. They all laughed and split up, starting their scan of the road, slowly moving along working along in their designated pairs.

"Is the guy from the Beemer okay?" Sam asked as he and Jake strode up the road on their side, to where the skid marks began.

"Cuts, bumps, bruises, an airbag burn, and he spent a night in the hospital to follow the concussion protocol."

"Did he total the car?"

"Oh, yeah."

"Well, shit."

They walked further along the road, scanning the ground. On the other side, Dan and Pere were doing the same.

"Well fuck a duck, look there," Sam said, pointing.

On the paved shoulder of the road there was a clear spot and a design of a circle and runes—dark ones, meant to harm—chalked inside the circle. Within the rune, a bit of white material shone like a lightbulb against the dark macadam. Even though it had rained heavily here too, the lines and the material looked pristine.

"We got something!" Dan called from across the road.

"So do we," Sam answered.

Jake looked at their position. Two feet beyond where he stood, the skid marks started, and beyond their parked cars he could see the path Kevin Torkes' BMW had taken into the trees.

# CHAPTER TEN

"I bring this meeting of the Citizens Against the Witches Walk to order," Calvin said, tapping the small gavel on the table. "First order of business?"

A hand went up in the small group in front of him. They were meeting in the fellowship hall, so it was echoing and made the fifteen people sitting in front of him seem scanty and useless for the fight they were waging.

"I'm very concerned about you wanting to bring in other people, outsiders, to picket with us or protest or whatever."

"I understand that, Mrs. Proctor. It does seem like it's a bit much," he soothed, even as he wanted to roll his eyes. Marion Proctor always wanted to second-guess everything. Then again, she and Estelle Hestworth had been neighbors for thirty or forty years. "But while our sentiments are pure, our numbers are small. If we're to make any impact on the Walk, stopping it in its tracks—" he smiled as someone tittered over the inadvertent allusion to walking. "Then we need more bodies."

He winced at that wording too. What was wrong with him today? Everything he said made him think about the poor woman in the car. Part of it was soothing. It reminded him that he'd helped, he'd found something important, he'd been a part of the community again, in a good way.

The other part was horrifying. The blood. The broken glass, the broken bones.

The fact that the woman was missing.

"I'm sorry, Mrs. Proctor, I lost my train of thought there for a moment," he apologized. "What did you say?"

"It's all right, young man," she said with a warm note of concern. "You've had a difficult few days." There were nods all around. "I said, perhaps it's time to realize that we're not making much headway at all, and give this up."

"No!" Calvin roared the words, and everyone shrank in their seats. "I'm sorry," he said, still angry but modifying his tone because he couldn't lose them. They were his lifeline to sanity in this insane community where witches ruled. "That was uncalled for. You're right, Mrs. Proctor, it's been a difficult couple of days."

There, that had done it. People relaxed. Tuned back in. He'd almost lost them with his intense reaction, and he couldn't afford that. He tried to make his voice soothing, practical, emotionless, like Brother Walthers. "As you know, I'm passionate about the cause, and I feel we should push on. Should we put it to a vote?"

There were nods all around. Some more enthusiastic than others. Dammit. He was losing them.

"Before we vote, I do want to apologize. I've not been focused on our mutual efforts for the last few days, with the accident and the mystery of the missing woman." He let his voice tremble. He needed their emotional response. It would keep them engaged. "I don't want my distraction to affect our efforts and if you feel I should step back, for now, and perhaps let Brother Twombly lead, I will certainly agree."

Twombly was the next most vocal member of the group, but he was also universally disliked, even though people were too polite to say it.

"No, no, Brother Parris," Stuart Reaton protested immediately. "We do understand, and I, for one, still feel you are most capable in your leadership."

Again, nods all around, more emphatic, this time. No one wanted Twombly leading the group.

"Well then, a vote?"

They fell in with him, of course, to continue the work. Even old maid Marion, as they'd always called the frumpy shopkeeper, didn't vote against him. She abstained. Her furious face was a balm to his soul. He felt redeemed in having swayed everyone but her back to his side.

"Thank you, Brothers and Sisters," he said. "I'll be in touch with the Brethren Holy Baptist leaders and those from Christianity First. Now, let us close with prayer."

#### 

Things were heating up in Haven Harbor.

The Walk was almost upon them, and Mari was busier than ever. She and Pere had avoided one another, in one way. In another, they were closer than ever because they were having a text and phone affair.

He texted her several times a day. She texted back. Sometimes it was just a hello, or a comment on the day. Sometimes it was just emojis.

She'd taken a chance a couple of times. She'd started it, which felt weird, but he was quick to respond.

They hadn't seen each other alone. They were always surrounded by a dozen other people, dealing with Walk management issues, but she was fiercely aware of it every time he came into the room. Gus, on the other hand, was in and out, but ceding more and more of the activities to her.

Lydia, who was present at a lot of these meetings, was

giving her a raft of shit about being a prude.

"Just go for it, Mari," she teased as they sat in Thyme4Lunch, catching a quick sandwich the day before Mari was to head to Salem for the following day's Walk kickoff. "The Gods know Pere is hot, and he's obviously attracted to you, and you to him. What's the problem?"

"You know the problem," Mari hissed, trying to look around, without anyone noticing she was looking around. She really did not want her love life—or lack thereof—to be all over the local gossip mill. The town was bad enough for gossip that wasn't even there, as it was. She'd heard one rumor that said that Calvin Parris was being considered as a suspect in Geneva's disappearance by the Massachusetts State Police investigator. Another rumor said that Jake and the MSP were calling in the FBI, since Geneva was still among the missing.

The new auditor was supposed to arrive next Monday, the day after the Walk was over. Although what he or she was going to audit, Mari had no idea.

"He's not your boss, Mari. You're your own boss."

"He is my boss, because I serve at the pleasure of the council."

"Yes," Lydia responded, patiently, as she had two or three times already. "But he's not the only person on the council and he'll rotate out of the chairmanship next month. Go for it," Lydia said, wiping mayo off her cheek, and smiling. "Then I can live vicariously."

"Right. No." Mari shook her head in a definitive negative. "It's too risky."

"Life's risky, Mari Beecham," a woman said, walking up to the table. She was tall, and, while she looked young, something about the eyes made her seem world-weary. She was just a little heavy-set, with bright blue eyes and dyed red hair. It looked good on her and had probably been her natural color. The only way Mari knew it was dyed was the faintest hint of bright white roots. "Lydia's right. Go for it."

"Excuse me?" Mari was utterly taken aback that a complete stranger would come up to the table with personal advice.

"Go for it. Life's short, as the commercial says. Play hard." The woman smiled at Lydia, who nodded, speechless for the first time in Mari's acquaintance. "Lydia Webb. You do so very well with your shop, we're all proud of you, you know." The woman turned back to Mari. "And you. Grab life with both hands and you'll make it. You'll walk through the fire and flames and be happy," she said fiercely. Her eyes turned dark now, and Mari stared. They'd been bright blue only a moment before, but now they looked stormy and turbulent. "If you don't, you will be consumed."

In another lightning shift, the woman's eyes returned to blue and she squeezed Mari's shoulder once, quite firmly, and walked out.

Belatedly, Mari realized that everyone in the restaurant had stopped talking and were all staring at the woman as she moved to the door. A man jumped up to open it for her and she nodded regally before going out into the sunshine and disappearing around the corner.

Silence reigned for another half a minute before the entire place burst into chatter at once. Surreptitious looks Mari's way had her putting down the remains of her sandwich and staring at Lydia.

"What the hell was that? Who the hell was that?" Mari said, glancing at the door before returning to her focus on Lydia.

"Oh. Dear. Gods." Lydia said, staring at the door.

Lucille Birkland bustled to their table and slid in next to Mari. Mari made room before she even realized it was Lucille.

"Well now, that was a wonder. What did she say to you, Mari?" Lucille demanded, then turned her gaze on Lydia and chuckled. "Lydia Webb, close your mouth before you start catching flies."

Lydia's teeth snapped together and she focused on Lucille. "Will not. And wow."

"Yes, indeed," Lucille agreed. "Not very often we see Regina anymore. She never seems to leave her own domain. And she never comes in any of the shops these days. That said, she did and she has today. So," Lucille turned back to Mari. "What did she say?"

Mari repeated it, with Lydia chiming in. "Interesting," Lucille said, nodding. "Well, you better get on with that embracing, Mari, or there'll be hell to pay, sounds like." She leaned in and kissed Mari's cheek. "And don't worry so much. We're not that prudish around here."

She bustled out, giving a word here or a shoulder touch there, as she moved through the crowd to the door. Talk in the restaurant resumed a more normal tone, with only the occasional glance Mari's way.

"Lydia, you better tell me what the hell is going on."

"That was Regina Mather."

"And?"

Lydia's head whipped around from where she'd been staring at the door again. "I keep forgetting," she said, suddenly, smiling. "You fit in so well here that I keep forgetting you don't know. That was THE Regina Mather. She was an actress, really popular when she started as a teenager, then blazed through to stardom even as an adult. She made a huge splash in Hollywood under the name Regina Black. The whole town was abuzz with one of our own hitting the big time."

"Oh, I remember her movies. I loved them."

"Yep. Then she started writing and directing, won an Oscar before she was twenty-five. Even bigger splash. Then she had what Hollywood termed a mental breakdown five years ago after an incident at her house in the Hollywood hills. Drugs and alcohol were reputed to be the problem, she went to rehab, supposedly. What it really was, was there was a murder at her house. A producer. It's still an open case." Lydia said it with complete confidence. Mari remembered the speculation, the stories. "Whatever happened that night, it changed her. She still writes movies," Lydia said, picking up a French fry, then putting it back on the plate. "And still does a cameo now and then, but mostly she lives in her family's huge old house out on River Bluff Road, looking out over the marshes toward the sea, supposedly with a houseful of ghosts. They say she's always out there alone, writing screenplays." Lydia lowered her voice, making what she obviously thought was a spooky face. "Probably going slowly mad."

Mari snorted. "Right. Get a grip, Webb." Lydia laughed too, and Mari resumed her interrogation. "What did she mean, embrace life?"

Lydia grinned. "I think she means you need to get it on with Pere Hestworth."

The encounter was all she could think about when Pere called her that night. He called her almost every night, since during the day they were never alone.

She was giddy every time his name popped up on the caller ID. She chided herself for being so school-girlish. When he called that night, she was more nervous than usual.

They'd been talking for an hour, however, before he brought up Regina. Then Gus.

"So maybe I won't have to resign from the council after all," he teased. "Will you listen to Regina's wisdom?"

"Stop," she said, blushing at the heat in his tone, the desire. How anyone could infuse his voice with that much sex was a mystery to her, but man, she felt that resonant voice all the way to her toes. "I'm trying to be good."

"Oh, we'll be good," he teased. Ever since he'd checked her for spells, he'd been so much more lighthearted about them being together. More open.

"Pere," she protested. "Tell me about your day," she insisted, trying to get him—and herself—off onto something innocuous.

"I had more meetings that any one person should be forced to endure," he said, laughing. "Mostly with Gus in attendance while you were off in Pennyfield, and Mouldon, and having lunch with all their people."

"Thanks. I had such fun." She dropped the sarcasm for seriousness. "I'm worried about him, Pere. Gus is there, he's present. He's doing the job, has everyone running, and everyone else seems to think he's acting normally."

"But you don't." His tone said he agreed with her.

"He's too quiet," she said, leaning back on the pillows, absently petting the ecstatic Pepper as she did. "Everything's too quiet." She let herself shudder, since no one could see it. The dreams were more vivid this last week. Fire and smoke and death.

"I know. Jake and the guy, Emerson, from MSP think so too. Geneva hasn't turned up, no more accidents. Nothing."

"Well, there was Kevin's car."

"That," Pere said, and she heard the irritation in his voice, was something different. "I think that's dark magic, and directed at you, like the cross and blood on your front porch. It was your blood in the car, on the bandages, keyed to the runes on the road. Someone expected you to be in that car. They got Kevin because part of you—your blood—*was* in the car."

"That's what Jake said."

"I know, we talked it over. It was aimed at you, and so far it's CAWW and Gus who have it in for you."

"And Gus is behaving like a choir boy."

"Never that," Pere laughed again. "If you'd only known him, and his brother, like I did, you'd never, ever say that."

"What's with the brother? Where's he now?"

"All I know is Carl moved to Canada sometime right after college. He had some serious trouble with the law.

192

The rumor was that he's got outstanding warrants for his arrest, but I don't know if that's true. Never bothered to ask. He's not been back as far as I know, much to their mom's lamenting woe."

"I met Mrs. Wilkerson last week. She doesn't seem like a lamenter," Mari quipped.

"No, she's a tough nut, that one. Pure New England steel." Pere paused, and she could hear him shifting around. "She's always looked down her nose at most of the rest of us, so she's not well liked, even though she's a member of both the main Haven coven and the Sea Witches Coven that goes out on the shore for their rituals."

"Great, bet she hates my guts, then."

"Probably," he joked. When she protested, he laughed and added, "She's all right. I'm sure she's worried though, about Gus." His voice grew serious. "I am too. I'm not a fan, but he's not himself, either, as you said."

"The FBI guy has been in the Walk office three times."

"I know. He was out at MicroMechanics asking me about Lissa. She's been released, by the way, and evidently headed straight for the Hamptons without so much as a call." He said the last with a flippant note. "I'm crushed."

"Pere," she chided. "I'm glad she's okay."

"Me too, and good riddance. How about I drive over?" he said, dropping his voice to a purr. "Regina said––"

He broke off, and she heard him shift. "Pere?"

"Someone's trying to break into MicroMechanics. They've broken through the protective spells. Call Jake, tell him to meet me out there."

There was a thump, and the line cut off. Mari immediately dialed Jake, reporting what Pere had said. The minute she ended the call, she threw on clothes and shoes and grabbed her keys. "Hold down the fort, Pepper. I'll be back."

The scene at MicroMechanics was all flashing lights

and crackling radios. As she pulled in behind Pere's car, she could see Jake, Emerson, the investigator from the Massachusetts State Police, and the new guy in town, Agent Suarez from the FBI.

The Walk endpoint grounds were roped off, but the tents were already set up, the high-end portable bathroom-and-shower trailers in place, and an air of readiness sat on that section of the grounds like a cloak. At the edge of the parking lot, an ambulance sat with its back doors open, and a man in a security guard's uniform was being treated as he sat on the bumper. She strode up to him.

"Wayne, are you all right?"

She'd met the young man, hired from Mouldon and trained by a firm in Boston, at one of the meetings with the MicroMechanics team. He looked at her with glazed eyes. "Oh, hi, Ms. Beecham. I'm fine, really. Just a bang on the head." The EMT looked at her and raised one eyebrow.

"Maybe you should go see Dr. Samuels over at the hospital," she said, and the EMT nodded vigorously where the guard couldn't see it. "I wouldn't want you to not be 100 percent for the Faire kickoff tomorrow night and the Walk arrivals on Friday."

That pushed the right button, because he agreed to be taken in for a once-over. The EMT mouthed, "Thank you" before helping the young man onto the gurney for the ride. She'd assured him that they'd have someone on duty for the rest of the night for the Walk grounds.

She'd leave that in Jake's hands.

Walking over to the cluster of men at the front walk to the building, she overheard Suarez exclaim, "I don't know how you even knew to come out here."

"It's a software I developed," Pere said. "It works with the alarm system."

She saw Jake and Pere exchange amused glances and realized that no software had alerted Per. It really had been magick with a k, as Lydia was fond of saying. Spells.

Wardings. Magick.

Her heart skipped a beat and a sense of something huge swamped her.

Magick was real. It really worked. Dear God in heaven.

Magick, the wrong kind, had caused Kevin's accident, if you believed Pere and Jake, and she did. They'd found spells there too, on the road.

She frowned. She still needed that one explained.

And magick had warned Pere about MicroMechanics.

Part of her wanted to totally freak out. What the hell? What was she doing here, with real witches and magick and weird screenwriters popping into restaurants to tell her to sleep with Pere?

Holy blazing shit!

*Not the time for a breakdown, Marisol.* That stern inner voice sounded like her Grandmother Hachette. *And isn't that just another kick in the Hachette-descendant-pants?*

"Stop it," she muttered to herself, yanking her imagination back into place and locking it down. Magick or no magick, real or not, she had an event to run, whether Gus was being helpful or not. People who'd signed up to walk were already asleep in Salem and arriving in droves for the Faire and Gala over the next few days, and the event *would* go on whether magick was real or not, and whether Mari was freaked out about it or not.

So. Time to focus on that.

"Gentleman," she said as she neared the group of men. To Pere, she added, "Mr. Hestworth, I'm sorry for your trouble."

"Ms. Beecham," Pere said cordially, but she heard the repressed smile. Jake wasn't hiding his amusement at the two of them very well.

"So, to sum up," Jake continued what he'd been saying when Mari arrived. "The alarms cut in, notifying Pere, and he called me. I rolled hot, as did my patrol officers, the only two I had on duty tonight since I need everyone on duty starting tomorrow. Two of the sheriff's team came in from the county patrol. They found Wayne, from Mouldon Security, out cold over by the fence, and that stack of boxes and smashed glass at the front door.

"Wayne said he thought he heard the glass break and the full alarms sound, and he knows all the lights on the grounds came on, but he didn't see who or what peeled out of the parking lot or what direction they went."

Jake's radio crackled and he stepped away, saying, "This is Chief Strongbow, go ahead," as he moved out of earshot.

Mari had just asked about the boxes scattered all over the sidewalk when Jake hurried back to them.

"Emerson, Suarez, you may want to come with me. A woman was attacked with a knife at the transit station in Mouldon. The chief there knew we'd had a problem, and he called me, to see if this might be our guy."

As one, the three men turned to cars, Jake shouting to his officers to secure the scene and the evidence.

"This is not what I meant when I said call Jake. I meant for you to do that and then sit tight," Pere accused as he moved closer to her.

Mari was no longer intimidated by the black scowl and sinister look Pere had leveled at her. Instead, she went on tiptoe to kiss his cheek. "Just looking out after Regina's favorite local son."

He frowned even more. "She didn't say that."

"That's what she meant," Mari said, laughing a little at his embarrassment. She turned to look at the front door with its shattered glass, and the scatter of boxes and debris that the two officers were, even now, collecting with gloved hands. They were carefully putting everything in heavy duty paper bags, and setting them aside after writing on them and sealing them with tape. Gathering evidence.

"What's in the boxes, do you know?"

Pere shook his head. "They have my name on them, but they're not components, and there's no return address."

In the glare of the spotlights, Mari could see the small boxes plainly. They looked familiar. Her visual memory kicked into gear and she said, "They look like the boxes Gus had stored in the new space, and the ones he told Carol always went in his office."

Pere shifted to look at her, then at the boxes. "Isn't that interesting?"

"Hey Chase," he called to one of the officers, moving in a little, but staying out of the way. "What's in the boxes?"

Chase looked up from where he was writing on another bag, then looked quickly at the other officer. Mari knew, from having met them both during the committee meetings, that the older officer, Richard, had been with Jake longer than Chase.

When Richard nodded an ok, Chase held up a clear baggie full of pills.

"Drugs."

#### 

"It's all your fault," Carl shouted, holding his cheek where the glass had cut him. "I told you not to break the glass, just to dump the boxes and scatter stuff around. You fucking blew it, as fucking usual."

"I did not, you idiot," Gus lashed out, his fist catching his brother right on the other cheek also cut by the flying glass. "The fucking glass *exploded* when I barely touched it, and you're the one who rammed the door and knocked out the guard. By the moon, Carl, what the hell were you thinking? You could have killed him if he'd hit one of those concrete parking bollards."

"Fuck you," Carl flung back, and fists flew. "You. Don't. Know. What's. At. Stake." The words were punctuated with blows as Carl let loose the fury and tension within him. He only stopped when he realized Gus wasn't moving. "Get up," he snarled, cursing. "You know she's going to kill us both for this. She and the big boss are *not* happy at you saying you want out, want to quit. If we don't keep the supply line going, we are dead men."

The big boss, with his dead eyes and silence, scared Carl more than the woman ever had.

"I said," Carl snarled, "Get. Up."

Gus didn't move. He just lay on the floor, bleeding.

"C'mon, Gus," he said, disgusted with his brother's acting. Gus had always known how to scare his little brother. "Get the fuck up. We have to go."

Gus didn't move.

####

Mari settled into her room in Salem. It had been reserved the year before, of course. She and Pere were next to each other, which was great, because there wasn't a space to be had at any hotel, B&B, motel, campground site or Inn in Salem or any of the smaller, surrounding communities. The Walk would begin in fifteen hours, at midnight, and witches, believers, New Agers, and a whole lot of people who supported freedom of religion, had come out for it.

To Mari's amusement, the parade of people in and out of the lobby had looked like cosplay at one of the more interesting science fiction/fantasy conventions. The streets, as she'd walked to the hotel from her reserved parking space, were just as colorful.

The dark spot in her day had been the really big knife stuck in the front tire of her new, not-red rental car. She'd called AAA, and Jake, of course, but even though Jake's tech, Missy, had come, and taken the knife and put it in an evidence bag, she said they probably couldn't trace it.

Knowing there was someone out there, following her to Salem with a knife like that, freaked her out. Whoever it was, was watching her. Tracking her.

*Snap out of it.* She reminded herself that she wasn't alone, and wasn't planning to *be* alone. There were thousands of volunteers, and she now knew most of the

Haven Harbor committee members and shop owners.

*It could be one of them.*

"Stop it," Mari snapped the words into the empty room. "There's nothing you can do that you aren't doing. Jake's in charge of the creepy people. You have to be in charge of the Walk until Gus shows up. Focus."

With the Walk starting at midnight, the approximate time the renegade witches had left Salem for their desperate journey northward, each of the team leaders had several hours of mandatory down time during the afternoon. Now that she'd gotten to the hotel, she was ready to take that down time. She had to be sharp for when the big start to the event kicked off.

But running through the details kept her mind off the other, darker things that tried to crowd in.

The walkers would reach Pennyfield about eight or nine in the morning, like their long ago counterparts, and would be directed to their tents, or be driven by friends back to their hotels, only to start the next section of the walk at nine that night.

For the next section, they'd go from Pennyfield to Mouldon, stay the night, and then the next day, at three in the afternoon, they'd make the last, more celebrational leg of the trip from Mouldon to Haven Harbor. Jake and his team would be there with lights and smiles for the stragglers, as would the sheriff and his men, and all the extras hired from Salem and Boston and other Massachusetts towns to direct traffic. They'd keep back the protestors and keep the peace. Then the Witches Walk would conclude with a huge party at MicroMechanics.

At each stage, Pere, Lucille, Mayor Bart, and Gus would give a talk, pull names for door prizes, tell about the witches of Haven Harbor, and generally encourage the group.

After the party, everyone would get a rest, go to the Faire and boost Haven Harbor's economy. On Saturday night, with great fanfare, the annual Witches Walk would conclude with the Witches Walk Gala at the Old Haven Mill Inn.

She couldn't wait.

####

Jake met Mari and Pere at the hotel in Salem, having called ahead offering to bring dinner. Once there, Jake broke the bad news bluntly over black coffee and Subway sandwiches in Pere's suite.

"Gus is missing."

"What? How? How do you know? Why?" Mari's mental staging of the event halted with a screech.

"What happened?" Pere reached for her hand, gripped it. She twined her fingers with his. This was no time to worry about what Jake or anyone else thought, she needed the contact.

*Shit, shit, shit!*

"There was evidently some kind of fight at his house. The place is busted up pretty badly. There's blood. Not sure whose blood it is, yet, but I can follow the fight— how they moved and that there were two people in the room."

Her earlier feeling of dread redoubled. The scenario of a faceless man with a knife merged with her worries about fire and smoke and danger.

*Where the hell was Gus?*

They'd been expecting Gus all day as they worked handing out packets, shirts, Walk numbers, water bottles, directions and more. Things were moving smoothly, and so when Jake had called and suggested he bring dinner for the three of them to meet in Pere's suite, they'd agreed.

"I think we keep the news under wraps for now," Pere said, glancing at her for her opinion.

"Yes. Our people know to keep their mouths shut. We'll just tell them he's not well, for now." Her event-management brain had kicked into overdrive, and she drilled down on that to keep her imagination from driving her crazy. "Pere, you'll kick off the Walk, with Mayor Bart and the Mayor of Salem. Lucille will be there, of course, and most of Salem's town council too."

"The FBI and MSP are on scene at Gus's house," Jake interjected. "They're going to want to talk to both of you."

"Of course," they both agreed at the same time.

"We've been here all day," Pere added, even though Jake knew it.

"Yeah, and your knuckles aren't bruised," Jake said, gesturing with his sandwich.

It took Mari a few minutes to figure out what they, in their male-bonded-shorthand, were saying.

"Of course he didn't do it," Mari defended, squeezing Pere's hand and facing Jake. "What the hell?"

Jake laughed, but his answer was directed at Pere, not Mari. "Mountain lion you've got there, friend, watch out."

"You know I will."

Jake rose, stretching. Mari could admire the sheer male attractiveness, but he really didn't do anything for her, not like the man who continued to hold her hand.

"Mountain lion?" Mari was baffled by the change of conversation.

"There used to be mountain lions—also called pumas or painters— around here, in colonial days. Not many, but they were here." Jake smiled whimsically, "Maybe we should see about inviting them back. Suarez said there was a bear sighted on the Mall in DC, but they got it and trucked it out to western Maryland."

"I am not a cat," Mari said realizing Jake was calling her a mountain lion for being protective of Pere. She was trying to decide if she should be offended or not. Switching subjects seemed to be the better part of wisdom. "And you'll let us know when Suarez and Emerson need us?"

"Of course." Jake paused at the door. Turning back as he held it, he said, "Mari, do your best not to be alone, okay? I don't think whatever's going on with Gus and the break-ins and all has anything to do with Geneva's disappearance. Or whatever happened to Lissa. But there were the problems at your house and the multiple attempts on your car."

"What about Kevin?" She heard Pere's subvocal growl at her question, but she needed to know.

"I think we might end up laying that at Gus's door, or his brother's," Jake said, letting the door swing shut again when he heard people in the hall. "Those runes didn't write themselves."

They'd shown her a picture of the dark runes that had been drawn on either side of the road in Pennyfield. The runes had each held a drop of her blood. The white fabric had been the bloody paper towels from when she cut her hand on the mug.

The trigger, Pere said, had been the bandage she'd worn, which had come off in Kevin's car. It lay on the passenger side floorboard when he and Jake checked out the wrecked car at the impound lot. They were sure the trap had been meant to catch her, but Kevin had taken the Interstate to Pennyfield for their date, and driven her home again the same way. But he'd taken the back road after he left her because there had been an all-lanes-closed wreck on I-95.

It was Mari's good luck that they'd not gone that way initially, since the trap would have caught her in the car. But it was bad luck for Kevin, since it had still caught him, thanks to Mari's blood being in the car, even though she wasn't.

"Law of Correspondence," Mari said, feeling terribly guilty that her blood had been the weapon that had hurt someone she knew. She and Kevin didn't have chemistry, but she certainly didn't wish a car wreck on anyone.

"Exactly. But the two women, even if they were run off the road by an SUV because of the whole same-kind or color-of-car coincidence? It's related, and there's more to it. I can't figure out how, and that pisses me off. I think someone is using whatever Gus is up to, to cover their own tracks."

"Nasty tracks," Pere commented quietly, and the two men exchanged meaningful glances.

"Yeah. So stick together whenever you can" was Jake's only comment as he left the room.

"What did that mean?" Mari demanded, her belligerence a symptom of her fear.

Pere turned to her, reaching for her other hand. Holding both hands, he drew her in. "Jake is smarter than your average small town cop."

"Not to knock small town cops," she said, annoyed with him for changing the subject.

"I'm not changing the subject."

"Stop reading my mind."

He laughed. "I wasn't, or at least not intentionally." He frowned for a moment, then shrugged. "No disrespect to the police in general, but Jake's a different breed, literally. As a descendant of both witches and spirit-talkers, if he's got a hunch, you can bet there's something to it."

Mari nodded, remembering Jake's comment about hunches.

"So he had Lissa's wounds re-checked. What forensics in Boston found was that the wounds from the glass were superficial. She lost more blood than she should have because someone used a knife to lengthen and widen the wounds, make them bleed more. They aren't sure why their suspect needed the blood. With Lissa, it was just that, blood. But with Geneva, there was a lot of blood, just like with Lissa, but this time, the suspect took Geneva's body too. That's why the MSP and FBI were so quick to come out here when Geneva disappeared."

"So you're saying Jake's right. Someone's covering their tracks with the antipathy toward the Witches Walk?"

"They're looking at Calvin."

Mari pulled back in horror. "One of us? Someone

from town?"

Pere wondered if she realized that she'd automatically allied herself with Haven Harbor. He still had visions of smoke and fire and death when he touched her. He still knew that she, and now he, faced something terrible. The knowledge was sobering, but it couldn't supplant the desire he had for her, or the wonder that she seemed to feel the same way.

"Yeah," he responded without giving his thoughts away. "It pisses me off too. Calvin's all set to protest at the Walk party on Friday night, and has gathered a bunch of outsiders, some real hellfire and brimstone types, including Brethren Holy Baptist."

"Crap."

"I said something a great deal more colorful," Pere growled. "Marion Proctor isn't a big fan of the Walk, but when she found out Calvin was bringing in the Brethren, she was flat-out pissed. She hates them. They picketed her uncle's funeral at Arlington, at the gates, anyway, since they couldn't get in." He shook his head over that. "She said she didn't let on to Calvin how mad she was, but she came to Jake right away. She'll side with the witches before she has any truck with the Brethren. That's a direct quote, by the way. Oh, and since she's the official president of the group, although Calvin's the leader, she went right to the courthouse and dropped the CAWW lawsuit against the Walk."

"That's great," Mari said, but she was still focused on the possibility of a protest. An ugly one. "Calvin won't be happy about that. Can't someone talk to him?"

"Marion said that Pastor Walthers sat through the last meeting, carving with his pocketknife the whole time, listening to the plan as Calvin laid it out. She said that at the end, Walthers stood up, put his pocket knife away and tried to talk Calvin out of what he was doing."

"No go?"

"No. And I think Calvin will be out of a job and out of

Haven Harbor, but the damage is already done. The Brethren, as they say..." He dropped his voice to a spooky, deep tone. "Are among us."

"Great. Just great." Mari spun out of his hold, pacing the short confines of the main room of the suite. Hers was smaller, so she was grateful to have the space. She had to think. "Can we call in any more off-duty assistance, security-wise?"

"Jake's on it. He's got ahold of a veterans group that's going to form up and come, and Marion Proctor's so fired up, she's got the ecumenical council on high alert, ready to go." Pere smiled at the image. "She's a warrior, that one, underneath it all."

"Dammit, dammit, dammit. I wanted this Walk to go off smoothly, without a hitch, so that Gus could have his last hurrah and be willing to leave the event with some dignity."

Surprised, Pere sat down. This he had to hear, and she obviously needed to walk off the mad. "Why?"

"Why?" She spun around, her eyes sharp with temper. He felt his heart shift, quake a little, and settle.

Dear Gods. He was in love with her. He pressed a hand to his chest, rubbing there, as if to relieve an ache he didn't quite understand, but she was on a roll and didn't notice. His grandfather had always said that Hestworths fell with a thud when it came to love. Pere realized he was proof of that. Now that he was sure he wasn't influenced by his mother's spellwork, he'd fallen for Mari Beecham, despite his grim visions of what her presence might mean for the town and for the Walk. She was smart and lovely. All the things he'd said to her before. But she also had taken the town into her heart, and the town, as evidenced by Regina Mathers's appearance, seemed to be feeling the same about Mari.

Mari, thankfully oblivious to Pere's revelations, was still talking about Gus.

Just as well. He didn't know what the hell to do with

the knowledge at this point.

"If Gus leaves in disgrace, then he's always going to be a thorn in the program. There will always be talk, there will always be those who look at me, or anyone who follows me, as less than. There will always be the 'well, when Mr. Gus ran the event...' people. Good or bad, if a director leaves in disgrace, it affects the event for years."

"So you're not so worried about Gus, personally?"

"What? No, not really," she admitted, hands tugging at her hair. "He's a classic bully, but he's a businessman in a small town that counts on its business people to make the event work. We need him, we need everyone."

Smiling at how she'd once again aligned herself with Haven Harbor, he rose and went to her.

"Don't look at me like that," she said, her flow of words cutting off as he drew her in.

"Like what?"

"Like you want to devour me, and cherish me and—"

"Love you?"

She paused, staring at him. "Yeah," she finally said, her voice husky. "That."

"We've got three hours," he said, not answering her unspoken question.

"But—"

"They'll get us if there's any news. We'll only make people worry more if we start rushing around trying to cover for Gus."

"True," she said, relaxing just a little as he glided his hands up and down her back.

"You need to rest. Everything's on you now, for the next few days. Take the time."

"Yes," she said, her voice catching a little as she raised her arms to twine them around his neck.

"Take it with me," he said, and his heart started pounding as he waited for her answer. It hadn't mattered before, not with anyone. Not like it did with Mari.

"Yes," she said, stretching up to kiss him as she had

done not so long ago in her kitchen. Everything in him fired hot as he gathered her in, gathered her up. He wanted to kiss every inch of her gorgeous, compact body, he wanted to twist his fingers in her dark hair and kiss her until they couldn't breathe.

"Yes, that," she murmured, curling one leg around his, pressing closer.

He hadn't said it out loud, he knew he hadn't. Part of him chilled a little at the thought that she was in his mind.

The other part didn't care. If this was a spell, he was its willing captive. He pushed away the tinge of smoke and lightning that crept into his mind.

Bending slightly, he shifted his hands under the luscious curves of her backside, lifting her easily so she could wrap her legs around his waist.

They continued their dance of tongues and heat, and he groaned when she pushed her hands into his hair, then down his back.

"Naked," she gasped. "I want you naked."

"Working on it," he said. He wanted her naked too, rising over him, snug under him, her smile, her scent, her laughter surrounding him.

"That too," she managed as he set her on her feet on the bed. She pulled off her light sweater, and started to unfasten her bra.

"Wait, let me." She stopped, and smiled. He slid his hands across the smooth perfection of her skin, gripping the hooks and sliding them open one by one.

"My skin isn't perfect," she said, a blush highlighting her cheeks.

"Yes, it is. I'm looking at you and I say it is," he said, tugging lightly at the straps of her bra, sliding it off her arms and tossing it to the side. "It's perfect to me, and that's all that matters."

"Yes," she said. "I'm very agreeable with you, Pere Hestworth," she teased, unbuttoning his shirt. "That won't do. You need someone to argue with you, keep you on your toes."

"Sold," he murmured, bending his head to run the tip of his tongue around her taut nipple. "Or hired. You have the job."

Her only answer was a moan, her hands buried in his hair, holding him to her breast as he teased first one nipple, then the other with firm strokes of his tongue. She was warm honey, her taste already an addiction. He let his hands fill with her gorgeous breasts as he found her mouth again. But his mind hazed when she ran her nails lightly down his chest, reaching for his belt buckle.

Mari couldn't believe she was here, in Pere's arms, finally. She wanted him desperately. Her body was already primed for orgasm from the moment he started kissing her. When he'd lifted her, again, like he had the other night, carrying her to the bed, she'd nearly come undone right then.

His mouth on her body was almost more that she could handle.

"Let me," she said, when he would have opened his belt himself. She slid the leather through the buckle, undid the button, the zipper. He was visibly aroused, the long hard length of him pressing the fabric so she had to have a care when she tugged at his trousers, his underwear.

"Mari," he growled as she let her fingers wrap around him. Thick, she thought, her mind already considering how he would fit into her. He was perfect. Thick and beautiful. She thought she said so, but couldn't be sure. She wanted to taste him.

"No, if you do that, I'll be done before I've even started."

"But," she protested.

"Later. Much later," he said, tugging her back to him, kissing her until her mind blurred and her body hungered. She fought to pull off her own neat black pants. Why had she worn a belt?

She wrestled it open, then dropped the pants to the

bed, kicked them off.

He picked her up and, wrapped around one another like a hot blanket, they fell to the bed hands smoothing and caressing, fingers exploring.

When his long, clever fingers parted her wet folds, she gasped, breaking the kiss to arch up, take in the rocketing sensations that threatened to overwhelm her.

"More," she demanded, as he slipped a finger inside of her, sliding it in and out until she felt the wetness of her own arousal on her thighs. "More."

He slid a second finger in, stretching her just a little, preparing her for his girth.

"We need—" she gasped.

"Protection." He finished the sentence, and slid his fingers back into her so that she had to muffle the scream of sheer sensation against his shoulder. She rode his hand as the orgasm rocked her, felt him band his other arm around her, holding her close as the shivers of pleasure wracked her with delight.

"Condom," he growled.

"Yes, now," she demanded, then managed, "Please."

He laughed, that open, full-bodied laugh she'd come to love.

Heart full, she acknowledged the emotion. Yes. Love.

"Good," he said. "Makes us even."

She didn't have a moment, or a brain cell left, to question what they were even on because he'd sheathed his gorgeous cock in a condom and she wanted every inch of that inside her. "Now, now, now."

"Your wish is my command," he managed before she captured his mouth and straddled him, rubbing her wet center onto him, sliding up and down his body while he groaned and tried to flip her.

"No," she insisted, "I want to ride you, to see you."

"You're killing me, I won't last."

"Then we'll just have to try again," she said, and rose up, folding back her inner petals with her fingers so that she could slide down onto the tip of him, slowly, oh, so slowly. "Oh, Lord," she breathed, feeling another orgasm building fast. "Just taking you in, I'm going to come."

He groaned and she slid lower, feeling him stretch her inner muscles and knowing the wave was rising. She wanted all of him when she climaxed, every inch.

"Come here," she said, pulling him over on top of her. "I'll ride next time." Arching up, she let him take control. He was careful, but she didn't want or need him to be. "Please," she said, pulling at his hips, moving him further inside. "In. Now. I want to come around you."

The last word was a moan as she felt her body clench around him, felt another orgasm break over her. He slid out, leaving her momentarily bereft, before filling her again. The pleasure was almost blinding.

"More," she said, sliding her hands into his hair, bringing his mouth to hers, lifting her hips to meet his thrusts. "More."

The full power of the orgasm hit her then and she cried out, twisting under him, pulling him deeper and deeper.

His body took over as his mind hazed and when she cried out again, pleasure in her gasp of his name, he let himself fly too.

Heat and light and breath rushed out of him and through him and he decided if this was death, that was okay.

#### 

"I rushed you."

They both said it at the same time.

Breathing still uneven, Pere, braced himself on his forearms, worried that his weight was too much. In answer, she pulled him tighter. "No, I rushed you," she said again.

His heart continued to pound and his breathing was ragged, but he managed to laugh. "I'll take my revenge later," he said, leaning down to kiss the tip of her nose. "I've only begun to explore."

"If that was just beginning, I'm in for a lot of orgasms." Her eyes were closed, and she wore a deeply satisfied smile.

"As many as I can manage before you rush me again," he promised, his voice so husky even he marveled at the emotion in it.

"Oh, goody," she murmured, petting his shoulders and neck and as much of his back as she could reach, without ever opening her eyes. "I think I'm struck blind," she said matter-of-factly, "but I don't really have enough energy to care."

"Your eyes are closed."

She opened them. "Oh, that." A satisfied smile curved her lips and lit in her eyes, and he felt himself harden again at the sight. "What's sight to a woman who's felt the earth move?"

"Important?" he teased.

"Yeah, yeah," she teased back, then her features sobered. "You're really beautiful," she said on a whisper. "All fierce planes and angles." She traced a finger over the black arch of his brows, down the line of his nose. "And magick. And wonderful. Who could have guessed what I'd gotten myself into when I answered the Witches Walk request for proposal for a Director?"

"No one, but you're the one, Mari. The right one."

She wasn't sure what he meant by that, but the depthless care in his gaze told her he meant everything. It scared her, and yet it didn't. She'd kissed a lot of frogs in her dating days. Pere Hestworth was no frog.

"Ribbit," he said softly.

"Stop that," she protested. "No fair."

"You do it too, you know."

"Do not," she exclaimed, wriggling a little.

"Wait, I'm crushing you," he said, shifting to his side and pulling her close.

She sighed, sorry to lose the most intimate of connections.

"I know, me too."

He did know, she realized, feeling the warm, powerful presence of him not only next to her body, but in her mind. It wasn't an intrusion. It was like a handclasp, companionship.

"I need to clean up," he murmured, and she heard the deep relaxation in his voice. She smiled. "I'm not going to sleep," he said, sleepily. "I'm just—"

"Relaxed."

"Mmm-hmmm." He ran the hand that held her to him up and down her back, making patterns and circles and whorls against her skin.

"That feels so good."

"Mmmm. Relax. Rest. I've got my phone set."

"Mine too," she said, letting her eyes drift shut, feeling sleep steal over her.

They both jerked awake at the sound of their phone's alarms.

"Good God," she said, pushing her hair out of her eyes. "I fell asleep."

"So did I," he said, fumbling for his pants and his phone. "Why do I use that ring-tone? I hate that ring tone."

She laughed as she got off the bed to grab her phone from her jacket where it still sat, draped over the back of one of the chairs in the sitting area.

She felt bouncy and energized. Even the thought of all the craziness and Gus being missing didn't dampen the feeling. She nearly skipped into the bathroom and stopped short at the sight of him, naked and absolutely magnificent.

"Wow. You are so built," she said before she could censor the words.

He threw back his head and laughed. "That's supposed to be my line."

She frowned, looking in the mirror. Her body, flushed and happy, her breasts already tight with need because he was looking at her, didn't look *built* to her. He appeared in the mirror behind her, his taller form looming over her, his hands sliding around to cup just under her breasts. The feel of his hands and the way he was looking at her made her want to purr.

"Is that a banana in your pocket," she murmured, rubbing her backside on his rigid erection. "Or are you happy to see me?"

"Very, very happy," he said, bending down to kiss the curve of her neck as he slid one hand down to caress her curls. Her body jerked as he slid a warm fingertip over her clitoris, already flushed and ready for his touch. "Mmmmm. How do you feel about making love in the shower?"

"I feel like it would be an effective way to get clean while also pandering to both of our obvious needs," she said, putting on a prim, lecturing tone.

"I'll take that as a yes," he said, managing to kiss her deeply at the same time he slipped one of those lovely, long fingers through her center and dipped it into her body.

She bucked into him, driving him deeper.

"Screw the shower," she said, boosting herself onto the sink. "Come here."

The sink was the perfect height, given how tall he was. "Mari, your back," he began, but she was already tearing open the condom he'd set on the counter. He sucked in a sharp breath when she bent her head, nearly prone on the counter, and swirled her tongue around the head of his cock before rolling the condom over him.

She made it a ferociously sensual act, cupping him, rolling her fingers around him and pulling him forward.

"Come inside me," she said, shifting back to give him access, all temptress, everything beautiful. The mirror reflected his desire back at him, and showed him the line of her back, the gorgeous dark fall of her hair. She guided him in, and she moaned and let her eyes half-close as he slowly slid into her wet heat. "That feels so damn good," she growled, shifting her hips and taking him deeper. He braced his hands on the counter and let her play, let her move.

If he took control, it might be too short again, too fast. He wanted her to come, to orgasm over and over while he watched.

She met his gaze. "I'm going to come," she said, a little desperately. "Move for me, bring me up."

He couldn't resist her, and didn't want to. He slid deeper and let his fingers play with the bud of her clitoris through the wet curls. There was plenty of lubrication, so he didn't worry that he would hurt her, or press too hard. She was pushing into his hand, undulating her hips to a primal rhythm as she pulled him in, hard, and threw back her head and moaned long and loud.

Her body clenched like a fist around him and it was all he could do not to pound into her, drive his hard cock in, over and over. But if he did, he'd come and he wanted to draw it out, see her come at least one more time before they had to face reality.

"Ohhhhh, that was so good," she said, shifting forward again to draw him in. He gritted his teeth at the wave of pleasure that engulfed him. She rolled her hips and drew an answering moan from him.

"Mari, you're going to make me lose control."

"Good."

"I don't want to hurt you."

"I'm pretty sturdy," she said, rolling her hips again, pulling back, drawing him out, then rolling her hips again so he sank back. "Try me."

The counter just wouldn't work, his splintering brain realized. It was great, on one hand, but the disparity in their heights meant he might hurt her if he pounded into her as he longed to do and as she was demanding.

"Come here, siren," he growled, gathering her up without ever breaking contact. Walking was a little challenging, but evidently pleasurable for her, because she kept making little mmmmm sounds of pleasure against his chest that were about to drive him mad.

He eyed the leather footstool that served as a coffee table in the sitting area. He was thinking that it was just the right height. She opened her eyes and looked over her shoulder.

"Mmmm, the ottoman?"

At his assent, she said, "I like the way you think. Put me down for a minute."

Before he did, he took her mouth in a kiss that nearly dropped them both to the floor. Gods she made his head spin. She wiggled and he had to tighten his grip on her hips to keep from taking him over the edge.

"Here," she said, unhooking one leg. Reluctantly, he lifted her and let her slide down his body. "Oh, I want you back inside me," she said. "Quickly. I'm about to come just thinking about you pounding into me."

"Mari, I don't want to hurt you."

"You won't. Trust me. Trust us." She knelt on the ottoman, looked back over her shoulder. "Please?"

With a groan he moved to her and she guided him in. She was tight and wet and so hot that he thought he'd explode.

"Make love to me, Pere. Now. Be with me."

"Yes," he said, shifting his hips to roll his cock inside her. She groaned and bucked her hips into him and that snapped his leash. He pulled out and came back in harder than before, a firm, urgent stroke.

"Yes, Pere, yes. I want you."

He stroked out and in, harder, more insistent. "Yes. More," she demanded.

When she looked back over her shoulder and repeated, "more," he was done.

He set a hard, demanding pace and she met him stroke for stroke. He felt her quiver, heard her gasp as her body clenched around him. Lost in her, his spine locked and his body spasmed in one of the most painfully pleasurable orgasms he'd ever experienced.

She moaned and backed into him, locking them together in a haze of aftershocks. He wondered vaguely if he'd ever get his knees to unlock. Ever be able to move.

"Good God," she rasped. "Wow."

His alarm beeped again, and he wanted to smash it, and barely stopped himself from doing something to it magickally.

"I don't want to move," Mari groaned.

"I'm not sure I can," he admitted.

She giggled. He laughed. Within moments, they were both laughing and he was helping her to stagger up from the ottoman. Together they wove their way to the bathroom like New Years' drunks, happy and sated, intoxicated with one another.

"Shower sex may have to wait," he said, turning on the water. "If we start up again, we'll be very, very late."

"Not an option," she said, trying to sober up. "It's important that we're there."

"Yes, but this was important too," he said, cupping her cheek and bending to kiss her softly. "Thank you."

"You're welcome, but why are you thanking me?"

"Because you're beautiful and generous and sexy and I want you again, already."

She kissed him again, and looked down. "Wow. You weren't kidding." Eyes lighting back on his, she grinned and it was a smile full of feminine power, and delight. "I'm impressed."

"Your fault."

"Oh, goodie," she said, and ducked behind the shower curtain. He laughed and handed her the soap. It was a near thing when she got out and he decided to dry her off.

"Not a good idea," she panted, pushing at his chest. "Shower, or so help me—"

"What?" But he gave in and stepped into the still-running shower. Sluicing off, he found himself grinning hugely, feeling buoyant and expansive in a way he'd never felt before.

Even facing some difficult things, and still with the worry about Geneva Banks disappearing, he knew he'd found something precious, something real.

He pulled on fresh clothes and found Mari shaking out her formerly neat wool trousers. She gave him a rueful look. "They're incredibly wrinkled. Good thing this event starts at night."

They grinned at one another.

"I'd say I'm sorry, but I'm not."

She pulled them on, did up the zip and button, fastened the belt. "Neither am I."

#### 

"I can't support this, Brother Calvin." Pastor Walthers sat at his desk, bent over with his knife in one hand and a smooth piece of wood in the other. He rubbed a thumb over the cut he'd just made, letting the next shaving fall gently into the wastebasket. He looked up, meeting Calvin's gaze. "I know you feel strongly about it. And I understand. I support you in your journey of faith, but I cannot condone bringing in outsiders."

"I appreciate your candor, Brother Walthers. I do feel strongly that I must press on. I don't want to bring you any embarrassment, so I've brought this." He laid an envelope on the desk. "It's my resignation."

"Much as I hate that you're doing it, and why, I'm going to have to accept it. The deacons and the membership will roast us both if I don't." He sighed, letting another smooth curl of wood fall into the basket. "I'm too old to go on the warpath, Brother Calvin, but I wish you the best."

He rose, folding the knife into itself. He stepped around the desk. "I really do wish you the best of luck," he said again as he opened his arms, embracing the younger man. "Go with God."

"You as well, Brother Walthers. You as well."

Calvin stepped back, cleared his throat. "I'll clear my things out of the other office tomorrow."

Walthers nodded, not trusting himself to speak.

He stepped to the window in time to see Calvin get into a van marked with the logo of the deeply despised Brethren Holy Baptist. With sorrow in his heart, but a firm conviction of what to do next, he shook his head and turned to take the wastebasket down and empty it.

## CHAPTER ELEVEN

The official start of the Walk went without a hitch. The spotlights and happy crowds surged forward as the ribbon was cut and there was laughter and celebration as the Eleventh Annual Witches Walk got under way.

Mari and Pere helped close up the Salem Walk office, and Mari and Carol hauled the remaining packets and t-shirts to the Pennyfield Walk station. With a certain level of publicity about Lissa Halliday's accident and Geneva's disappearance, there were some Walkers who'd signed up but who hadn't shown up to participate. Thankfully, their contributions would still fund the Walk, and any donations they brought in would still go to the First Amendment Freedom Fund, which worked to defend people who were facing difficulties due to their religious affiliations.

Mari hoped that some of the Walkers who hadn't picked up would join the group at Pennyfield the next afternoon, or at Mouldon the following day. Carol said there were people who paid every year, but didn't pick their shirts and packets up till Mouldon, only walking the last bit, but still bringing considerable funds.

Mari's phone rang with the tone she'd assigned to Jake. "Hey," she said by way of hello. "Everything okay?"

"All good so far. Everyone's on the path. We've got some joggers who've already pulled way ahead of the pack, but that happens every year. The torches are lit all along the route, so its fine."

"So, how can I help?"

"Not help. Just information. I wanted to tell you that the guy they caught in Mouldon did attack that woman at the transit station, but he's alibied for the night of Lissa Halliday's accident and Geneva's disappearance. He was in jail. Thought you'd want an update."

"Great," she said, feeling a shiver run up her spine. "That means someone's still out there, with a knife." And whoever it was, he was still taking his pique out on her car. She had been quick to reassure Jake that she was fine, but knowing that someone had been that close again, right there, following her, gave her the creeps.

"Yeah, so be careful. Remember, try not to go anywhere alone."

She looked around the parking lot, which was quickly emptying out, but there were two or three people she could identify. If she called out, those people would help.

"I'm okay," she reassured Jake as she turned back to her task. Pere was still with the Mayors and council people from the other towns, and Carol had gone to finish her tasks. Everyone was concerned about Gus and the negative publicity, and rightly so. However, they all seemed, so far, to feel like the Walk was still in good shape and that they everyone would have to move forward as best they could.

"There are still people here," Mari said, as she loaded her suitcase into the car. She hadn't even opened the bag because she'd been in Pere's room. That made her smile, so that when she pulled out of the parking lot, she was smiling at the cops directing traffic. "Carol just left," she said, answering Jake's query about who she'd be meeting. "But I'm already in the car and the doors are locked. I'm heading out."

"Be careful. I'll keep you posted if there's anything else."

"Thanks." They hung up, and her phone rang again before she could put it down. She pulled over to take the call.

"Hey," Pere's deep voice made her shiver in a good way. "Did you leave already?"

"Yes, I'm headed for Pennyfield."

"Alone?"

"I just left a dozen volunteers. I was on the phone with Jake, and I'm in the car with the doors locked. It's okay. I'm good."

"Okay." Pere's voice still held concern, but she let it warm her. He cared. It had been a long time since a man cared the way Pere did. "Did you talk to Jake?"

"Yes," she shifted back into traffic once she'd gotten her hands-free working. "I'm headed to Pennyfield, but there will be tons of volunteers there, so I'll be okay."

"Okay. Ping me by text when you get there. I'll see you in about an hour."

Warmth curled in her belly. "Yeah, see you there."

He clicked off without a goodbye, but she didn't need it. She'd see him in a few hours. Then they'd start the madness all over again.

When she got to the Pennyfield headquarters, there were plenty of volunteers milling around. She didn't worry about the car, or its tires, thanks to the sheer volume of people. Since she had so much help unloading the packets and t-shirts, it wasn't long before she was turning her car toward the B&B.

Carol had already headed on to Mouldon. On one hand it seemed silly to stay in Pennyfield when it would

221

only take her forty-five minutes to drive home, but the room was booked. Pepper was with Adele at the clinic, and Mari needed to be ready to address any issues that might arise when the Walkers arrived in Pennyfield in the early hours of the morning.

There were volunteers all along the route, and volunteers from the staff who would make sure every registered Walker got to the Pennyfield campsite and checked in. Many of those same staff would also re-walk the route, extinguishing the torches.

The Dower House B&B in Pennyfield was pleasant and airy and the rooms surprisingly spacious. The innkeeper, Alicia Remington, met her at the door.

"Welcome, welcome. I'm Alicia, but you probably remember that," she said, smiling. "I was sorry to hear that Gus wasn't going to be with us. I do hope he feels better soon."

"As do I," Mari said, trying to keep her voice level. "Thanks for your concern."

"Of course. This is such a wonderful event, any way we can help." She winked. "Really great for my business, of course. I have a full house for both nights. People who don't like to sleep in the tents, nice as they are, and of course, we have a lot of their family members. I've got some members of the press in the coach house rooms, which are separate from the main house."

"Good to know," Mari said, appreciating the subtle clue that there would be reporters at the breakfast table.

"They're out now, talking to Walkers along the route, I believe, but breakfast should be lively."

"Indeed."

Alicia unlocked a lovely room, handing her the key. "Get some rest. Do you want a wakeup call?"

"That's probably a good idea. Breakfast is at seven, correct?" At Alicia's affirmative nod, Mari added, "then if you'd give me a wakeup call at six?"

She only had to wait an hour for Pere to arrive. She'd

texted him as he'd requested, so he'd known she was in safe. While she waited, Mari changed into sweat pants and a t-shirt, and set out her clothes for the next morning. Stroking a hand down the wrinkled black pants, she found herself grinning with delight.

She heard Alicia's voice again, and Pere's deeper one, almost exactly an hour after she'd texted him. Mari waited till she heard Alicia go back down the broad stairs after escorting Pere up, before she opened the door. Pere slipped in, dropping his duffle to the floor. Within the next breath he had her in his arms and backed up to the door, mouth pressed to hers.

"I missed you," he rasped when they came up for air. "Just a few short hours and I missed you."

"I missed you too. I kept thinking about you." She kissed him again. "You looked good up there, with the mayors, the council. I was proud of you."

He smiled, resting his forehead on hers. "Thank you. I couldn't see you in the crowd."

"It would have been hard to, especially since I was trying to be eight places at once."

"Doing what?"

"Problem solving, helping with numbers, lost items, that kind of thing."

"Gus always made a volunteer handle that."

"They did, for the most part. The Salem team is outstanding, but they're two hands short. Kevin's still out, and one of the ladies is on bedrest, as of this morning."

"Is she okay?"

"Some early contractions, nothing serious, or so Trista Reynolds assures me. But I filled in wherever they needed me."

"No wonder they already like you better than Gus."

She laughed. "It's the way I like to work. Pitching in. Making the job flow smoothly."

He pulled her close, walked her over to the small, feminine-looking settee in the curve of the house's turret.

"Yeah? Well, what's the word from Carol and Lucille?" Lucille and Mayor Bart had helped start the Walk in Salem, then immediately headed to Haven Harbor to open the Faire. According to Carol and Gus, the Faire wouldn't be very active tonight, but would be in high form by noon tomorrow. Business and activity would increase on Thursday, and Friday would be huge. Saturday would be quieter, if the past notes were accurate, with the Faire closing at three to allow everyone to be ready for the Saturday evening Walk Gala, which closed the event.

Carol, Adele, Winona Aylesworth and several other committee heads had already checked in with her to let her know everything was in good shape at the Faire.

"They had some picketers from CAWW, but no Calvin," she said. "Much to my surprise."

"Mmm," Pere said, nuzzling into her hair as he pulled her down with him onto the settee. "Tired?"

"Not really," she said, turning to him, then rising a bit to kick off shoes, then come back and straddle him. "I have some ideas of how we could get tired, though."

"A sleep aid. I like that."

She kissed him long and deep, and his brain turned off every worry and focused only on her.

They made love on the settee, and again, in the shower. By the time they were done, they were both drooping.

Mari turned down the covers on the bed. She'd managed to pull back on the t-shirt featuring the logo of one of her previous events. Oddly shy, she turned to him.

"Stay?"

He'd pulled on his shirt, unbuttoned, and trousers, but he was happy to take them back off. "I'd like that."

"So would I."

Desire stirred again as they slid into bed and turned off the lights, but both of them dropped into sleep within minutes, despite their raging attraction.

Pere's hands woke her to a deep, languorous arousal before it was light. In all, Pere and Mari had only slept a few hours, but they'd need to be there to greet the earliest walkers as they arrived at the Pennyfield site. Although there would be volunteers there for the runners who always clocked the mileage in good time, she and Pere had agreed that they needed to be visible, and there to greet the actual Walkers. Gus, Adele and two other committee members had done it the year before, but with everything so unsettled, Pere had decided to do it, supporting Mari.

"Morning," she murmured as they came together, "is a lovely time of day."

"Mmmm," he agreed, sliding along her curves and pulling her knee over his hip so she lay half on top of him. He was enjoying the way her skin heated under his hands and the restless movement of her body as he ended each long stroke with a light caress at her inner thigh. The connection they shared when they were this close, when he could hear her thoughts and feel what she felt, didn't worry him. Even the ever-present hint of smoke and danger didn't dampen his desire.

It only made him want her more.

"You're teasing me," she said, letting her hands slide down his body, finding him hot and ready for her. "I'm going to have to return the favor."

He bit his lip when she wrapped her hand around him, slid her strong fingers up and down the shaft of his cock, gently tugging, with just the right amount of friction to drive him mad. When she shifted and curled down to take him into her mouth, he had to fist his hands in the blankets to keep from thrusting upward, into the wet heaven that was her mouth.

"Mari," he growled, trying not to come.

"This time," she whispered, leaving his cock with her mouth but not her clever, warm hands. "I get to play."

She took the time to let him put on the condom, but he was all but helpless in her hands as she rose above him, elegant and gorgeous in the dim light. She glided up, then down over him, taking him in, slicking him with her heat as she slowly settled all the way down onto him.

"You're so big," she said. "You fill me up."

"I don't want to hurt you." She was petite, perfect to his eyes, but there was nothing fragile about her.

"You don't," she said on a groan. "You make me feel so damn good."

She rose again, increasing the pace, and he helped, lifting her hips and rising to meet her. He fought the urge to turn her and drive into her, letting her set the pace, but when she crested, and gasped as her first orgasm hit her, he gripped her hips and kept the pace as she quaked in his arms.

"Pere," she moaned his name and he felt his heart and his cock swell as the pleasure built for them both.

"Again," he insisted, letting one hand caress the firm globe of her backside, while he slid the other in a downward stroke along the sensitive shaft of her clitoris. "Come again for me."

"I want to scream it feels so good."

"Oh, Gods," he said, wanting her to scream with pleasure too, but knowing it would bring people running. "Don't scream."

"I know," she panted, pressing into his fingers, riding his cock harder and faster. "But I'm going to come, hard."

He reared up to take her mouth, which drove him deeper into her and brought more pressure to bear on her sensitive inner trigger points. He caught the almost-scream in a kiss, and when her wild tongue tangled with his, and her hands gripped in his hair, he felt his own climax blaze through him.

Arching up, they came together, muffling one another's cries as the flood of sensation overtook them.

They collapsed together into a tangle of sweat-damp limbs and tangled sheets. His heart thundered and he could feel the frantic beat of hers as well.

"You're beautiful," he murmured. "So beautiful."

"So are you," she said, running her fingers down his

side, letting her splayed hand rest at his hip. He'd never thought of his hip as an erogenous zone, but her hand, just lying there was a sweet torture all its own.

"I don't want to move," he murmured, his mouth pressing kisses along her jawline.

"I don't either."

"My alarm's going to ring soon."

"Mine too."

With a long sigh that pressed her beautiful breasts into his chest, she lifted up. She crossed her hands on his chest and rested her chin on her hands. "Time to go be adults, I guess."

He laughed, and couldn't believe the husky, happy sound was coming from his chest.

"Yeah, I guess. And I guess I should go shower in my room, pretend that I didn't stay here all night."

"Probably."

They sat, just like that, cocooned in the warm glow of their lovemaking for just a few more minutes. "All right," she finally spoke again, just as he was wondering if she'd fallen back to sleep. "Let's do it."

####

When Mari came down to breakfast, Pere was already at the table talking to two of the other volunteer coordinators who'd stayed at the Inn as well. She only recognized one of them, but nodded to both and introduced herself as she sat down with them. She smiled at Pere as well.

"Good morning, Pere."

"And to you, Mari. I trust you slept well?"

Not by even a twinkle in his eye did he betray that he had more than a passing interest in her sleeping habits. Mari laughed inside, but hopefully she didn't show anything either. She wasn't sure she had quite as good a poker face as Pere.

"Well, for what little I slept." She included the volunteer coordinators in her smile. "I tend to get so keyed up when the event's actually going on that I don't get much rest."

"So true," one of the women said, and droned on for a few minutes about her sleep interruptions during Walk week.

Alicia brought out more food and provided to-go cups of coffee for all of them as they moved out *en masse* to go to welcome the walkers.

"I feel like the other shoe is going to drop," she said to Pere as she was about to get into her car.

"I know. I wish we knew where Gus is."

With that thought, they parted company. After thirty minutes greeting the incoming walkers, Pere headed back to Haven Harbor to work with Jake and Lucille to handle any Faire issues. Mari stayed at Pennyfield for another hour and a half, surrounded by volunteers as she greeted the last few stragglers and helped with packet pickup for latecomers. To be safe, she texted Pere before heading on to Mouldon with the remainder of the t-shirts and packets.

Dan, the handsome librarian who was Pere's friend, was waiting for her at Mouldon. When he spoke, it was with a quiet nonchalance that had her revising her opinion of Pere's friend.

"I'm here as your security, for now, until Pere or Jake gets here." He nodded to one of the volunteers who smiled at him. Still speaking quietly, he continued. "There's trouble brewing with Calvin Parris and the Brethren Holy Baptist people. They're setting up to block the bridge for the last of the walk tomorrow."

"Great. Just great," Mari groused, but didn't let her voice carry. She was sure Dan could hear just how frustrating it was to know that there was nothing they could do about the protest.

The day crawled by, with Dan her constant shadow. On one hand, she accepted his watchfulness, and appreciated that people cared. On the other hand, it was driving her nuts to have to be so vigilant.

With only a few texts from Pere, and a lot of putting out minor fires with Walk logistics, the day dragged. Mari was more than ready by when the time arrived to wave the walkers off toward Mouldon. Today, the walkers would spend most of the Walk in daylight. Even with September nights being cooler, it was sunny and dry during the day and the Walkers were a happy group, by and large.

She heard what seemed like ongoing debates and fresh introductions as she and Dan moved through the crowd to the head of the path that led to Mouldon. The old railroad bed had been turned into a trail and, like the path from Salem to Pennyfield, kept the Walkers off the roads, and away from traffic.

Jake met her in Mouldon, along with the Mouldon Chief of Police, Michael Borton. His force was just two full-time people, and a part-time dispatcher for nights and weekends. Like Pennyfield and Haven Harbor, they hired on extra help for the Walk.

When she and Jake were alone for a moment, she turned to him, but he shook his head before she could speak. "Nothing on Gus or Geneva. Calvin is in the wind," he said.

"What?"

"We can't find him. Pastor Walthers said he resigned and was going to hook up with the Brethren for the protest. I can't find him with them, either, however."

"What does Lydia say? Or Madame Sabina?"

"Nothing's clear for anyone, and believe me, I've asked virtually everyone to keep an eye on you, the Walk, and the Faire."

"Crap."

Borton headed back their way, so Jake finished his news in a quiet voice. "Emerson and Suarez got a warrant to search Calvin's apartment and car, since he's a potential for what happened to Geneva." Mari must have looked surprised, but Jake smiled grimly. "It wasn't as hard to convince the judge as you might think. Calvin had

Geneva's blood on him and was the last to see her before she disappeared. He's flown the coop." Jake shrugged. "Warrant issued." He looked around, nodding to people as they passed by. "They also questioned some of the Brethren, but they claim they don't know him and don't have anything they can tell us other than that we're going to hell."

"And the car?"

"The car was at the church, so Missy was able to get that in right away. The apartment was empty."

"Empty?"

"Totally."

"Freaky," she said, just as Borton rejoined them.

"I think we're ready for the hordes," Borton said cheerfully, checking his watch. "We should have the first of the runners in pretty soon."

The rest of the afternoon was a blur of greeting walkers and putting out proverbial fires with the Walk volunteers. There were a few walkers who'd overdone it and had to be taken to the local hospital. More had blisters or skinned knees treated in the medical tent set up at the Mouldon site when they arrived.

Dan arrived to take over from Jake just as the band tuned up and brought people to their feet for dancing. For every dancer, there were at least double the number already sacked out in their tents. By eleven, the site was quiet. Mari and her shadow headed to the small roadside motel, Mouldon's main overnighting spot.

All of the B&Bs in Mouldon were full, and had been booked for months, but the motel was clean and neat, if not fancy.

"I'll be next door," Dan said, waiting until she'd unlocked her room and stepped inside. "Until Pere can get here."

The FBI and MSP arrived first.

"Ms. Beecham, may we come in? We have a few questions that you might be able to answer."

Since she'd met both Emerson and Suarez before, she stepped back, letting them in. The questions weren't new, but they were focused on Calvin this time, rather than Gus or Lissa or Geneva.

"I don't know him at all," she said firmly when she'd answered the question, stated a different way, for the third time.

"But you've had contact."

"Only once and only at a distance. Lydia Webb, owner of the Besom Shop, pointed him out to me in the restaurant, The Judge's Chambers. Once."

"We found evidence that indicated he might have an unhealthy interest in you."

"In me? As the Walk director?"

"Among other things."

That stopped her in her tracks. If Calvin Parris had been watching her, or following her, she hadn't caught on. What did that say for any intuition she might claim?

"We think he might have been behind the cross painted on your porch, the blood, and the attempted break in."

Relief coursed through her. "So he wasn't stalking me or anything?"

"We did find a journal in his car, and it indicated an above-average interest in you." Suarez shifted in his seat and glanced at Emerson. "However, there was no indication he intended to follow through on any of his ideas, which did include stalking you."

A knock at the door brought another rush of relief when she let Pere into the room.

They tossed ideas and concerns about Calvin and the protestors around for a few more minutes before the two agents rose to leave.

"We'll have a man watching the hotel tonight," Suarez said, glancing from Pere to Mari. "We don't want anything happening on our watch."

*A not-so-subtle warning.*

Pere laughed softly when she'd closed the door. "Big

brother is watching us," he said, coming up behind her and wrapping her in his arms. "Wonder why they didn't watch over us last night?"

"Calvin wasn't in the wind last night. He's who they're after, right?"

Pere considered it, and nodded. "With that and Gus missing and blood at his house, they're watching everyone more closely."

"Damn," she said, just as softly.

"I want to be with you tonight, but—" he murmured the words along the curve of her neck. The minute he touched her, his vision-sense lit up. He couldn't quite tamp down the knowledge of fire, of blood and screams.

"But," she echoed him. "We'll have to be good."

He dropped his head down to kiss her collarbone, then back to her neck, at the curve where it met her shoulder. It was a sensitive spot and heat sprang full blown in her body when he let his lips rest there, flicking the spot with his tongue.

"Don't make a mark," she said, on a sigh.

"I didn't, but I want to," he said, laughing. "Like in high school, making a mark, claiming you as mine."

"Are we going steady?"

"You bet," he said, turning her to face him, eyes serious, gaze intent. "If I knew where my class ring or letter jacket was at the moment, I'd give it to you."

She laughed. "Thank you. I've never had either one from a guy, so that would be a new experience."

"Now that's a challenge. I'll have to find them," he murmured, closing the distance and kissing her.

They forced themselves to part, with Pere walking boldly out to his car to get his bag, and moving into the room next to hers.

Within seconds, he texted her.

*Get a good night's sleep, beautiful. See you bright and early in the morning.*

There were little feet emoticons pacing across the

screen under the words.

*You too,* she texted back, and sent a pumpkin to punctuate it.

*Hey,* came the immediate response. *Will you be my date for the Gala?*

Grinning, she texted back an enthusiastic *Yes! Happy to go with you.*

He sent her pumpkins and sleeping smileys, and signed off. Mari went to sleep alone, watched over by several federal officers, but with a smile on her face. In the night, the smile faded, and she dreamed of fire and smoke and death.

# CHAPTER TWELVE

She didn't remember the dreams until the next afternoon. She was beginning to feel like they might make it, they might get through the Walk without any more surprises or disappearances or scandal.

Mari should have known better to even think it.

"Mari, how are you holding up, dear?" Lucille Birkland and her friend, the back-patter, Winona Aylesworth, appeared out of the crowd of volunteers at the MicroMechanics volunteer tent. Pere had ordered pizzas for the volunteers and the hot cheese and pepperoni had hit the spot.

"I'm doing well, Mrs. Birkland, thank you. Hello again, Mrs. Aylesworth," she said as Winona delivered her usual back pat and a smile.

"Do call me Lucille, my dear."

Winona patted again. "Yes, and call me Winona. We don't need to stand on ceremony any longer, young lady.

You're family now and have stepped into the job brilliantly in young Gus's absence." She frowned and patted herself this time, as if reassuring her heart. "I do hope they find out what happened to him. I cannot get a single clue with the cards or dowsing."

This time it was Lucille who did the patting on Winona's arm. "I know. I haven't either, and we've all tried something."

"I hope he'll turn up soon as well," Mari offered, knowing it sounded simplistic next to what they had to offer.

"Have you seen that agent from the FBI?" Lucille said, changing the subject. Mari could have sworn she hear Lucille giggle. "He's got these adorable dimples when he smiles."

Mari laughed but Winona just *tsked*. "As if Mari has eyes for anyone but young Peregrine Hestworth."

Mari felt the blush color her cheeks and Lucille proved that Mari had indeed heard a giggle earlier by giggling again, louder and longer.

"I know that, Winona, but even if she's taken, she's not dead or blind. Suarez has the most adorable dimples you've ever seen."

Mari couldn't help it, she giggled right back. "I've never seen him smile. How did you get him to smile?"

"I told him I was going to ride George Ratcliff's white mare naked down Main Street in front of all those picketers, while wearing a long white wig."

Mari goggled. "You did not!"

"I did," Lucille huffed out a laugh. "Not that I'd do it unless there was no other way to get them to leave. Nor would I give them the show for free, but it did give me the chance to see Suarez's dimples."

Winona was laughing, hands braced on her hips. "That's not the whole story, at all," Winona scolded, then turned to Mari. "This all started when she told him she'd provide a distraction if he would push them all off the bridge into the Merrimack River."

"That was the best I could come up with," Lucille said. "Feeding them to the river." Then she sighed dramatically. "Suarez declined, alas, to send them to the water Gods."

"Yes," Winona agreed, "But he did inquire as to the nature of the distraction."

"And thus, we got to see the dimples."

Mari shook her head, laughing along with the two older women.

"Oh! Here they come!" Winona crowed, shading her eyes with a hand. "The first of this year's crazy runners."

"Winona disapproves of running," Lucille informed Mari, also shading her eyes and standing on tiptoe to spot what Winona had seen.

"Why?" Mari asked, more for form than for interest in the answer.

Winona *tsked* again. "Have you ever seen a smiling runner? A happy one?"

"Well," Mari began, then stopped, thinking about it. "Now that you mention it. No."

"There you go, then."

The first of the runners came into the camp and were welcomed by the legion of volunteers. Salem's volunteers always came onto the Faire when their part was done, and many of the Salem volunteers continued to help out in Haven Harbor, both with the walkers and with the Faire. The same with volunteers from Moulton and Pennyfield, so there were plenty of experienced hands on deck to get the first wave of walkers settled with a hot meal and a good seat for the band which was already warming up.

Now that they were in Haven Harbor, Mari had her walkie-talkie and was getting regular updates about the protest at the bridge and the line of townspeople, church matrons and elders, deacons, veterans and students who had formed a formidable, happy line between the walkers and the Brethren. Facebook, it seemed, had brought more than enough good spirits to block the hate-spewing

Brethren.

Lucille popped up at her elbow again, as the clouds brought night a little more quickly. "Any word on where our errant young pastor is? Pere told me they impounded his car, and searched his apartment."

Mari controlled her instinctive jolt, but was pleased when her voice stayed even. "Nothing so far. He may have taken off, you know."

"It would be smart," Lucille mused. "If he had anything to do with that Halliday woman or the auditor."

"Yes, but on the other hand, I hope they catch him so we can find Geneva."

Lucille's face tightened in anger. "Yes." After a moment, she put her hand on Mari's arm. "You realize we might not find her in time?"

Mari nodded, not sure if her voice would wobble or not when she spoke.

Lucille nodded, and then, unexpectedly smiled. "I see someone heading your way, young lady. If I were you, I'd plant a big wet one on him."

Mari scanned the crowd, and within moments she'd spotted Pere striding toward her in the gathering gloom.

Lucille laughed and strode away, calling out to someone she knew, and heading off a volunteer who was moving Mari's way.

"Hey," Pere said, stopping right in front of her, so close that she could smell his aftershave, feel the intense heat of his body.

"Hey."

"Can I kiss you, or will that tarnish your rep?"

"Kiss me. You'll make my rep."

He smiled, that slow, smoking hot smile of his, and bent his head to lay his lips on Mari's. The kiss was slow, and a little fierce, a promise of pleasure and delight. Her insides quivered at the intensity, the welcome he infused in his kiss.

Whistles and catcalls broke them apart, but Pere was

grinning. He wrapped an arm around her shoulders. "Any more pizza?"

She put her arm around his waist and they walked to the volunteer tent. "Hot batch just delivered. Were there problems at the bridge?"

Pere laughed, shaking his head. "No. You should have seen it, Mari. In fact, I think you'll be able to since I'll bet someone recorded it."

"What?" she demanded with a grin, impatient for news.

"Some jackass from the Brethren started quoting Bible verses, and damned if Marion Proctor didn't step up in front of him and fire back with…what do you call it?" He waved a hand, searching for words. "Chapter and verse. Matched him quote for quote and then went on her own extremely loud rant about how the New Testament was the New Covenant, or some such, and that going by Old Testament nonsense was backward and unChristian because Christ said go by the new covenant. I was educated and impressed all in one speech."

"Oh, wow." Mari was astonished. "What got into her?"

"Don't know," Pere said, making a beeline for the stacked, steaming pizza boxes. "I'm starving." He didn't speak again until he'd loaded a plate with several slices. "She seems to have seriously found her mad when Calvin Parris wanted to bring in outsiders."

"He just screwed up all around, didn't he?"

Pere nodded. "Seems like it."

The walkie-talkie crackled at her belt and she pulled it out. "This is Mari, go ahead."

"We've got a problem at the Besom Shop tent. Over." A young-sounding voice said. "Could use some official back up."

"I'll go," Pere said, wolfing down the last half of a slice. "You've got Winona and Lucille here with you. Anyway, I'll bet it's Barry Tang. He likes to come into the Walk Faire and try to sell delivery from his restaurant, which would be okay, since his food is great, but he doesn't pay for a spot in the Faire. Worse, if he sees someone who he thinks is Chinese too, he'll start telling them not to go to any of the Faire vendors, but to visit his mother's shop in town for good Chinese herbs or potions."

"Grrrrreat," Mari drawled the word. "That's a pain."

"Yeah, it really was until Dan was there a couple of years ago. Dan learned Chinese, somewhere along the way. He gave Tang a raft of shit for his behavior, in Chinese. Tang's been cool since then, but…" Pere stopped, stuffing the last of the pizza in his mouth. Gone was the icy, distant CEO. This was a man, a friend, a good guy. Her lover.

"Yeah, and I'll prove it later," he whispered in her ear as he gave her a peck on the cheek. "Oops, got pizza sauce on you," he said, rubbing it off with his thumb. "See you in a bit."

She watched him go, delighted with him, and with life. It made her heart catch a little that they seemed to be reading one another's minds. But, it felt…wonderful too.

She was walking over to rejoin Lucille and her sidekick Winona when her radio pinged again. "Base to Mari, over."

"This is Mari, over."

"Jake called, you're needed at the inn. Something about Gala prep? He said he'd meet you there, for safety."

"Got it. On my way."

She waved at Lucille and called, "Headed to the inn!"

Lucille nodded and turned back to what she was doing.

Mari drove around the long way, per Walk protocol, coming at the Old Haven Mill Inn through the residential streets. Knowing she'd be meeting Jake at the inn, she wasn't worried as she parked in the dusky evening light. Seeing the enormous banner that stretched from one end of the inn to the other, she smiled.

"Welcome to the Witches Walk," she read it out loud. "That is so incredibly cool."

She checked her watch and was reaching for her walkie-talkie to ask Jake if he'd been delayed. A sound made her turn, so the blow caught her on her cheek and temple and she crumpled to the ground.

####

"Dammit," Calvin hissed as two bulky men with the Brethren symbol on their shirts helped him lift Mari into the waiting van. "I hit her wrong. We need her awake."

The bigger man leaned in close, peered at the growing bruise on Mari's temple. "You did okay," he said, straightening back up. "She'll come round."

"Good." The smile Calvin Parris wore would have scared lesser men, but the two men who shared the back of the van with him smiled the same smile.

####

Jake met Pere at Lydia's tent, only to find that the deeply drunk, belligerent customer—not George Tang—had been corralled and carried off by his friends with florid apologies all around.

"He didn't like the future Mimi read for him in the cards. The more she told him, the angrier he got," Lydia said ruefully, rubbing the back of her neck. She'd been restless for the last hour, feeling the shifting weather that would bring the storm Estelle Hestworth had predicted for Gala night.

"You handled yourself, champ," Jake said, giving her a light, friendly punch on the arm. "Didn't need me at all."

Pere flinched, and his face went white before he dropped to one knee. "Mari," he gasped.

"What the hell?" a passerby exclaimed, rushing over to help.

"Don't know," Jake lied, grabbing the radio at his belt. "Jake to medics, Besom Shop tent on the double."

"He doesn't—" Lydia began, her gaze slanting to the stranger.

"I'm okay," Pere said, struggling to his feet, leaning heavily on Jake. "We have to find Mari."

"Let's get him inside," Jake said, handing Pere's stumbling form off to Lydia. "Thanks for your help," he reassured the good Samaritan. The man left, but not without looking back over his shoulder a time or two. The EMTs arrived within a couple of minutes.

"I'm okay, dammit," Pere cursed, struggling to rise even as he pressed a hand to his temple and groaned.

Lydia looked surprised. "Do they have a bond?" she hissed at Jake. "Mari and Pere, do they have a bond?"

"Looks like it," Jake answered tersely.

"Well shit. Kept that one under wraps," Lydia muttered, as the EMT pulled an ammonia capsule out and snapped it under Pere's nose. Pere jerked, but the glazed look cleared and he pushed the tech away.

"Mari. We have to find her. Somebody hit her."

"On it," Jake snapped, pulling the official police radio off his shoulder, rather than using the Walk radio. "All officers, alert, alert, alert. We're looking for Marisol Beecham, the Walk director. Five foot one or two, black hair, brown eyes. Wearing a scarlet Walk Admin shirt, jeans, walkie talkie. Last seen at the MicroMechanics Walk area. She's driving a blue sedan, rental, New York plates."

The Walk radio crackled. "Jake? Jake? It's Lucille."

"Go ahead, Lucille."

"I just heard your broadcast. Mari got a call from you to meet her at the inn."

"Got it." He glanced at Pere. "It wasn't from me."

He re-keyed the police radio. "All officers on duty, who's closest to the inn?"

"Jake, its Chase. I'm closest, I think."

"Go there, get me a visual on Mari Beecham, she may be down or disabled."

"On it."

To Pere, he said, "Come on." Then he hauled Pere up and supported him as they hurried toward the Blazer. Down one aisle of the Faire, lights flashed as a couple took a selfie with a ginormous stuffed cauldron they'd won at one of the booths.

It took two heartbeats for Pere to realize the woman was Jake's wife.

The man she was wrapped around, cheek pressed to cheek, was obviously not Jake.

He shot a look at his friend as he continued to stumble toward the car. Jake's jaw was set like granite, his eyes like glittering obsidian.

"Not now," Jake ground out, and it sounded as if his teeth were splintering. "That is old business. Mari comes first."

Pere said nothing, but gripped his friend's arm when they got to the car and Jake helped him into the seat. He was recovering his equilibrium, but slowly.

They had pulled out of the lot, easing through the crowd with a few whoops of the siren, when Jake's official radio signaled.

"Strongbow, go ahead."

"Chief, I found her walkie talkie." A hesitation. "There's blood."

# CHAPTER THIRTEEN

Mari woke to the smell of gasoline, but her thoughts were distorted and unclear.

Her head pounded and she really, really, *really* wanted to throw up. A logical part of her decided that would be a bad idea, given the gag in her mouth.

Heavy clouds scudded across the nearly full moon, and her thoughts fuzzed again. Lydia had called it a special moon, the Full Harvest Moon. It was supposed to be a good omen and bring prosperity. They always had the Walk under the waxing moon and the Gala on the night of the full.

*Witches,* she thought with wobbly amusement. *Crazy for those dates and symbols.*

She tried to smile, which broke open the cut on her cheek and temple and sent a headache roaring like a storm to pound in time with her heartrate. It also snapped her out of the weird half-conscious state.

It wasn't just the moon illuminating the rough clearing in the woods. A van was parked sideways on the road, its headlamps shining across the clearing. What it lit was the stuff of Pere and Mari's nightmares.

"She's awake," an unfamiliar voice said.

"Good. Let's get this started and get gone." That voice sounded a little familiar, but she wasn't sure.

Mari managed to open the eye that seemed to be working best. The other one was swollen and hurt like a bitch.

"Calvin Parris," she managed to garble, around the gag.

"Be silent, witch!" he roared, spinning toward her as he brandished a large crucifix. Mari was momentarily puzzled by the crucifix. Calvin wasn't Catholic. But her mind cleared again and she realized that she too was hanging from a cross. Her arms were tied to the rough, wooden crossbeam, and her knees and waist were tied to the main shaft of the cross. All around the edge of the clearing, in a circle around the cross, was a line of kindling and split firewood.

*What the hell?*

"For the crime of witchcraft, and aiding and abetting the witches of Haven Harbor, Mouldon, Pennyfield, and Salem in growing their numbers, I, Calvin Parris, a man of God, and these two witnesses, sentence you to death by burning."

"Wait, what are you talking about, death?" one of the other men said, sounding shocked. She managed to turn her head just enough that she could see him. He held a big, round, red can of gasoline, and he had paused in the act of sloshing it onto the ring of wood that surrounded her. There was a clear space between the cross and the wood, maybe twenty feet of empty grass.

"Keep working," the other unknown man growled. He was stacking wood, finishing the circle on Mari's other side.

She got the gag in her teeth and pulled, twisting her

neck this way and that. It hurt like fire, but whoever had tied the knot wasn't a local. She'd learned that most of the locals knew their knots. But she was grateful for it, because the gag was loosening.

"How dare you?" she said, the minute the bandana was free of her mouth. "I was born in Oregon and raised in the Unitarian Church. I'm here to do a job, nothing more. Turn me loose at once."

She'd heard a cop give a talk once and he'd said that sometimes, if you sounded like an authority figure, no matter how bad your position, you might be able to talk your way free. One of the men took a hesitant step forward.

"You're a witch who consorts with the devil," Parris hissed, blocking the other man's forward motion with a gesture. "She's a servant of evil. Don't listen to her. Keep pouring the gasoline on the wood. We will burn her."

The witch scene from Monty Python flitted inappropriately into her mind, and she almost muttered "...very small rocks." She and Babs loved quoting that scene to one another, line by line.

It wasn't very funny at the moment. Panic hit her because she couldn't seem to keep her mind from wandering. Her cheek hurt and so did her head. What had they hit her with?

"Hey, Brother Parris," the big, hooded man with the gasoline said with a note of alarm in his voice. "You've got the wood back here going all the way up to the cross. You can't do that."

"I'll burn the witch," Calvin shouted, crossing the circle of cut wood to stand in front of the man. "And you will help me."

"Oh, hell no," the man said, setting down the gas can and backing up, hands raised. "Scaring the heathens and circling her in fire is one thing. Burning her alive? Oh, hell no. I didn't sign up for killing."

The other man looked unsure now. He'd been caught up in Calvin's rhetoric, seemingly mesmerized by the waving crucifix and her "sentence" as a witch.

"He's Catholic," she said, on sudden inspiration, her thoughts clearing again. "Catholics are the only ones who use a crucifix. You follow a Catholic? One who worships the Pope?"

She'd read the Brethren Holy Baptist followers hated Jews and Catholics nearly as much as they hated homosexuals and blacks. Protestants didn't use crosses with the figure of Jesus hanging on them. Just the plain, unadorned cross. An empty cross was a reminder, her Grandfather Beecham had said, that we all could be called upon to make the sacrifices God required.

Mari preferred to think of the empty cross as a symbol of the resurrection. Either way, even if it wasn't true, if she could use it to drive a wedge she would.

She winced as she felt another sharp pain in her head. She could feel the blood dripping off the side of her jaw. Her shoulders ached like spikes were being driven into the joints. But she was still alive, and by God she was going to fight.

If she could get the two men to abandon Calvin, she might survive.

"Only fire can cleanse the unrighteous," Calvin intoned, and he used a lighter to light a torch he held, having laid the crucifix aside when she zinged him with Catholicism.

She didn't want to be a sacrifice. She wanted to be with Pere.

*Pere! Help me!* The inarticulate cry came from the deepest part of her. She didn't want to die, not here, not now. Not when she'd just realized she loved Pere Hestworth, witch, town council chairman, and CEO of the town's biggest business.

Her brain was playing tricks on her because she could all but see a woman's tall form slipping through the woods. Man, her head hurt. It was so hard to think straight. She looked for the woman again, but saw nothing but trees and darkness.

"You're nothing but a killer," she yelled at Calvin, playing on what the other man had said about not signing on to kill anyone. "What have you done with Geneva? Why did you hurt Lissa?" she coughed as the smoke from Calvin's torch blew into her face. "Why did you kill Geneva?"

"I didn't kill that woman," he declared. "Distract me not, witch!"

"Killer!" she taunted. "You killed her and hid her body. Where is she?"

"I didn't touch her. I found her car," he said, "but I didn't touch her."

The man who'd been squeamish about the fire backed further away. It wouldn't take much more to get him to run. Fleeing people attracted attention. Surely someone had missed her by now? They were all supposed to check in on a regular basis. She hadn't been alone, except to go meet Jake.

Her head pounded again, with another wave of pain, and she retched. Nothing came up, but the pain of it cleared her mind and she went cold all over.

That's how they'd gotten her. She thought she'd be safe, meeting Jake. Somehow they'd gotten him away, or it had all be a ruse.

She was going to die here.

To burn. She wasn't even a witch, just like the people in Salem, so long ago.

"You can't kill her, dude," the nervous man said, still holding up his hands like he hadn't been a party to all this. "We just protest. We just scare people into remembering that God is a mighty and terrible God."

"They'll blame you," she said, calling to the man. "If I die, you're responsible."

"You will die," Calvin said, firmly. To the nervous

man, he said, "Leave if you have no stomach for God's work." To the other man, he said, "Will you stay, Brother, and witness the glory of God freeing this poor soul?"

The man nodded eagerly and Mari felt a cold, sick revulsion shudder through her.

"Good." Calvin turned his back on the nervous man and, still holding the torch, bent to pick up a worn Bible. "In the name of the Father, I condemn you of practicing witchcraft. In the name of the Son, I condemn you of practicing witchcraft. In the name of the Holy Spirit, I condemn you of—"

*"Stop this, at once!"*

A statuesque woman strode out of the trees, her face a study in flickering light of the torch and the van's headlights. To Mari's intense satisfaction, she carried a shotgun. Regina Mathers.

The woman she'd seen in the trees had been real. Relief coursed through her. Her mind wasn't working like it should, but she hadn't hallucinated that.

"You," she said, gesturing toward the nervous man with the barrel of the gun, "cut her loose."

The nervous man didn't move. Regina discharged one barrel toward the vehicle. The buckshot pinged and bounced and punched through the plastic of the van's bumper like an ax.

"I said," Regina intoned, using her theater training to make her voice boom across the clearing, "cut her down. Where's the knife? Someone has one."

Mari didn't know what to say, and her head was pounding again, making Regina waver in her sight, which was making her feel sick again.

"Parris has a knife," Regina said. "And it has blood on it. I can sense it from here."

"Another witch," Calvin hissed. "Witch!! I carry no knife."

"It's in your outside jacket pocket, you idiot." She gestured with the gun again. "Get the knife" she said to the nervous one. "And go cut her down."

Nervous Guy moved behind Calvin and felt in his pocket. When his hand came out, a long, slim form glinted in the light.

Calvin looked briefly frightened. "That's not mine. I don't carry a knife."

"Looks like you do," Nervous Man said, unfolding the blade.

"I told you he had a knife," Regina said, and broke the barrel and loaded in a fresh shell. Before anyone could make a move, she had the shotgun reloaded and pointed back at Calvin and the guy holding the pocket knife. "What are you waiting for? Cut her down."

Nervous Man seemed to be having a change of heart. "How did you know Brother Calvin had a knife when he didn't know it?"

"I could smell the blood on it," she snapped. "Now get over there and cut her down."

"Don't do it, Brother," Calvin implored Nervous Man. "She's a witch too. She planted that knife on me. It's not mine."

The three men stood together now, and Mari, squinting from her one good eye could see they were about to try something. She was still having trouble making her mind work right.

Smoke and fire and wind and ash. The images kept rolling across her vision. Fire. Death. Lightning.

"Yeah, yeah, I get it," she muttered, struggling to focus. If something was sending her dreams and visions, they weren't being very helpful otherwise. "Smoke, fire, wind, ash. Dying here's possible."

"Mari," Regina called. "Stay with me now."

"I'm staying," Mari said crossly, feeling scolded. God, why wouldn't her brain work?

She felt the change, rather than saw it. Like a shift in air pressure before a huge storm. The wind began to stir the trees and a scent of rain filled the air. People formed out of the shadows. Some dressed in Walk t-shirts, others in jeans and t-shirts. One in a baker's apron. Oh! There was Estelle Hestworth. Mari nearly giggled because always-perfect Estelle's hair was had twigs in it. Leaves lay on her shoulders.

What was that sound?

Mari's head jerked up, and she drew in a deep breath, feeling a charge of a storm in the air. She looked back at Estelle. Little whirlwinds were circling her, stirring the leaves and twigs from the ground and tossing them up like a cloak onto Estelle's shoulders.

"Calvin Parris. Men of the Brethren," someone, one of the witches, called from Mari's right.

"Put down the torch, and step away." That was another voice, from the left.

"Spare our Sister, and we will spare you."

Calvin spun around to face the growing crowd of people. Mari could hear the sirens now. Sirens meant help. Sirens meant Pere and Jake.

Even with her vision wavering in and out, and her mind hazy, she knew sirens meant help.

*Pere!* She could feel him now. He was coming.

"I've got eight bullets in this gun," Calvin said, spinning around to face the crowd. He had the torch in one hand and now, a gun in the other. He was pointing the gun at the crowd. "I can get eight of you before I drop the torch." He must have smiled or made some kind of face because the witches of Haven Harbor drew back, just a bit.

"Where's Geneva, you fucker!" Mari yelled, suddenly incensed all over again that he'd been part of making her first Walk year such a disaster. "Did you kill her with that knife? There was blood on the knife!"

The woman—Mari lost her savior's name for a minute as her head ached and throbbed—No, she had it. Regina. Regina had said there was blood on the knife. Mari swiveled her head so that she could find the woman.

Where did she go? Shotgun woman. *Regina*, her brain

finally supplied the name again. Where was she?

Mari looked back at the crowd trying to spot the woman. All she saw was that the witches had now joined hands. They formed a semi-circle around Estelle Hestworth, who looked bigger somehow, and dignified, even with twigs and leaves still rising and falling around her, and tangled in her hair.

"For the last time you stupid bitch, I didn't kill the woman," Calvin shouted at her, before turning back to face the witches. To Nervous Man, he hissed, "Finish spreading that gasoline, you idiot."

Mari felt a touch on her knee, right above the ropes and jerked, hard.

"Shhhh," came a whisper. "It's me, Regina."

"Calvin, stop this before anyone gets seriously hurt," Lucille Birkland called. Mari squinted at the crowd. She hadn't seen Lucille come into the clearing. "I've known you since you were four, and this is not you. This is wrong, Calvin."

"Shut up you old biddy. I hated you then and I hate you now. Witches, all of you," he spat the words. "Unclean. Filth!"

"And proud to be the witches of Haven Harbor," Estelle said, drawing herself up to her full height. "Christians were persecuted once, long ago. You would think it would make them more sympathetic to those who are different, but," Estelle lifted her hands and shrugged a *what can you expect* gesture.

"She's trying to keep him talking," Regina whispered as the ropes at Mari's knees fell away. Her arms hurt worse now that her legs were free, and she sagged forward. She was tied to the cross bar, and the weight of her body pulled on already sore arms.

Calvin brandished the gun. "Shut up, old woman."

The sirens roared to a peak, and the Blazer skidded to a stop in a spurt of gravel. Jake and Pere leapt from the car. The spotlight from the cruiser lit up the whole clearing, and, unfortunately, revealed Regina behind her.

"Get away from her, bitch," Calvin said, whipping around to turn the gun on Mari and Regina. "Or die with her."

"*NO!*" Estelle cried, and Calvin whipped back around, leveled the gun, and fired, just as Pere flew into him in a driving tackle.

There was a crackle of the hottest lightning Mari had ever seen and it struck the ground behind the witches. The bolt fired the clearing with light and the smell of ozone.

"No!" cried Jake, rushing toward Pere. "There's gasoline!"

But it was too late. The torch flew from Calvin's hand as the bolt struck, and Pere hit him. It lit the wood in the large circle where the men had laid it.

Flames followed the gasoline around the rough fuel until Mari and Regina were nearly encircled. The flames hadn't found the secondary trail of wood to the cross where Mari was tied yet. Nor had Nervous Man managed to get gasoline onto all the wood, but it was obvious the wood was dry and ready to burn. It was only a matter of minutes before the whole circle of wood was aflame, whether there was gasoline on it or not. The trail of stacked firewood that led to the cross might not be fuel-soaked, but it would still burn.

She struggled in the ropes, and Regina hissed at her to be still. Mari complied, but squinted, trying to see through the dancing flames. Where was Pere? Where was Calvin?

A figure arose, and she could see the gun in his hand. He pointed it downward, and laughed. Calvin.

That meant the man on the ground was Pere.

Calvin fired.

Mari screamed and the clearing turned into Hell.

Lightning roared, and rain pounded down as if it were being dumped from truck-sized buckets overhead. Regina clung to Mari, still working at the ropes with her own knife.

"Don't fuck with the weather witch," Regina spluttered through the drenching water. "Never, ever, *ever* fuck with the weather witch's kid."

"PERE!" Mari cried. "PERE!!" Calvin had shot him! Was that him, lying so still? Where was Calvin? Trying to focus, Mari felt for Pere, felt for the bond they seemed to share.

And found him. Relief cascaded through her.

"Here!" he answered, leaping over the smoking wood circle with his hand clamped to his side. "I've got her," he said, as Regina cut the last bit of rope. Mari sagged in his arms, unable to keep her balance, or find her feet.

"Thank you," she tried to say to Regina, but got a mouthful of water as she looked up at the taller woman. The fires spluttered fitfully as the rain soaked into the dry wood. Even a gasoline-fed fire couldn't continue with the saturated wood. The rain diluted the fuel on the ground and on the wood, subduing the fire that remained.

Hair plastered to her face, Regina just nodded, and winced, ducking to help as Pere staggered under her weight, and his injury. The lightning continued to strike.

"*PERE!*" Jake appeared and dragged at Pere's arm. "I'll get Mari. You have to help your mom. Estelle called the Gala-day storm early, now she can't stop it."

"Shit." Pere hesitated, just the barest fraction, and Mari's heart swelled and nearly broke at the same time. He would choose her, if he had to choose.

"Go, help your mother," she rasped a shout, suppressing a shriek of surprise as another bolt struck the trees. And another.

"You go too. I've got her," Regina hissed at Jake, and even as she said it, Jake's officers hurried to help. Chase carried her over the still-smoldering wood to a stretcher, held by EMTs she vaguely recognized from safety meetings.

"No! Let me see," she near-screamed as thunder

roared continuously through the night. Mari batted at the hands supporting her, blocking her.

In the light of the cruiser spotlight and headlights, the lights from the Brethren van, and the strobing lighting, she could see Estelle. With her silvery hair wild in the wind, Estelle stood at the center of a twisting ring of debris that rose to create a mini-whirlwind around her body. It funneled up into the sky as lighting struck again and again, from cloud to cloud, jerking down to hit a tree and blow it to toothpicks.

Those hits came closer to the town's witches with each passing minute. Yet, they stood firm.

"Get her into the ambulance," someone shouted, at Mari's ear.

"NO!" Mari said, shoving at them. She didn't know why, but she needed to be here, needed to help if she could. *Pere, I love you. You love your mother. Help her!*

A wordless flow of love and relief and energy jolted through her. "Hands," she rasped, gripping Regina's hand, and feeling her jerk. She grabbed the EMT, yelling, "Get everyone to join hands, send energy or whatever to Pere and Estelle."

Everyone hesitated, just a second.

"*MOVE, people!*" Mari yelled in her best imitation of her father's drill sergeant voice. People jumped, and moved closer. They joined hands, linking themselves to one another, and the line of witches, to Jake, and then to Pere.

Mari felt the sharp, hot shock, like an electric charge, when Pere took his mother's hand. Mari decided they all must have heard him talk to her, an echo down the line of linked hands.

*Mother. Control it, don't let it control you. I'm fine. Mari is fine. The situation is contained. I love you.*

He was on his third repeat of the words, and growing more desperate, when the storm suddenly lessened. Mari felt the relief that flowed back and forth up and down the line of joined hands and hearts.

The rain slackened suddenly, and the clouds thinned with an unnatural speed. A brisk breeze took the rain off over the trees and the roar of it hitting the water of the river and the marsh was a drumbeat like no other.

The sudden quiet, broken only by the rain pouring into the river, and a distant, light, rumble of thunder, was almost too much to bear.

It was the EMT who broke the chain. She let go of Regina's hand and grabbed a stethoscope to begin checking Mari's vitals, easing her onto the waiting gurney.

Regina enclosed Mari's hand in both of hers, breaking the chain on her side to do so.

All along the line, people were dropping hands, or turning to hug each other. They milled around and spoke in hushed tones, until Pere shifted.

"Mercy?" Jake yelled to the EMT next to Mari. "Pere needs you."

Mercy jerked her head at the other guy, yelled back. "Tom's coming, I'm with Mari Beecham."

"*Mari!*" the voice that called out next was the best thing Mari ever heard.

"*Pere! I'm okay!*"

"Good," he called back and there were chuckles in the crowd now.

Suddenly he was at her side, and Jake was there too, gently depositing Estelle on a second gurney the other EMT had run to get from the waiting ambulance. They turned that cot immediately and headed to the ambulance, racing away with sirens going and lights flashing.

"Good thing we brought the second rig," Tom said, popping in the earpieces to a stethoscope and listening to Pere's heart.

Jake's officers led the two Brethren thugs toward a cruiser. Mari couldn't see very well, but it looked like they were shaking and having trouble walking.

"Did your mom hit them with the lightning?" Mari

said, gripping Pere's hand when he moved to stand beside her, hovering behind Mercy as she worked.

"No, just Calvin."

"He had a knife," Regina said to Jake. "It was covered in blood."

"But he said he didn't kill her," Mari put in, turning to Pere. "Geneva. He was insistent about that. Calvin said he didn't kill her."

"This is going to be one hell of a report," Jake snarled, wiping rain and mud off his face. "Pere, let's get you in the ambulance."

"I'm not moving until Mari does."

"Federals," someone called, and like magic, the crowd faded into the trees, and slipped off down trails and over neighborhood fences beyond the trees.

When Emerson and Suarez arrived, with their own lights flashing, there were only eight or ten people left in the clearing. Mari was puzzled as hell, but Regina bent down and murmured, "They'll have a hard time figuring all this out as it is. More people equals more problems with the story. Better to have the professionals handle it, and only a few people to question."

"Ms. Beecham," Mercy said at her other ear. "I want you to close your eyes now. I know you're conscious, but we're going to get you and Mr. Hestworth into the ambulance and fly on out of here like the witches we are," she said, obviously trying to inject some levity into a tense situation. "No need to deal with the badges tonight, okay?"

Mari nodded and Regina squeezed her hand. "I'll come see you at the hospital."

Mari's eyes flew open. "The Gala," she gasped. "The Walk!"

"Shhhh," Lucille Birkland said, moving up to stand with Regina. Winona was there too and she patted Regina first, which seemed to surprise the tall woman, then reached over to pat Mari's cheek. "You rest. I'm a lawyer.

Between that and the rest of the people here, we've got it covered."

#### 

Mari didn't know anything else until the sun coming in the windows woke her. She was in a stiff, white-sheeted hospital bed. The blanket was nubby and warm, but everything looked institutional and stark, despite attempts to soften the walls with harbor scenes and pictures of boats with red and blue sails.

"Ugh," she groaned the word, and suddenly Pere was by her side.

"Mari?"

"Hey," she managed and was surprised to find her voice was still slurring a little.

"Hey, back. You're at the hospital."

"Yes, Captain," she muttered, frowning at him.

He frowned back. "Captain?"

"Captain Obvious. This is no Ritz-Carlton, even I know that."

He grinned and her heart blossomed at the sight.

"Your mom?"

He sighed and closed his eyes briefly. "She'll be all right with lots of rest and a few months without doing anything even remotely magickal."

"That was pretty awe inspiring," Mari said, waking up more with every passing minute. She could almost feel the mists of the drugs or whatever peeling away. "God I feel like I got hit by a truck."

"Fist." The sudden fury in his voice could have set the room on fire.

"Huh?" She struggled to sit up and he helped her, putting pillows behind her and raising the bed. "Nurse Hestworth. I like it," she joked, to ease his mood.

"I suck at nursing almost as much as I suck at being a patient."

The door creaked open and a man walked in, clipboard in hand. "Jesus, Pere, couldn't you have at least waited until rounds were over to sneak out?"

"Sneak out?" she peered at him and realized he too was wearing hospital gear. In his case though, he had on what looked like scrubs, and a bathrobe. "Pere. You were hurt. Why aren't you in bed?"

"Because I'm with you," he said, temper edging every word. "And I wasn't waiting for you, Sam, to tell me I could come up here and see her."

Sam rolled his eyes and moved to Mari's other side. He cocked his head to one side, then met her gaze. "You feel like crap, I'm sure."

"Great bedside manner, doc," Pere chided.

"Shut up, Hestworth. I'm talking here," he said, never taking his eyes off Mari. "You took a very large fist to your face, which has my friend here eager to beat the hell out of someone, for which I don't blame him. You have a concussion, and a fractured cheekbone. Your tongue is probably hurting and swollen, because you bit it at some point. You have burns from flying embers from the fire, and some pretty nasty contusions on your wrists and arms from the rope. You didn't dislocate a shoulder, but I'll bet it feels like you did, even so."

As he ran through the litany of injuries, she began to feel every one of them.

"So much for the damsel and the knight getting to celebrate being alive," Sam concluded, opening the chart. "But I'm glad you both are. Alive, that is."

She whipped her head around to glare at Pere and immediately wished she hadn't. "What happened? You got hurt. What did he do?" Parts of the previous night were shadowed in her mind. Others, unfortunately were crystal clear.

"He shot me, then I—"

"He *shot* you? That little *fucker.*"

Both men sucked in a breath, then burst out laughing. "Ow, ow, don't make me laugh," Pere complained, clutching his side. "Oh, my Gods you should have seen your face."

Mari frowned, which made her head and jaw hurt all over again. "Shut up," she said petulantly, relieved that he was obviously going to be okay, despite getting shot. "Jake better be sending him to prison for-freakin-ever."

When both men went quiet, she stopped. Then it hit her.

Lightning. The memory of Regina saying, "Don't ever fuck with the weather witch's kid."

"He's dead, isn't he?"

They nodded, and she sighed. "Regina said something about that, but it's blurry. I think I went sleepy-sleep pretty soon after that."

Sam smiled now. "Yeah. You went under pretty fast, but that's not unusual, given what you'd been through. That, and you were the anchor."

"The whatsit?" Anchor? Her brain supplied the image of an anchor, but she couldn't for the life of her connect the dots. How was she an anchor?

"I'll explain in a bit," Pere said, mock-glaring at Sam. "Aren't you done yet?"

"You can hang out with your girlfriend for ten more minutes, but then you have to get back to your own bed, you hear me?" Sam was smiling, but Mari could see the seriousness underlying his light words. "Gunshot wounds are nothing to screw with, even if was a through and through." Sam turned to Mari. "It didn't hit anything vital, but he's gonna be hurting on that side for a while."

"Got it," Pere agreed, and he turned to Mari, waving a hand in a shooing motion toward Sam. "Now scram."

"Mari, you okay with flowers?" Sam was talking to her as he back-walked to the door. "I've been getting calls since you came in. I held them off until I could ask if you were allergic."

"I love flowers," she said, gazing into Pere's eyes.

"Great. Oh, Adele said Pepper is fine, and she'll take good care of him till you're back on your feet."

Relief coursed through her. "Thanks, Dr..." she hesitated. Pere had called him Sam, but she didn't even know his last name.

"Samuels. But call me Sam."

"Thanks, Sam."

"Go away, Sam," Pere snarled.

"Yeah, yeah," he said, pulling the door open. He stopped and scowled at Pere again. "Ten minutes, or I pull rank."

"Got it. Go away."

The door shut on quiet hinges, and Pere leaned down and kissed her carefully. "He's right, it does suck that we can't jump each other's bones and rejoice in being alive."

She smiled against his lips. "Yeah. That blows."

They kissed for a few minutes, but the bending down hurt Pere and the kissing hurt Mari, so they stopped. "I want more," he murmured.

"I know. But you only have five more minutes."

"Sucks," he repeated, slipping into the chair at the bedside, but continuing to hold her hand.

"Tell me what happened," she said, needing to know.

"We realized you were missing and Lucille directed us to the inn. We found your walkie-talkie, your car, and your blood." He gripped her hand so tightly it hurt, but he realized it before she could speak, and loosened his grip. He pressed a kiss to her fingers in apology. "Sorry. Jake pulled everyone in to search. He had a bad feeling, and that's never good."

"So I hear," Mari said, smiling. Jake's hunches. "Looks like our fire and smoke thing came to pass."

"Yeah, I guess so." He shuddered, staring blindly at the bland wall. "I almost lost you."

"Yeah? I almost lost you too," Mari said softly, squeezing his hand, only then feeling the bandage that wrapped it. "What happened to your hand?" She spotted the other, bandaged hand. "How did you hurt your hands?"

He winced and said, "Well, there was this weather witch. She kinda lost control…"

"Oh, dear. Your mother is not going to be happy about that," Mari said with a grimace. Part of her was amazed that she was taking this all so calmly. Maybe she was getting used to Haven Harbor. "I don't know her well, but she prides herself on control, that you can see at a glance."

"She does. And no, she won't be happy, not at all." He paused, standing again, and gazing down at her. "I think she'll be happier when she realizes I'm getting married."

"She will?" Mari said, surprised. Then her brain caught up. "You are?"

He got down on one knee next to the hospital bed, which was awkward, but endearing. "If you'll have me. Mari Beecham, my love, will you marry me? I know we've not known one another long, but—"

The grin that split her face hurt, but she didn't care. Joy and giddy excitement rushed through her in a wave. "I will most definitely have you, Peregrine Hestworth."

"Oh, thank the Gods," he said, rising to kiss her gently again. "I was worried."

"You were not," she teased.

"Actually, I was. We've put you through the wringer from the first day you got here, Mari. After all that, I'm glad you love me enough to stay."

"Come here," she said, pulling his head down to kiss him more firmly. "I do love you. I love Haven Harbor and all its witchy quirks. It'll still take some getting used to, I know, but hey, I'm up for it. We'll figure out the rest."

"Good," he said, kissing her back.

It was too easy to get lost in his kisses, even with the pain in her cheek and jaw. But she managed not to, and gently pushed at his shoulders. "Doc said ten minutes, my love, and he's given us fifteen. You need to rest. To heal."

"I know," he said, but added, "I don't want to leave you."

"I know," she said, and she did. She could feel it. "I'm not far away."

The bond thing. That was pretty freaky, but she liked it.

"I like it too." He grinned. "I know, it'll take me some time to get used to it too. Wait till I tell my mother."

"Oh boy," she managed, as it dawned on her that his mother had almost obliterated several acres of New England. "That could be a little dangerous."

"No," he said, still smiling. "She likes you."

When Pere slipped out of the room a while later, she realized he hadn't explained the thing about the anchor. A nurse came in as soon as he'd gone and within minutes, Mari was asleep again. This time with a smile on her face.

When she woke, it was to find the room filled with flowers. It looked like a greenhouse had exploded. The riot of colors and scents and cheer was fabulous.

There was a light knock and when she called a "come in," Lydia popped her head in the door.

"Hey girl, you up for some company?"

"Do you have Chinese?"

Lydia laughed. "No, sorry, Sam confiscated it."

"Damn."

"Don't worry, I'll get you some. Until then, wanna hear the goss?"

"You bet."

Lydia stayed for an hour, catching Mari up on the Walk and how the Gala was going to go off without Gus, Mari, or Estelle. Carol, it seemed, was stepping up, and with a lot of help from Winona and other town leaders, the Gala was going to be awesome.

"I've got every faith in her," Mari said, smiling.

"I'll tell her that," Lydia said. "It'll make her night."

It was Lydia who broke the news that they'd found

Gus's body.

"Jake thinks it was his brother. Carl was always bad news. He was dealing drugs in college, and everyone says he skipped to Canada to avoid being prosecuted. Jake's still unraveling everything, but he thinks that Carl involved Gus and the Walk in one of his schemes, and when he tried to get out of it, and untangle the Walk's finances or whatever, Carl killed him."

Mari's heart ached. She hadn't been Gus's biggest fan, but no one deserved to be killed by his own brother.

"I'm so sad for their mom, their family."

"Yeah," Lydia said. "Me too. And for the last of the bad news, they haven't found Geneva yet either. They found a knife on Calvin, and as Regina supposedly told them it was blood-soaked, they tested it. Since they already had Geneva's blood they were able to tell it was hers on the knife. Looks like Calvin was the culprit behind Lissa and Geneva's accidents."

They talked non-stop for about thirty minutes, and only when Lydia left did Mari realize she hadn't told Lydia about Pere, and the fact that they were now engaged. Nor had she found out about the anchor.

Visitors popped in and out like bunnies out of a burrow all afternoon. There were so many people that she never had one moment that seemed right to say, "Hey, Pere and I are engaged!"

It was making her seriously cranky. And she kept dropping off to sleep without any warning at all.

By the time everyone stopped popping in and headed to get ready for the Gala, Mari had flowers on every surface and more magazines than she could possibly read in a year. She had the nurses re-gift most of the magazines, and, when the room got too full, she asked if the nurses would like flowers out at their station and had them drop some of the corporate arrangements with longer-term patients who hadn't had visitors or flowers recently.

Mari checked the clock, feeling useless and a little dejected. Once again, through no fault of hers, one of her events had sucked wide. She wouldn't be surprised if they gave her her walking papers.

She was feeling distinctly sorry for herself as the time for the Gala kickoff rolled around. She had wanted to go with Pere and dance in his arms. She had wanted this event, finally, to be a success.

"Cinderella story," she muttered, trying to get comfortable in the annoyingly hard, flat bed. "Dancing with the handsome prince." She wanted to roll her eyes at the fact that she too had bought into the girl-as-princess mythology. She sighed again.

"Why the sigh, my dearest fiancée?"

She felt like her whole being lit up. Pere was here.

*It's freaky, and princess, but I like it.*

"You're back! Hey!" She scooted over in the bed, which hurt, but she didn't care. She patted the side of the too-firm mattress, wanting him to come sit with her.

"I missed you." He bent down and kissed her lightly. "I did come back up, but you had a room full of people," he said, perching on the bed. "Now, why are you sad?"

"I'm just being a grump. I didn't get to spill our news to anyone," she said, frowning. "And then, I didn't know if you wanted to make it public yet. And I don't get to dance with you tonight. And the Walk bombed because of me. My rep as an event planner is going to have a black cloud hanging over it," she lamented. "The council will probably fire me."

"Not a chance in hell," he said firmly, then smiled. "That's a lot of cranky." He ran the back of his hand over her cheek. As she had that first day he'd done it, she decided that cheek rubbing thing was a secret weapon. It just melted her.

"Hey," she said with surprise, gripping his fingers and pulling his hand down to look at it. "Your bandage is off."

"I paid a visit to Madame Sabina, at her request. One

of her people does healing by touch. Between that and one of Lydia's salves, I'm down to a gauze pad and some tape," he said, showing her his palm.

"That's pretty cool." She sighed again, and caught herself at it. "Dammit, I'm lucky to be alive, I shouldn't be moping and sighing. I just wanted to do this event justice. Do it right."

"You have. It's going to go down as one of the most successful in years, despite the troubles, and you've now cleared the way for it to grow." He laughed. "But if anyone is entitled to a big ol' mopefest, it's you, since you don't get to enjoy the fruits of your labor. How about this, though," he said, standing up and pulling a box out of his pocket. "You didn't get to share our news, but if you're okay with it, Lucille would like to announce it at the Gala tonight."

Mari thought about it for about two seconds, then nodded. "That would be great."

"Good." He seemed relieved. "We won't have to be there, but everyone can know in one fell swoop."

"Efficient," she said, appreciating that she wasn't going to have to tell everything over and over. "And Lucille will make it sound good."

He nodded. "My mother's awake, so I told her our news when I saw her earlier."

"Oh, Pere, I'm so glad!" Mari said with relief. She really liked Estelle Hestworth. It took her a few seconds to remember her earlier apprehension, and then process with a clear mind that Estelle was going to be her mother-in-law.

"Mari, are you okay?" Pere asked, taking her hand, alarm lighting his features. "You just went white."

"I just realized that the really scary lightning lady is going to be my mother-in-law."

Pere paused, just a second, then threw back his head and laughed. "Gods I love you," he said, when he could manage it. Even wincing and gripping his side, he still laughed. "Wait till I tell her. Scary Lightning Lady. Perfect."

"Stop," Mari protested. "Now you're making fun of me."

"Not much. Okay, just a little," Pere agreed. "Will this make up for it?" he asked, pressing the small box with its gaily frothing ribbon adorning the top, into her hand. The ribbon bore the Besom Shop logo.

"You got me something from Lydia's?"

"No, but she wrapped it for me."

Mari undid the ribbon and opened the box. Inside the larger box was a smaller, worn velvet ring box. The nap of the velvet was soft, and a little threadbare around the edges. She carefully opened the lid.

"Oh, wow." Her eyes shot to Pere's. "I mean really, wow."

The ring inside was a center ruby of at least two carats. Dark as blood, it was offset with citrines and diamonds.

"It was my great-great-grandmother's ring, I think." Pere shifted from one foot to the other. Mari hid her smile. He was nervous. Pere was never nervous. "One of the Aldens. Someone who was related to you as well," he went on. "Mother thought you'd like it, but if it doesn't suit you, I'll get you a diamond or whatever you want."

"Oh, no, it's perfect." She loved rubies, always had. And this made her feel like she was not only loved, but belonged. "Put it on for me?" She wasn't sure if she could take it out of the box without dropping it, her hands were shaking so much.

He slid it on. It was a little big, but not much. "It's beautiful, and so are you," he said, leaning in to kiss her. When she tugged at him, he lay down on the bed with her, holding her close. "I love you, Mari Beecham. I'm glad you're going to marry me."

"I hope you like dogs," she said, "because Pepper is a non-negotiable roommate."

"Love them. Let's get another one to keep him

company."

She smiled into his eyes. "Excellent idea," she said. "I'll get you a dog on one condition."

"What's that?" he said, nuzzling the curve of her neck, making her shiver with anticipation.

"You ask me to the Halloween Ball."

"Done. Will you go with me to the Halloween Ball and the Yule Ball and the Walk Gala for the rest of our lives?"

She smiled, feeling her heart fill to the bursting point. Here was home. Here was family.

"I'd be happy to, Mr. Hestworth."

"Excellent. I'm so glad to hear it, Ms. Beecham."

They kissed until they had to stop so Mari wouldn't hurt, but she really didn't want to, even with the pain. To distract herself, she linked their fingers and settled into his embrace.

"Now," she said, sighing a little with happiness this time. "Why don't you tell me what an anchor is?"

"It's a big metal thing they use to keep ships in place."

"I could hurt you, Pere Hestworth," she mock-warned.

Pere smiled, but he answered seriously this time. "When witches do a big magickal working, they have one or two people act as the grounding point for the magick. Usually, of course, it's done in a circle, with a lot more control than we had time for last night."

Mari considered it and what she'd been reading and learning. "Okay, I get that. But?"

"No one expected what happened. There was no preparation, no ritual, no planning."

"No time for it, not with that storm," Mari said, nodding.

"But you formed the circle all on your own, Mari," he said, his hand cupping her cheek, the heat of him warming her through to her heart. His near-awe at her flowed through whatever weird bond or connection they had, enfolding her in love. "You set the anchor and got the link started. It was the only thing that let me ground mother's energy, to save her, and probably, most of us in the clearing."

The catastrophe that could have been, with lightning arcing from person to person, fire and smoke and death, blinked across her mind in a series of fast-action slides.

"Holy cow!" It was all she could think of to say. "That's just freaky."

"Yes, both of our dreams—nightmares, really—were about last night. The fire and death I sensed when I touched you, the lightning. They were all foreshadowing last night's events."

"Wow."

He laughed, and it sounded more than a little strained. "Yeah. I can't dwell on that, or it stops my heart," he admitted. They held one another for a moment before he continued. "Being the anchor means managing the power. You did it, untrained and unprepared." Now she could feel his pride, and his fear for her, mixing together. "It's why you keep falling asleep, and why Sam is insisting you stay another night. You used up, and managed, a hell of a lot of wild energy."

"That is just so," she yawned suddenly, feeling one of those sleeping fits creeping up on her now. "Freaky."

"Sleep," he said, and she nodded, helpless to do anything else. "I'll be right here."

"Always," she murmured, smiling, and dropped into the warm dark.

## EPILOGUE

The water was calm after the wicked storm of the previous evening. Pastor Walthers could see the lights from the inn, awash in people and color, a celebration of the Walk coming to fruition for another year. The Gala was in full swing.

It was sad, really, how little the people who lived in Haven Harbor knew about their town and the evil that had spawned it. He'd learned so much, in so short a time.

Leroy Walthers smiled as he slid the woman's limp body into the boat. He'd wrapped her in a painter's tarp, but it showed where the blood had leaked out of her to stain the tough fabric.

"The sea will wash away any evidence," he said, patting the cloth. "The Master has fed and grows strong once more."

The Bible that was his constant companion now rode next to his skin, zipped inside the tough windbreaker he wore. His suitcases were already loaded into his car in the park on the other side of the river. He'd contacted the Reform Church Administrative offices and they would send a replacement pastor immediately. He'd told them he felt unable to continue with the disgrace and death of his protégé, Calvin Parris, and with the renewed weight of grief over his wife.

They were all sympathy.

His assistant would continue to manage the drug trade admirably from where she was. He didn't need to be nearby for her to do the job correctly.

It was really too funny. All of it.

He smiled as he considered what the townsfolk would think if they knew.

Since he'd found the letters, the wonderful, powerful letters tucked safely in the Bible, he'd grown strong again. He was determined and powerful in a way that he'd not been since before his beautiful wife had had died in his arms, leaving him so alone.

He'd felt so lost, so rootless, until he found the letters.

Then when he'd given in to them, let them feed on him, he'd learned how to profit from the fear of the witches. When he let that same power from the letters feed on the blood of the two women, he'd learned so much more.

So very much more.

"Always be the power behind the throne," he murmured, starting the engine and letting the boat putt-putt-putt out into the river. He'd taken the boat from Gus's house, of course. Stupid Gus, who couldn't control his business or his brother. A weakling.

"Never let yourself get caught," he continued his litany, speaking aloud the things the letters had taught him for the first time. It felt right to do it, out on the free, open water. "Have a scapegoat handy at all times."

Poor Calvin. He'd never seen it coming.

####

Jake didn't have the heart for the Gala this year. Too much had happened. Too much had yet to be resolved.

He'd just turned his office computer back on and decided to get another cup of coffee when he felt it. It was a hard twinge in his chest, like a bowstring or a harp string had been plucked, hard. Or like a hard hit from an opposing linebacker, right to the chest.

"What the hell?" He rubbed his sternum to ease the ache. It came again.

The sound of running feet had him jumping up, despite the pain. He whipped open his door.

Jim Stansfield skidded to a stop in front of him, his tuxedo limp and drooping with the speed and heat of his run. "You gotta come. The river. Boat. Bad. Now," he panted, tugging on Jake's arm and trying to pull him down the hall. "Now."

"Slow down, buddy," he soothed. "What's going on?" Jim was rubbing at his chest too.

"No time. The City Wards," he continued to tug at Jake with one hand, panting out the words as he rubbed at his chest with the other. "The magick ones. I'm Holly King this year. I hold the Seal. The old evil is crossing the wards in the river. Right now. By boat."

"Holy shit. They're real? Nevermind. What do you need?" Adrenaline surged and Jake rode it.

Jake had never been chosen as either the Holly King or the Oak King, one of which was picked at Yule, the other at Midsummer. He'd never paid much attention to the celebration, other than thinking it a quaint bit of witchy fun.

Obviously a gap in his education.

"Come with me. We'll…need…gun. Salt." Jim heaved in great gulps of air as Jake snatched his jacket and a long, silvery shotgun out of the gun cabinet in his office. "Don't know what else until we get there." Jim at last managed a full sentence even as another twinge hit them both.

"Let's go."

####

Pere felt the twinge in his chest, and looked at Mari. She was sleeping quietly in his arms, but as he shifted, just a little to rub at the spot, she woke.

"What's wrong?"

"I don't know." He considered getting his phone, calling Jake. She smiled at him and he decided that whatever it was, someone else would have to deal with it tonight. Just for tonight, he needed to be a man, alone with the woman he loved. "Do you think you can stand up for a few minutes?"

"I'd love to get up," she said, her smile widening. "I'm sick of this bed."

He helped her get up, get away from the cords and wires, all of which had now been disconnected because she'd been allowed to sit in the chair for a little while. He steadied her as he led her to the window.

"I'd ask you to dance with me, but I think we're probably both too unsteady."

She smiled, hugging him carefully. "You're being kind. You're steady, I'm not."

He kissed her. "Okay, you're right."

"Smart ass," she said, but without heat. "Why are we at the windows?"

"Give it a few minutes, you'll see. We have one of the best vantage points from here."

"Vantage points?" she said, puzzled. He saw her face change to delight as she figured it out. "Oh, the fireworks!"

"They launch them from Founders Park, so you can see them best from the Gala ballroom, and from here, since the medical center is on the bluffs."

Within seconds, a brilliant orange and gold blossom of fire lit the sky, then another.

Pere watched them for a few moments, but then turned to look at Mari. Here, finally, was his match, his partner.

She turned to him and smiled.

"You're my own personal fireworks," he murmured. "Beautiful Marisol Beecham. I'm glad you came to Haven Harbor."

The glitter of the fireworks beyond the windows matched the light in her eyes. She stood on tiptoe, gingerly stretching her arms to link them around his neck. "Me too, Peregrine Hestworth." She smiled. "Now kiss your fiancée."

"Your wish is my command."

####

Jake and Jim raced out of the building. "Do I need the Coasties?" Jake demanded as they jumped into the Blazer and headed for the Marina. The streets were nearly empty, thanks to the Gala.

"No. They won't understand."

"As an alibi, Jim, not for help," Jake cursed as he nearly spun out taking a corner.

"Oh, yeah, maybe." Jim kept rubbing at his chest. "By ash and rowen, that hurts."

Jake could still feel the thrum in his own chest, but like a constant, dull throb. Jim must be feeling something more by the look on his face.

They peeled into the police dock at the Marina. Wherever the Marina guard was, he wasn't nearby. Jake tossed Jim the shotgun. "It's got a salt load in both barrels."

"Got it."

Jake wrestled open the door to the Haven Harbor Police shed above the police dock. It creaked heavily. He found the boat keys more by feel than anything and beat feet for the boat Jim was already climbing into.

"Is everyone feeling this throb? This ache?" Jake asked, as he backed the boat out of the slip and turned it into the open water of the river.

"Yes, if they were here for the midsummer ball, or Yule Gala. The King and the Court have it the worst. We're the focus of the Ward."

"Shit. Okay. Where to?"

"Toward the mouth of the river. We can't let him get past the second Ward or he'll be loosed on the world."

"Shit, who is it? What is it?"

Jim shook his head, hanging on as Jake hit the throttle. "I don't know who, exactly. Just that they must have contacted the Old Power. The evil that ran us out of Salem, and tried to kill us once we got here. The City Wards circle the town, following the water. The bridges have extra protection, but all of it is only triggered by the Old Power. Because when our ancestors got here, the Evil they knew still stalked them."

"Well, hells bells," Jake swore, using even stronger curses in his mind. Here he was, in the middle of the river with Jim Stansfield, owner of the local garage and body shop, and only one shotgun full of salt. "Piece of cake," he muttered. "Just like in *Supernatural*. Go after the bad guy ill-prepared."

Jim must have heard him, because he laughed. "Yeah, exactly. They told me about this when I took the crown, but hey, no one's had to actually do anything in about a hundred fifty years, so no problem, right? Last time there was something was around the Civil War. Nobody said anything about your chest feeling like somebody was splitting it open with a five-pound sledge."

"Fuck."

"Yeah."

Tuning into that note of pain in his chest, he felt the answering throb of the evil before he spotted the boat putting along in the shadows, headed for the Atlantic.

"There," he hissed, throttling back. "Ahoy the boat!" he called. If Jim was right, the far side of the inlet, bordering the marsh, marked the second of the two town Wards.

He hit the lights and whooped the sirens, attracting some partygoers in the larger marina houses to come out to see what was going on. Pre-gala or instead-of-gala parties in those houses tended to be wild, and often meant calls for Haven Harbor's police.

He hoped none of them needed him tonight. Picking up the radio, he called the Coasties. If this got ugly, he wanted backup. With the police-boat spotlights on the now-accelerating boat, he could see the long, thick roll lying in the seat well.

"If that's not a body, I'll eat my badge," he said.

"Shit, shit, shit," Jim cussed. "He's fed on blood."

"I'm not even going to ask," Jake snarled, anger rising that this thing—whatever it was—was trying to get away with murder in his town. All of his duty officers were either on patrol, or on Gala duty. If things went sideways out here on the river, he and Jim were screwed. *Shit.* "Jim Stansfield," Jake said, yelling to be heard over the roar of the engine. "I hereby deputize you as a peace officer of the Haven Harbor Police Department, officially under my hand, this September, shit, whatever the hell the date is."

"What? Deputize? What the hell? Is that legal?"

"Yes, it's still legal," Jake snapped, avoiding a channel marker. "Even if it isn't usual. It means if I tell you to shoot that fucker with that shotgun full of salt, or with my service revolver, you do it. My deputizing you means you don't go on trial for murder." He keyed the mic. "Coast Guard two-ten, this is Haven Harbor one. Repeat, Haven Harbor one requesting assistance."

"Haven Harbor One, this is Coast Guard two-ten, where do you need us, over?"

"Mouth of the river. I've got a small boat, attempting a body dump. One white male visible, body visible, over."

"Well shit, Jake," came the reply, before protocol reasserted itself and the official tone returned. "On the way, Haven Harbor One."

"Make it fast, Carter."

"Got it."

"Small boat," Jake called with the loudspeaker now.

He was gaining on the smaller, less powerful boat. "Cut your engine and prepare to be boarded. Keep your hands where I can see them."

In answer the boat engine revved and the boat cut across their path, heading for the channel that led to the Atlantic.

Clutching his chest, Jim staggered. "Dammit, he's about to breech the Ward."

"Steer!" Jake ordered, pulling his service revolver as he let go the wheel.

"Coast Guard, suspect is running your way," he called it in, then switched over to loudspeaker. "Small boat, stop your engines now or we will fire on you."

Jake's first shot was high, whistling over the head of the man driving the boat. Even with the lights, trained on the boat, the shifting waves and shivering shadows seemed to cloak the man's features and body. He couldn't tell who it was, and he couldn't let him get away.

"Call another warning," he said, bracing himself as Jim hissed in pain. Jim kept the boat steady though, and grabbed the mic.

"Small boat," Jim's voice roared through the speaker. "Stop your engines now or we will fire on you."

"Good enough." Jake took aim, not letting himself be distracted by the sight and sound of the Coast Guard cutter speeding toward them from the mouth of the river. He squeezed the trigger, letting the feel of the wind and the weapon guide his aim. Time seemed to slow down and he could almost see the bullet as it left the barrel. The roll of the tide, the catenary, hadn't spoiled his aim. He had the guy.

The bullet sped toward the suspect, and somehow, at the last minute, the man held something up, and the bullet plowed into it.

The second shot hit the boat's engine and it died. The man dropped into the river with an almighty splash as if he too had been hit, although Jake hadn't fired a third shot.

Within seconds, they pulled alongside the boat and Jake leaped into the seat well, narrowly missing the body. The Coasties were only seconds behind.

"Aaagh," Jim groaned, clutching his chest. "Shit. He's crossed the Ward. Dead or alive, he's crossed it."

"Hellfire and damnation."

#### 

"So that's the story," Jake said, as he, Sam, Dan, and Pere sat among the flowers in Mari's room the next day.

"Pastor Walthers. What the hell?" Dan said, looking bewildered. "Why?"

"Why not?" Sam said, and cynicism dripped from the words. "I've met a lot of preachers who sold drugs and sex right along with redemption."

"Sam worked in California for a while," Pere said to Mari. "He's jaded."

"Right," Sam drawled. He smiled at Mari. "Don't listen to him, Mari. I'm a happy, optimistic guy."

The snorts of laughter from the other three men clued Mari in that he was totally teasing.

"I'm glad to know," she said, and the men focused on her. "I hate that this man pushed Calvin into what he did. And that he was somehow influencing Gus as well. And Geneva." She had to stop, catch her breath and steady her emotions. "But, I'm glad to know. Calvin was so adamant that he hadn't hurt either of the other women. It really had the ring of truth."

Jake stood up, and came over to kiss her cheek. "I'm glad you're going to be okay, Mari Beecham." He smiled at her, but she could see the shadows and sorrow in his eyes. "Save me a dance at the Halloween Ball, you hear me?"

"I will."

"Me too," Sam said, also rising. "I need to get back to rounds."

"Guess that means I should go too, and leave you lovebirds alone." Dan kissed her cheek as well. "Heal well, Mari. We need you."

Near tears at the affection and respect these men had shown her, she waited till they'd left to pull tissues from the box and dab her eyes.

"I really love Haven Harbor," she blurted, when Pere looked at her.

"But do you love me?" he said, smiling. He understood her. He got her.

*Priceless.*

She felt the love swell in her heart. Man, did she love her some Pere Hestworth.

"You bet I do. Why don't you come over here and let me show you how much?"

With a smile that threatened to outshine the sun glinting on the water of the Merrimack, Pere gathered her into his arms.

"Anytime, my love. And forever."

## EXCERPT: *A MIDNIGHT PROMISE*

*October, The Year of Our Lord, 2016*
*Boston, Massachusetts*

"Goddamn dog," the man cursed. Although the dog lay unconscious, maybe dead, the man and his companion were bleeding from multiple bites. They'd incapacitated the dog, or so they thought. But even in his drugged state, the dog had attacked.

Two of the man's companions finished in the back of the house and came out with their slight burden. With silent nods, they moved to the waiting sedan with it's blacked out windows gleaming in the security lights mounted on the house.

In the cloudy dark of the October night, the long, sleek car sped away with a little girl lying unconscious and bound on the back seat.

"Throw the damn thing in the back of the van, Turk."

he growled, keeping his voice low.

Within minutes, they, too, had pulled away from the elegant Back Bay home. The nanny and the housekeeper, tied and drugged in the spotless kitchen, had never seen any of them. The gas they'd used had put the women out within seconds.

"Let's go," Turk said, climbing into the driver's seat. "We're at time."

The op had been calculated down to the second. They'd built in a safety margin, but dealing with the fucking dog attack had eaten every minute of the margin.

It was a silent drive northward out of Boston's elegant neighborhoods, and through the northern suburbs. Taking a quieter rural road, they maneuvered through late night traffic in Salem, and out into the emptiness of rural Massachusetts. On the dark, deserted road between Pennyfield and the Merrimack River, they stopped to dump the dog. This far from Boston, no one would connect the body of a dog, dead in the road, with the missing girl's guard dog.

Mick snapped on a pair of rubber gloves then used his boot knife to neatly slice off the dog's collar. That, he tossed into the van. With a quick twist of his wrist, he cut off the end of the dog's tail. Then, with a grunt, he lifted the dead weight of the German Shepherd.

"Jesus, what the hell do they feed this dog, bricks?"

"Toldja he was heavy," Turk said, grinning from the driver's seat.

The patter of rain on the windshield was a welcome helper. In fact, the storm was absolutely perfect. People didn't look around when they drove in bad weather. The dog wouldn't be found until morning, if then.

Mick laid the dog on the slick, black macadam in the middle of the northbound lane and ran back to the van.

He saw Turk look in the rearview mirror and checked behind them. Headlights were a faint wink of light in the distance. In a few minutes the Shepherd would be history, and he wouldn't have to kill the dog. He wasn't squeamish about people, but animals weren't on his hit list.

"You're brilliant, Mick," Turk complimented with laugh.

"Yeah. No blood in the van, no dog anywhere to be found. When the cars are through with him, all anyone will see is another flattened, road kill farm dog."

He dropped the bloody end of the dog's tail into a Ziplock, and that into a FedEx envelope. Dr. Michael Thompson, III, would receive the bloody tail in the morning. The ransom note would come in another FedEx, along with a lock of his daughter's long blonde hair.

They were in the money now.

####

Adele rolled down the driver's side window to let in the October wind. She was exhausted, and she needed the rush of air to stay awake.

She was grateful that her sturdy truck was easy to drive, even on the rain-slick road. She'd been helping with a foaling racehorse and her arm felt like a limp spaghetti noodle. The life of a vet wasn't for the weak or squeamish, she thought, realizing she still had blood and hay stuck on her sleeve.

"Dammit, I changed my shirt." That meant she had to wash two shirts, and her pants, and probably the door of the truck. Ugh.

She couldn't wait to get home to Haven Harbor. The vets up here in the upper, more rural, part of Massachusetts had a loose network amongst themselves. If any of them needed an extra hand, or coverage on a tough case, they supported one another. George Barrett had called her that afternoon, frantic that he might lose both the mare and the foal.

"That was actually yesterday, Adele," she said, talking to herself to try and stay awake. "Hell. Another night of short sleep." She and George had worked with the mare for almost nine hours, getting the foal turned and the mare settled enough to give birth. Adele, with her strong, but much narrower arms, had ended up getting the foal to turn. "Veterinary medicine," she intoned, laughing at herself. "Not for sissies." She grabbed her water bottle for a swig. The icy water helped, but damn, she needed to get to bed.

Off in the distance, she saw taillights, and wondered who else was out on the road this late. Her cell pinged with an incoming email, it popped up on the dashboard's display.

Dan Nutter. He was reminding everyone about a coven leadership meeting on Tuesday.

Heat uncurled in her gut. She wasn't sure what the hell she was going to do about her serious hankering for the quiet librarian. Gods, he was not only smart as hell, he was built like Adonis, straight out of a woman's Chippendales fantasy. They'd had one dance at the Witches Walk Gala and she'd nearly melted in lust.

But a librarian? What the hell was that about? Did she get the hots for a CEO or another small business owner? Oh no, not her. She got all googlie-eyed and wet-pantied over a director of libraries. Of course, he was also a medium who talked to the spirits that roamed around town, but what would be weird and grounds for commitment to a psych ward in any other place was normal for Haven Harbor.

"Get a grip, girl. It's not like he's working at Seven-Eleven or something." But a librarian? She knew he had some kind of mystery in his past, and he hung out with four of the most eligible bachelors in Haven Harbor. Make that three eligible guys—Mari Beecham had well and truly taken bachelor number one, Pere Hestworth, off the market.

She shifted in the seat, pumping the volume on her radio. "C'mon, girl. You can make it. Quit blinking those sleepy eyes," she remonstrated with herself. With only a few more minutes to go before she got to the bridge and Haven Harbor, she wasn't going to pull off the road for a nap. She wanted her own bed.

Adele rounded a curve and barely had time to hit the brakes as her headlights picked out the still form lying in the road.

"Effin bloody hell!" she snarled as she fought the steering wheel. The tires squealed and she shuddered to a stop, inches from the huge dog lying in the road.

The dog was a big, healthy-looking German Shephard. Cursing every unscrupulous dog owner in existence, she jumped out and ran to kneel by the unconscious animal. The male dog was still breathing. The respiration was shallow and slow, but it was still there. He was bleeding from somewhere, but in the darkness, she couldn't tell where. She ran her hands over him, not feeling anything torn or broken yet.

"Poor baby," she whispered, concentrating on the dog's life energy. It was faltering, but there. Underneath that temporary weakness was a deep well of fierce strength.

A car came from the north. It slowed as it approached, pulling up right by her. She raised a hand to screen the glare from the headlights as a tall, lean figure stepped out of the low-slung sports car.

"Adele?"

*Speak of the devil, and he shall appear.*

Relief and surprise flooded through her in equal measures, followed hard by heat. Dan Nutter's voice was pure sex, low and rich and deep.

"Hey," she managed to squeak out the word. "You've got the best timing."

"Not me. The ghosts told me you were in trouble. How can I help?"

Just as fast as the heat had come, a chill shivered over her. The ghosts that talked to Dan hadn't seemed to like Adele at all. But she wasn't going to worry about it if they'd sent him to help now.

"Help me get this big, beautiful guy into the truck. I have to get him to the clinic, and see if I can save him."

With an ease she envied, and with no concern for his clothes or anything else, Dan lifted the massive dog in his arms. She raced to open the door and yanked out one of the blankets she kept in a bag in the back of the cab. She threw the soft cover on the seat and stepped out of the way.

"I'll follow you in," he said, opening the driver's door for her before turning back to his car. She was about to say he didn't have to, when she realized she'd have to get the dog out of the truck and into the clinic somehow.

She peeled out, racing for Haven Harbor with her hottest fantasy guy hot on her tail.

The thought made her grin, despite her worry for the gorgeous, wounded pup riding silently behind her.

"He followed me home, mom," she said, snorting out a laugh. Countless children, including Adele herself, had cheerfully used those same words to plead with their moms about rescuing strays. In this context, the stakes were much higher. "Can I keep him?"

# ABOUT THE AUTHOR

Jeanne Adams likes calling North Carolina home, but for now, she lives in DC, with her husband, two sons, and three dogs. Jeanne's favorite holiday is Halloween and she starts planning the annual yard decor for each year as soon as the current Halloween is over. As an amateur genealogist, Jeanne was researching her husband's Adams relatives and discovered one had been accused in the Witch Trials in Salem. (He escaped...) Thus was the genesis of The Witches Walk.

On another spooky and suspenseful note, Jeanne used to work in the funeral and cemetery business, and knows a thing or two about getting rid of the body....bwhahahah! (She even teaches classes about it for writers!) She claims that's one reason she took up writing romantic suspense! Jeanne has written award-winning suspense novels for Kensington/Zebra Publishing since 2007, including the highly acclaimed DEADLY LITTLE SECRETS, and its follow up, DEADLY LITTLE LIES. An excerpt from DEADLY LITTLE SECRETS was featured in Cosmopolitan Magazine.

For updates on all Jeanne's work, check her website - www.JeanneAdams.com where you can sign up for her newsletter.
Follow her on Twitter @JeanneAdams
Follow her on Facebook at
www.Facebook.com/JeanneAdamsAuthor

# TITLES BY JEANNE ADAMS

SUSPENSE
DEAD RUN, Faithful Defenders #1
DEADLY DELIVERY (Novella)
CAPITOL DANGER (With Suzanne Ferrell, JD Tyler,
and Nancy Northcott)

HISTORICAL
BEHIND ENEMY LINES (WWII)

URBAN FANTASY
THE TENTACLE AFFAIRE

FORTHCOMING BOOKS
A MIDNIGHT PROMISE, Novella in WELCOME TO
HAVEN HARBOR (Haven Harbor 1.25), October 2016
A YULE TO REMEMBER, Novella in UNDER THE
KISSING BOUGH (Haven Harbor 1.50), November
2016
A SPIRITED LIFE, A Green Magic Novel, January 2017
THE RUM RUNNER INCIDENT, Slip Traveler #2,
March 2017

TITLES CAN BE FOUND AT ALL MAJOR
RETAILERS

64990442R00177

Made in the USA
Charleston, SC
12 December 2016